"It's time you learned to lean on me."

He kissed her again, harder this time, stilling her protests. She wasn't kissing him back—it was too much to hope for—but neither was she fighting him. He pulled back a little to watch her face.

He dropped his arms immediately. "Ach, Evelynne, don't look at me like that. It's over. I won't say I'm sorry, however. I'm not. I've wanted to do that for the last twelve hours."

"Yes," she snapped, "and I've wanted to box your ears more than once, and never gave in to the impulse. And God save me from men who think that every woman is theirs for the taking! You're no better than that red-headed coachman."

"Has he been trying to kiss you too?"

"Oh, I see. You're having a joke at my expense. I'm glad you find me laughable, my Lord."

"This Lord finds you to be many things, Eve. . . . " The earl's voice was soft and deep. "But never, ever, laughable."

Lord Monteith's Gift

Nancy Butler

A SIGNET BOOK

SIGNET
Published by the Penguin Group
Penguin Putnam Inc., 375 Hudson Street,
New York, New York 10014, U.S.A.
Penguin Books Ltd, 27 Wrights Lane,
London W8 5TZ, England
Penguin Books Australia Ltd,
Ringwood, Victoria, Australia
Penguin Books Canada Ltd, 10 Alcorn Avenue,
Toronto, Ontario, Canada M4V 3B2
Penguin Books (N.Z.) Ltd, 182-190 Wairau Road,
Auckland 10, New Zealand

Penguin Books Ltd, Registered Offices:
Harmondsworth, Middlesex, England

First published by Signet, an imprint of Dutton Signet,
a member of Penguin Putnam Inc.

First Printing, January 1998
10 9 8 7 6 5 4 3 2 1

This book is for my three tenacious muses—
Joyce, who inspired me to write it
Lisa, who critiqued it along the way
and Susan, who encouraged me to take
it to market

. . . and for Ginger, my own "Little Georgie"

Love that is hoarded moulds at last,
Until we know some day
The only thing we ever have
Is what we give away.

—Louis Ginsberg, *Song*

Chapter 1

$\backsim$

When a virtuous man performs an act of valor, soon all in his acquaintance are marveling at the deed. In truth, even virtuous men enjoy the well-deserved acclaim of their peers. However, if the man in question is of a dour, taciturn nature, then the deed often goes unannounced and, thus, unacclaimed.

So it was that that not one person who chanced to meet Robert MacIntyre, fifth Earl of Monteith, on that particular day in September, had any idea that they were in the presence of a bona fide hero.

He went along to his club for a late luncheon, as was his habit, dining with several casual friends, and then spent the rest of his afternoon at Jackson's Boxing Emporium, working out the stiffness from an old shoulder wound acquired during his military service in the Peninsular War. The earl then returned home to his Cavendish Square town house, where he allowed his valet to coax him into superbly cut evening clothes, before he made his way to yet another of the gatherings offered by the hostesses of the *ton* during London's Little Season.

And during that entire time, having joined in conversation with no less than twenty persons, ranging in rank from a royal duke sparring with his cronies at Jackson's, to his own Scots valet, not one word of self-congratulation passed Robert MacIntyre's lips.

But if the earl chose not to blow his own trumpet, it was a far different case with the beneficiary of his heroic deed. Gilly Marriott, an open-faced, fair-haired lad of thirteen, was agog with wonder. And not, as some might think, because he had been snatched from almost certain death. Rather, his awe was directed at the dashing and courageous manner in which this rescue had been effected.

He ran straight home to the small Camden Town row house where his family lodged with the Widow Cooperall. She looked after the Marriott children while their older sister, Evelynne, was at work. The widow also tutored them in mathematics and reading, having once been a schoolmistress.

It was these lessons that accounted for Gilly's frequent absences from home. This morning, however, he flew back to Number Twelve, Camden Passage, lessons notwithstanding.

The neighborhood where they lodged was working-class in character, though not a slum by any means. Gilly knew what real slums were. He had traveled more than once into those forbidden territories, and not always by accident, for he had an entrepreneurial nature. There was often work at alehouses or about the docks. Gilly gladly did what he could to earn a few pence, and to ensure that his older sister was not the only contributor to the family finances.

This morning the street was lined with hawkers and vendors; before Number Twelve a pair of men argued over the price of some pigeons. Gilly scurried past them, leapt up the cracked stone stairs, and bulleted into the narrow hallway. He called out to the landlady and was answered from the rear of the house. He trotted through to the back landing, which gave onto a neatly kept garden.

Biddie Cooperall, a parched lady of threescore years, sat on a stone bench, conducting lessons with her two charges. Her frizz of white-brown hair was covered by a lace cap, and over her day dress she wore a simple pinafore. A Marriott child sat perched on either side of her, Joshua, ten, and nearsighted, holding his lesson book close beneath his pointed little nose, and Jeremiah, seven and willful, looking everywhere in the garden except at his grammar.

"Gilbert," she chided, "it's been hours since you walked your sister to the factory. I'd despaired of seeing you until dinner—we've had to start the lessons without you."

Gilly, breathless from his race home, tried to muster a look of regret.

"I'm sorry, Mrs. Coop. I'm afraid I got into a bit of a scrape this morning." His brothers turned their attention to him as one, and Gilly had all the audience he could wish for as he regaled them with the tale of his near demise and his subsequent rescue by a tall, dark-haired gentleman. Mrs. Coop tut-tutted with concern as Gilly's story progressed. Josh and Jemmy sat spellbound, envious that their brother should have been center stage in such a ripping good adventure.

"Well, I am relieved you are come home safe. But what your sister will say to this, I cannot tell," Mrs. Cooperall pronounced dolefully once Gilly had finished his tale. "And however shall she repay that gallant man who risked his own life to save you?"

Gilly pondered this a minute, and then said brightly, "I daresay we needn't repay him at all—he looked a gentry cove—" He frowned and silently took himself to task for speaking slang to a lady. "Er, that is, he looked to be quite well-off if the bit o' blood . . . um, horse, he was riding was any clue."

"Still, the debt needs to be acknowledged." She was adamant. "I believe your sister and I should pay a morning call to thank him in person. Is it too much to hope that the gentleman made himself known to you?"

"Well, not in so many words. But he did give me this." Gilly pulled an ivory-colored calling card, now rather dog-eared, from his jacket pocket. "He told me he could always use a game youngster in his stable, and if I ever wanted a job working with horses, to show this card."

Mrs. Cooperall made a little humphing noise in her throat as she adjusted her pince-nez to better read the engraved letters upon the card. "Never say that he mistook you for a servant, Gilbert. Your sister will be that upset."

"She's a fine one to care," Josh pointed out. "Going off to work in that smelly manufact'ry every day."

"It's only temporary," Gilly snapped. "And she's doing it, partly, so she can send you to school next year, Mr. High-and-Mighty!"

"Well, then at least I'll have some kind of profession." Josh cast an owl-eyed sneer at his older brother. "Not like *some* people who come creeping in at all hours, smelling of fish and ale."

It was only an instant before the fists flew. Jemmy knew better than to get in range, and so ducked behind a nearby apple tree while his elders battled it out. Joshua, in spite of his thin frame and nearsightedness, was an able opponent. He was as plucky as they come, Gilly would often assure his sister.

The skirmish quickly subsided when the combatants realized that Mrs. Cooperall was paying no attention to them. She was staring off into space, a bemused expression on her lined face, absently waving the gentleman's card in one hand.

Gilly set his squirming brother firmly aside and took a seat beside her on the bench. "Mrs. Coop, are you unwell?"

She shook herself back to the present moment. "Oh no, my dear, I'm quite fine. Just a little distracted. You've had quite an eventful morning, and now this." She fluttered the card slowly before them. Josh took it from her and read aloud.

"Robert MacIntyre, Lord Monteith." He screwed up his mouth. "What does it mean?"

"It means," Mrs. Cooperall said, plucking the card from his grubby fingers and carefully placing it in the small net reticule she wore at her waist, "that your brother was rescued by a gentleman of very high birth, one whose name has reached even our corner of London." She put an arm about Gilly's shoulders and gave him a squeeze. "Gilbert, you have perhaps become our deus ex machina, and, no, don't ask me to translate it, but your mishap this morning may yet prove to be fortuitous. Your sister and I will most certainly pay a call on his lordship."

She gathered up the lesson books and herded the boys into the kitchen for their dinner, wondering all the while at the strange workings of fate.

"Bless me if that rascal hasn't tumbled himself into the arms of the most eligible bachelor in London," she mused. "Now if his stubborn sister could only do the same, everything would be most satisfactory."

Evelynne Marriott often thought that the worst thing about Tillery's Pin Manufactory, barring the long hours, poor ventilation, and low pay, was that they employed only men. In truth, there were few tasks that were performed in the manufactory that could not be accomplished by a woman—no heavy lifting or dangerous climbing. Yet, in spite of this fact, Mr. Tillery refused to hire any females.

Evelynne's acquaintance with the pin factory had come about in a circuitous manner. She had been raised in the West Country, the only daughter of Sir Edmund Marriott, a gentleman farmer. Her early years were quite free of care. She spent her days tramping after her older brother, Edgar, across the wild moors of Devon. He taught her to fish and to ride, to sail a small skiff, and to shoot straight and true. When she turned twelve, she attended Mrs. Cooperall's Academy for Young Ladies in

Exeter, to learn some of the finer graces. She returned home every other weekend to the welcoming bosom of her family. Looking back, she often thought of it as a charmed time.

But then everything turned dark. Edgar, headstrong and restless, swore he was not cut out to manage an estate. He enlisted in a cavalry unit and went off to fight on the Peninsula. When he was killed at Busaco, her parents were despondent. Her younger brothers, of course, had a sense of loss, but Evelynne was completely devastated. Edgar had been her best friend, her confidant, the one person in the world who shared her joy of life, and her sometimes troublesome sense of the ridiculous.

Within a year of Edgar's passing, both her parents had died also, carried off by a severe epidemic of influenza. She suspected that the loss of their eldest son had greatly decreased their resistance to the disease. She tried to keep the farm running, but her father had left the property heavily mortgaged, and when she turned twenty, she was forced to sell to his creditors. Taking what little monies remained, she relocated with her brothers to London, expecting that in such a large city she could find some type of employment.

Mrs. Cooperall abetted her in this decision—the widow had closed her girls' academy several years before and retired to a small house in London. It was an ideal place for the Marriott family to stay until they could bring themselves to rights.

Once they had settled in their new home, Evelynne set about to find work. She haunted every employment agency in the city, first seeking work as a governess or paid companion, then finally as a seamstress, milliner's assistant, or shop clerk. But her age and lack of references worked against her. It never occurred to her that her rather startling, dark beauty was a liability, as well. She was unaware of her own attributes, often lamenting privately before her mirror that her deep gray eyes and unruly brown hair gave her a gypsy look. Edgar had told her she was a throwback to their Cornish great-grandfather, but as the only brunette in the present-day Marriott clan, she thought it most unfair that her brothers all were blessed with golden locks and celestial blue eyes.

When no offers of genteel employment were forthcoming, Evelynne cast her eyes on Tillery's Pin Manufactory. It was less than a half mile from Camden Passage, and the building looked relatively clean. Not like the "dark, Satanic mills" that Mr. Blake had written of, some of which Evelynne had seen on their journey from Devon. No, the pin factory seemed a logical choice.

However, Mr. Tillery's assistant, a pock-marked scarecrow of a man, refused to even consider her application for work, and instead ogled her shamelessly. He offered her employment of a different sort, whereupon she stormed from his office, making sure to tread heavily on his instep as she made her way out.

Weeks later, with their meager resources nearly depleted, Gilbert announced that he would have a stab at the pin factory himself.

"No pun intended," he informed her soberly, the weight of new responsibility clearly written on his young face.

It wrung Evelynne's heart to watch as her carefree brother lost his relaxed country manner. It would be his undoing to work in a factory—he was too young, too callow—and though, even in her fondest moments, she knew he would never be a scholar like Josh, nor yet a charmer like Jem, she had hopes for a better future for him. Perhaps work as an apprentice printer, or such. Anything would be preferable to the bleak lot of a factory boy.

That she had intended to barter herself into such servitude bothered her hardly at all. She was the eldest, and practical, besides. She saw her actions as merely the means to an end—keeping her family together and out of the workhouse. But Gilly's repeated insistence that a tall, strong lad could make a pile of money in the factory did give her an idea.

The very next morning, clad in a pair of Edgar's twill breeches, a cambric shirt, a pair of brogues that Gilly had outgrown, and a corded waistcoat unearthed from Mrs. Coop's attic, Evelynne embarked on her new career, "Ethan Marriott, pin counter."

To Evelynne's great relief, the scarecrow at Tillery's did not recognize her, perceiving only a tall, thin lad with an unkempt head of cropped hair, wearing a rather old-fashioned waistcoat. He had sent her forthwith to the shop foreman, who assigned her to the counting room.

That had been nearly three months ago, and every day, barring Sundays, Evelynne rose up at dawn, donned her masculine attire, and made her way, accompanied by Gilly, to the street opposite Tillery's. There her brother would hand her a wrapped parcel, prepared by Mrs Coop, which contained her dinner and a scone or two for tea break. She would smile reassuringly at

Gilly, and then make her way with a calculatedly boyish stride to the workers' entrance.

Evelynne never felt apprehensive when Gilly was at her side, for, in spite of his youth, he had been raised on farm work, and was strong for his age. But as soon as she was out of his sight, inside the dense, shadowed walls of the factory, Evelynne always felt uneasy. Even after conducting her charade successfully for three months, she still feared discovery.

Most of the men employed at the pin factory were rough-spoken laborers, of middle age, with wives and children at home. But there were also a number of younger men, who tended to hang about in groups, seeking targets for their uncouth humor.

And that was the crux of Evelynne's dilemma—in order to maintain her disguise, she knew it was best to have little contact with her fellow workers. Yet she couldn't afford to be totally isolated, for that was the surest way to call attention to herself. And she certainly didn't want to fall under the eye of Ollie Hooper, the smirking leader of the young rowdies. Fortunately, she was soon drawn into a group of gruff, good-natured Scotsmen, who shared her mealtimes and called her "wee laddie."

So she counted her pins, collected her pay, and tried to stay out of the way of the brash troublemakers. But more than once she had seen Ollie Hooper's darting little eyes follow her as she worked, and she had the unnerving feeling that it was only a matter of time before someone saw through her masquerade. And then, aside from the obvious consequence of losing her employment, there might be repercussions that were just too distressing to think on.

Gilbert was waiting for her in his usual spot, just under the spade-shaped tradesman's sign that read JOS. DIGGER, SHOVEL-MAKER. He was rocking from foot to foot, whistling a tuneless air.

"Come on, Eve!" he called out impatiently as she hurried across the street. "Mrs. Coop's got a fowl on to roast, and I'm fairly starving!"

"I'm sorry you had to wait, Gil," she said breathlessly as she crossed over to him. "It took me some time to finish up."

Gilly was at first too preoccupied with his own exciting news to notice the flush that colored his sister's face, or to realize that her breathlessness had nothing to do with hurrying across the street.

The fact was, Evelynne had just experienced a most unpleasant encounter with the dreadful Ollie Hooper. She had been working late, hoping to avoid passing him where he lingered near the factory's rear doorway. When all the other shift-workers were gone, and Ollie loitered there still, Evelynne realized with a jolt that he must be lying in wait for her. Nothing but to brazen it out. She pulled on her jacket and strode boldly to the dimly lit exit. As she tried to go past him, he caught her by the sleeve.

"Eh, lad, running home to Mama?" He leered down at her, his large hand grasping her arm through the woolen fabric. She could see his discolored front teeth and matted, dirty hair. Ollie Hooper did not improve upon close scrutiny.

"My brother is waiting. I must go." She tried to shrug away from his hold.

"What kind a' lad needs 'is baby brother to fetch 'im?" Ollie raised a gnarled brow. "You'rc a namby-pamby one, you are. Whyn't you come along wif me, now, and we'll 'ave us a pint at the corner pub. Might even put some spunk in your step." From the odors emanating from his person, it was quite clear he'd already imbibed a quantity of spirits.

"Thank you, no. Perhaps another time."

"Ooh, ain't we the proper little gent. 'P'raps annover time', indeed! Well, Ollie 'Ooper don't take no for an answer." He thrust her roughly before him through the doorway into the littered alley that backed the factory. "Stop squirmin', ye little weasel—Aagh!"

Evelynne's brogue had caught her tormenter squarely in midshin. He let go of her sleeve, only to wrap one burly arm around her middle and swing her against the far brick wall. He leaned into her.

"That weren't very polite, laddie. Ollie might be thinkin' you don't like 'im."

Evelynne drew a breath to speak, and at that moment he leapt back as if she had slapped him. His eyes widened, and his thick jaw dropped.

"Well, I'll be damned! You ain't no lad at all." His eyes narrowed, and he grinned in a manner that set Evelynne's heart in her throat. "Knew there was summat strange about you. Now, let's see what you been hidin' all this time." He began kissing her, his breath hot and rank, as he fumbled at the front of her jacket. Evelynne's fingers closed around a wooden stake that had become jammed between her back and the brick wall. Ollie's hands were grasping at her shirtfront, when she swung the piece of wood up and clouted him sharply on the side of the head. He fell back with a bellow of pain.

"Ye little bitch!" he roared and came at her again, arms outspread. She caught him midbody this time, putting all her strength behind the swing. With a satisfying "Ooph!" he fell to his knees, and as she watched, wide-eyed, he tilted forward and toppled onto his face.

"Thank you, Edgar." She breathed a grateful prayer to the brother who had insisted she know how to use a quarter-staff. At the time, she believed his motives had been purely selfish—she was his only available sparring partner—but his lessons had served her well, just the same.

She looked down at the stake in her trembling hand, and cast it from her, beyond the prostrate form of Ollie Hooper. Allowing herself one last look at the walls of the pin factory, her late place of employment, she straightened her clothing and ran from the alley to find Gilbert.

"A roast fowl? For dinner?" She echoed Gilly's words. "Then we'd best make haste." She hurried along the street, Gilly trotting to keep up. Once they had turned several corners, she could at last put behind her the phantasm of an enraged Ollie Hooper emerging from the alley and staggering in pursuit.

"Slow down, Eve." Gilly tugged at her arm. "Mrs. Coop will hold supper for us."

Evelynne took a deep breath. "I'm just anxious to be home." *Well it's not really a lie.* She walked on at a more leisurely pace. "What's the occasion for the roast? Are we celebrating something or is Mrs. Coop just splurging, what with the enormous rent we pay her?"

The grin he gave her held a hint of mystery. "Well, it's not exactly a celebration. Mrs. Coop said I was the 'deuced, hexed mackerel'—whatever that is—and now she's in high fettle because you're both to go and have tea with the gentleman who rescued me—" He halted in midsentence.

"Stap me for a rattle-pated clunch!" he moaned. "I've so much to tell you, and now I've spilt the best part first."

"Rescued? Yes, I think you'd better tell me." This was his

sister's no-nonsense voice. "Who rescued you, and from what?"

As calmly as possible, and with far less embellishment than he had used to lace the tale when telling his brothers and Mrs. Coop, Gilly related the events that had transpired that morning outside the gates of Kensington Park.

"You jumped into an empty carriage and tried to stop two runaway horses?" She repeated his words, as if hearing them a second time would enable her already overloaded brain to fully absorb them. There was a quiver in her voice as she spoke, and Gilly quickly sought to reassure her.

"I doubt it was as dangerous as it sounds. I probably wouldn't have been hurt at all." He knew it for a lie even as he spoke, for the pair of highly bred chestnuts had been quite crazed when they bolted. But the last thing he wanted was to upset his sister. Something was troubling Evelynne; he'd seen it in her face as she hurried away from the factory, and the tale of his adventure was probably not what she needed to hear right now. He suddenly wished he'd never visited the park that morning.

At the time he had been drifting with the regular crowd of hawkers and pedestrians, just outside the park's south entrance, his eyes drawn to a fine pair of chestnuts, hitched to a light racing curricle. They were being walked in a circle by their groom, while their owner, no doubt, was part of a small group of gentlemen blowing a cloud on the pavement nearby.

It may have been a bursting balloon, a stray bit of paper, or one of those phantoms that can only be seen by equine eyes, but something spooked the pair. Gilly saw them rear up as one, screaming and pawing the air, and in the next instant, they had thrown off their groom. They swept toward Gilly, toward the park entrance, the harness reins still knotted to the railing.

"I know it was a daft thing to do." He hung his fair head and looked contrite. "But, Eve, all I could think of was those lovely bits of blood and bone, flying through the park to their doom."

"Not to mention any luckless people who got in their way," Evelynne pointed out.

"Well, that too, I suppose," he murmured. Evelynne knew that saving human lives had never entered her brother's thinking. Horses, especially blooded horses, were the current deities in Gilly's pantheon.

"And after you'd jumped into the curricle?"

"Then everything started happening very quickly."

"I daresay it would." He missed her wry smile.

Gilly continued with a bit more gusto. "I'd got hold of the reins, but the horses were having none of it. At least I was able to steer them, if not actually slow them down. I did manage to keep us from colliding with an old lady in a barouche—so you were right about the people thing—but then she started screaming like a banshee, and—whoosh!—we were off again, even faster than before."

He stopped and took hold of Evelynne's wrists, warming to his tale, in spite of his resolution not to distress her.

"What happened next was like a miracle, Evelynne. Quite out of the blue, this dark-haired chap on an absolutely ripping stallion comes pelting up alongside us. He gets his horse right up beside the wheeler and manages to turn us in a circle. My pair realize they've been bested, and they just slow down and stop, as docile as you please. He was a centaur, Eve! A veritable centaur! You should have been there."

Gilly was breathless, and a bit shaken by the retelling. He was suddenly feeling exactly like a young lad who had had a very frightening experience.

His sister saw the stricken look in his eyes and knew he was, at last, coming to grips with the reality of his misadventure. It had not been an auspicious day for the elder Marriott siblings. She put an arm over his shoulder and said, "What you did was quite brave, Gil. I'm very proud of you. Papa always said you were a fool for horses, but I don't think it's foolish to come to someone's aid. I hope the owner of the curricle was grateful."

"Lord, no!" Gilly pulled back from her encircling arm with a wicked grin. "He came roaring up the path, all round and red-faced and fit to burst, claiming I'd stolen his precious pair, and should be carted off to Newgate, forthwith."

"He never did!" Evelynne was incredulous.

" 'Pon my honor! He had me by the scruff, don't you know, and my gentleman, that is, the dark-haired man, jumped down from his horse and laid his riding crop smartly across the fat fellow's arm, and said, 'Unhand the boy, Babbage! That lad's saved your horses, and the curricle, as well. Furthermore, I do believe he prevented your beasts from flattening Lady Clavering, for which her husband, the earl, will most likely be grateful."

Gilly stopped his narrative to gauge his sister's response to this spirited rebuttal. "Wasn't he topping, Eve?" he coaxed. "Well, wasn't he?"

"Yes," she concurred, but a little remotely. "I rather suppose he was." She couldn't find it in herself to completely squelch his hero worship. Lord knew, Gilly had had little inspiration in that direction since the death of his brother. And since the loss of their parents, he had acquired an almost jaded manner. She was glad in her heart for the return of his boyish enthusiasm.

But, unlike Gilly, she chose not to focus on the stirring picture of a dark-haired man executing a daring rescue. Rather, it was the vision of a thirteen-year-old boy flinging himself into a dangerous situation, which had then quickly escalated beyond his control, that twisted her heart.

Evelynne was no fool—she knew he often missed his lessons, spending his time prowling the streets of the capital, mingling with the street vendors and dock workers. She knew where the occasional extra pence in their money tin came from. Gilly was quick to claim that he could look after himself, and she had found it convenient to believe him. But the incident in the park proved to her that such was not really the case at all. Gilly needed looking after. For the first time since leaving Devon, she allowed herself to doubt the wisdom of bringing her brothers to London.

"You're out of charity with me over this, aren't you?' he muttered, worrying his lower lip. "I daresay I deserve it if you rip up at me."

"I daresay you do." She cuffed him gently on the chin as they went up the steps of Number Twelve. "If only for frightening me half to death with your narrow escape. But there's more to it, Gil." She halted before the front door. "Kensington Park is halfway across town, and how you came to be there, I shan't even ask. But this wandering about has almost brought you to grief, and it must stop. Last week it was skinned knees when you fell down the cellar steps of an alehouse . . ."

"I was unloading beer kegs for the owner!" he protested.

"And the week before that, you fell into the river, and, no—" She held up one hand. "Don't tell me you were just helping to cast off a ship. I want you at home, with Josh and Jem."

"You're not my mother!" He was sullen and angry now, and Evelynne recoiled at his tone.

"Stop it, Gilbert! I've enough to worry about without forever wondering what scrapes you're getting into."

"I'm sorry, Eve, but I'm not a child anymore." Gilbert's voice was plaintive. He pulled himself up, until he was almost head to head with her. "I don't need lessons with the boys. I need to be doing something useful. If I could just find a job of some kind—I know we need the money."

Evelynne thought, *You have no idea, my boy,* but said only, "Your well-being is more important to me than any money you could earn. And you do need lessons to get on in life."

"But I've learned a great deal from being out in the city. You could say I was a student of people."

He bore such a look of earnestness on his face that she smiled in spite of herself.

"Nevertheless," she admonished him, "you've studied quite enough in *that* school. I want you to promise me you'll stay with Mrs. Coop during the day. And I'll try to find you a position of some sort, one that will keep you out of harm's way."

He nodded silently, eyes downcast.

"Cheer up, Gil," she coaxed, opening the door and ushering him into the hallway. "I'll start looking tomorrow. And for tonight, well, we've got roast chicken, and maybe cobbler for dessert, and," she added with a twinkle, "I'm bound to admit that your dark-haired gentleman was truly heroic. I am all admiration."

Gilly's smile lit the dark hall. "Oh, I just knew you would be, Eve, because above everything you're fair. I only hope he knows how splendid he was."

"As for that," she said, following him up the stairs to their parlor, "I don't doubt he's told every soul in his acquaintance, and is presently being made much of by one and all."

Chapter 2

Robert MacIntyre, Earl of Monteith, was weary of being weary. He leaned back against the plush, upholstered squabs of his coach, long legs crossed and set at an angle before him, and wished for the hundredth time that season that he could miraculously be delivered to his home in the Highlands. But the coachman drove inexorably on to yet another gathering of the *ton*.

His current visit to London was necessitated by one thing only—politics. Parliament would be in session in a few months, and he was a member of that august body. There were issues he needed to investigate in the capital city, issues that were vital to him, as a Scot and as a man of principle. He had spent the past weeks in the teeming capital, rallying influential friends, seeking out various cabinet ministers, and attempting to win converts to his sometimes unpopular causes.

But it wasn't the days passed in political machinations that were the cause of his restlessness; rather it was the evenings and weekends. His leisure time seemed filled with an endless parade of pointless entertainments—luncheons, nuncheons, soirees, musicales, masquerades, galas, garden parties, and balls. Yet these shallow gatherings often furnished him with opportunities to connect with important politicians. He could spar with a member of the opposition over the punch bowl, or win the support of a fence-sitter by dancing with his simpering daughter. He felt a need to continue the rounds of parties, if only to further the political career that he had only recently begun to hone, but which already had come to mean a great deal to him.

As the coach rocked and swayed through London's dark streets, the earl thought back to his first visit to the great city.

At the age of seventeen, just prior to entering Cambridge, he had come to London, much against his family's wishes, He had felt little kinship with the city or its inhabitants. He had been a tall, rangy youth, uncomfortable with his height. And he was set apart, more so, by the severe, dark clothing that bespoke his family's strict Puritan beliefs.

He sought out no members of the *ton*, attended no sporting events, joined no clubs. He did not drive a racing curricle through the town, or parade his horsemanship in the park—though he frequently did both at home in Scotland. And, aside from a few excursions to the more historical of London's many sights, he did little to acquaint himself with the town.

And though young Robert MacIntyre may have taken little heed of the great metropolis, the same cannot be said of London, for the town, or more specifically, its match-hungry mamas took a very great interest in him.

Through his Uncle Collum, the Laird of Monteith, he was heir to a Scottish earldom, a considerable fortune, and an imposing castle in the Highlands. As such, he was reckoned a matrimonial prize of very high order. A hopeful mama might certainly overlook his gangling limbs, his thatch of unruly black hair, and his perpetually scornful expression, for the considerations of title, money, and land.

Nearly fourteen years had passed, and in the intervening years he had grown taller still, but somehow his ungainliness had turned to grace, his dark looks had become compelling, and his infamous scowl was now aped by dandies from Pall Mall to Piccadilly.

After taking a first at Cambridge in medieval history, he had coerced his uncle, the then-sitting earl, into buying him a lieutenancy in the army, just in time for the Peninsular Campaign against Bonaparte. His brooding nature didn't win him any popularity contests at first, but his level-headedness and fierce courage made him an outstanding officer. He had risen to the rank of major, been co-opted to Wellington's staff after a French bullet shattered his shoulder, and was finally billeted out when his Uncle Collum went to his just reward.

The new Laird of Monteith congratulated himself on having survived the bloody Spanish war. But upon returning to London, he discovered his ascent to an earldom had greatly increased his marital marketability. He found himself in numerous skirmishes with ruthlessly determined matchmaking mothers. The French soldiers weren't a patch on them. He began to yearn for his old army life on the Peninsula. Being plain Major MacIntyre had had its distinct merits, and sometimes he heartily wished the earldom had gone to some other deserving soul.

There was, however, one positive aspect to his recent inheritance. As a peer of the realm, the Monteith was able to take a seat in the House of Lords. He knew there were men of aristocratic birth who saw nothing laudable in that goal. A few friends had even scoffed at his ambitions, laying odds that he'd be fully back on the town once the novelty wore off.

It hadn't worn off, though, and his enthusiasm had increased tenfold. Over the years he had come to reject his family's strict brand of Puritanism, but he still believed strongly that if a man had an opportunity to be an influence for good, he had damned well better use that influence.

"Another night of mixing politics with idle pleasure," he murmured to himself over the sounds of the city beyond his carriage window. On this particular evening he was bound for a small, informal gathering at the Marchioness of Endsleigh's town house, an event that he knew from long experience would be neither small nor informal. He would dutifully mingle with the cream of society, perhaps dance a little, and then play several very predictable hands of piquet with his very predictable friends.

Those friends of his misunderstood his distaste for their chosen style of living. A few of the braver ones even chided him to his face, calling him a "prosy Puritan." But it wasn't really the lazy indolence of their lives that troubled him, nor yet their casual amorality. It was the boring sameness of their daily routine—day blending into day, week blending into week, until the whole season was a blur. And when he was in their company for any length of time, he became lulled into a kind of complacent acceptance. How the wild Highlanders who had been his distant forebears would have hooted to see him tricked out in his fashionable clothing, his behavior so constrained by the society around him.

There were few moments anymore when he felt truly alive, truly invigorated. Of late, all those moments had occurred when he was attending the House of Lords. There was a cause he was championing at present that was of particular import to him— the land rights of tenant crofters in the Scottish Highlands. He would be opposing many great landowners, Scottish and English both—for a number of English peers held Scottish lands, acquired either through marriage or conquest—and he would need to convince them all of the merits of his appeal.

Once Parliament reconvened, he would be speaking on the matter, and he had taken great care to prepare his case well—too well perhaps. His chief opponent, Randall Skelton, a baron who was part of the prime minister's set, had started to make thinly veiled threats every time they were in company together. Lord Skelton owned numerous holdings in Scotland, and his feelings toward his tenants were anything but paternal. The earl had been investigating the baron's finances and had turned up some surprisingly unsavory dealings. Clearly the earl was making his opponent nervous. There was some solace in that.

The Monteith had powerful and influential men on his side, the most significant being Sir Robert Poole, the noted orator and reformer. But there were times when the earl felt sure that his cause was propelled only by the sheer momentum of his own beliefs. For regardless of his staunch supporters, it was he who held the reins of this unruly political juggernaut.

Reminds me of that daft, gallant boy trying to stop Babbage's runaway curricle, he thought with a twisted grin. He realized he was beginning to feel quite as daft as that boy, and a lot less gallant. He hoped he wasn't losing his taste for righteous causes. Was his ennui becoming so pervasive then?

"Perhaps I am getting cynical," he muttered sourly.

But, by God, he *had* felt truly alive that morning in the park, racing neck and neck with the runaway pair. And the youngster in the threadbare jacket hadn't given an inch. Who was he to lose heart, when a street child showed so much raw courage? His last thought before he entered the brightly lit doorway to Lady Endsleigh's mansion was a silent, earnest prayer. *God give Parliament a hundred men with the pluck of that lad, and we'll cure the ills of this nation.*

It was after supper that same evening, after the celebratory fowl had been consumed to the bones, while the two younger children played at jackstraws in front of the fire, that Mrs. Cooperall broached Evelynne on the matter of reparations to the earl. The landlady had sent Gilly off to an early bedtime, partly in light of his adventurous day, and partly so he would not be an impediment to plain speaking.

"Of course I agree that we should thank him," Evelynne concurred with her elderly friend's edict. "Nothing could be fairer than that. A note, perhaps a small gift . . . though I imagine earls lack for very little."

"Nonsense!" Mrs. Cooperall chided, dropping her tatting into her lap to better make her point. "We must pay a call on his lordship and offer our thanks in person." She shook a bony finger at Evelynne and admonished, "I fear the past months in that dreadful factory have made you forget your manners, and your dear mother — and though I only met her those few times at my school, I just know she was a dear person—would be quite dismayed. There is no excuse for neglecting your obligations. And make no mistake, you are obligated to the Earl of Monteith. You must never forget that you are of the quality, however come down in the world.

"Do you realize, Evelynne, that the earl took your brother for a common street child? Why, when he gave Gilbert his card, he offered him a job in his stable." She pulled the limp card from her reticule, where it had resided all day, offering its talismanic comfort, and held it out to the girl.

Evelynne had been woolgathering during the landlady's discourse. Mrs. Cooperall all too frequently lamented over the Marriott family's sadly fallen state—it was her favorite theme—but this was new territory.

"The earl offered Gil a job?" Evelynne leaned from her chair and took the proffered card.

"Yes. Can you credit it? And Gilbert the son of a knight of the realm and a don's daughter. To be set to work in an earl's stable . . ."

"Robert MacIntyre, Lord Monteith." Evelynne said the words aloud, but the dull throbbing pulse in her ears was suddenly all she could hear. *Robert MacIntyre. Robert MacIntyre.* It wasn't possible.

Evelynne stood up abruptly, tucking the card in to her breeches pocket. "I'm afraid I need to go out. I've got some things to think through. Just a turn around the square. I'll be back directly."

And before Mrs. Cooperall could utter a word of protest, Evelynne had swung her jacket off its peg and disappeared out into the hall. The sound of the front door closing echoed through the small house.

The landlady was too busy "tsk, tsking" with dismay to hear

the door open and close a second time. Jem and Josh heard it, though, and smiled secretively at each other. There was no end of astonishing things their two elder siblings could get up to.

Evelynne did, in truth, walk several times about the small, shadowed square that lay opposite Number Twelve. The September night was chill, but she didn't feel the cold. She still wore her work clothes, brogues and breeches, for she hadn't wanted to keep the others from their meal while she changed. Evelynne sighed. Not changing for dinner was yet another of Mrs. Coop's warning signs of fallen gentry. But now Evelynne was glad she hadn't put on one of her threadbare gowns. If she went through with the plan that was forming with desperate haste inside her head, her masculine disguise would be much more appropriate.

She still couldn't credit the name inscribed on the gentleman's card. It was the very same name that had burned itself into her memory during a time of great loss. Could it possibly be the same man? She knew she could dig through the trunk of mementos she had taken away from their farm in Devon and find the letters, just to make sure.

Edgar had been an indifferent correspondent while he was away fighting in Portugal, and the post from the war-torn Continent was equally unreliable. So it was by an unfortunate accident of timing that Edgar's last letter to his family arrived a good month after his demise on the battlefield. And for that reason, his words were doubly precious to his sister. She had sat and read that last epistle over and over, until her mother called it morbid, and threatened to burn the cherished note. Evelynne had packed it away, but the words were always there in her heart.

"We have a ripping new officer," her brother had written in his offhand manner. "He is dark as the devil, and quite stern to look at, can wither a subaltern at a glance, don't you know. But he fights like the Highlander he is and stands by his men on and off the field. There isn't one of us who wouldn't follow him to Hell and back . . ."

And then at the closing of his missive, he wrote, "We're in for some heavy fighting. The Frenchies are camped all over the next hill, but no one doubts Major MacIntyre will see us through. It's hard to credit he's in line for an earldom, for if anyone was born to follow the drum, it's our Lamb."

Evelynne always wondered how a man who was described as "stern" and "dark as the devil" should come to be called Lamb by his men. And Edgar hadn't survived the engagement at Busaco to clear up the mystery. But a great many men in his regiment *had* survived, so her brother's faith in his major had not been totally misplaced.

There had been a second letter, months after her brother's death, from the Major himself, apologizing for the delay in offering his condolences. It seemed he had been seriously wounded in the battle and had only just regained the use of his writing hand. He'd called Edgar "a lad after my own heart," and he wrote, furthermore, that he was "at the family's service for any assistance in their time of need."

The letter was brief, but sincere, without any military platitudes. It was clear that the man had come to esteem her brother in their time together, and that he, too, had suffered a loss when Edgar was killed.

It was signed, "Major Robert MacIntyre."

It was uncanny. Two of her brothers falling under the spell of the same man. If it was the same man.

And he had offered her family his assistance. Of course, now that the major had come into his inheritance, he was no doubt petitioned daily for handouts. But, Evelynne thought, recalling one particularly plaintive line in his letter, what she had in mind to deliver to the earl was more of a gift than a petition. It might serve, it just might serve.

With a clear sense of purpose for the first time in months, she turned from the square and headed rapidly for the High Street. The shops and stalls were shut up for the night, but a few horse-drawn cabs stood idly by, waiting for trade from the Gatekeeper Tavern.

She was a bit intimidated by the thought of traveling through nighttime London in an open carriage, so she approached a jarvey who was leaning upon the door of a rather scarred closed carriage. She told him her destination, and when he looked skeptical, she held up the shilling she carried in her pocket for emergencies. He waved her inside the cab, and climbing onto the box, he turned his rawboned horse in the direction of central London.

Neither he nor the cab's occupant saw the lithe shadow that detached itself from the side street and nimbly hopped onto the cab's wooden bumper. Gilly clung gamely to an unlit and rather rickety lantern sconce, and wondered where the deuce his sister was off to in the middle of the night.

The earl's carriage came into Cavendish Square at a leisurely trot and drew up in front of his town house. The second coachman leapt from his perch behind and opened the door to his master. It had been a short outing—the two coachmen had remarked on it with puzzled mutterings as they made their way home from Lady Endsleigh's party.

The Monteith emerged from his carriage and cast a look up at the clear night sky. He couldn't help thinking of the men who still fought in Portugal and Spain, camped out under that sky. He thought, too, of the crofters on his Highland estates, out hunting the red deer with their grizzled coursing hounds, under that same sky. But if Lord Skelton had his way, there would be far fewer crofters in Scotland; they'd be replaced by profitable flocks of Merino sheep. And if Lord-bleeding-Skelton continued unchecked with his penny-pinching economic policies, Wellington's army would end up underfunded, underfed, and under the guns of the French.

With an oath, the Monteith strode up his front steps. Lord Skelton had been all unctuous solicitude at Lady Endsleigh's party, his sibilant voice particularly ingratiating as he had taken the earl's arm and walked with him along the length of the card room. The earl seethed as he recollected Skelton's smooth offers of cooperation. Looking to work together for England's good was he! Looking for a compromise was he! And then when the earl had shaken off the baron's overly familiar hand with distaste, Skelton had pronounced ominously, "Then let it be upon your head, Monteith!" and stormed out.

Minutes later, the earl had taken leave of his hostess, pleading another engagement, praying he could get away before the strong desire to throttle the smug baron overcame him totally.

The Monteith pounded on his front door. "Damn the scoundrel's temerity! How dare he threaten me!"

The hall clock was just chiming half-after-ten when he was admitted by his imposing butler, Wenders.

"You are early home, my lord," Wenders said with his usual composure, as he took the earl's cloak and cane.

"Yes, well, unfortunately Skelton chose to make an appearance."

"Most unfortunate," Wenders murmured soothingly. He was

aware, as were all in the earl's London household, of his master's political affairs. Lord Skelton had taken on the aspect of Beelzebub himself to most of the staff in Cavendish Square.

The Monteith started for the stairs. Wenders gave a discreet little cough. "My lord?"

The earl turned. "This had better be good, Wenders, if it's to keep me from my brandy."

"If it please your lordship, there's an . . . um . . . young person waiting to see you. It being a coolish evening, I took the liberty of placing this person in the library."

"A stranger? In with my books?" Monteith's already ominous expression grew even darker.

Wenders opened his mouth to make some sort of explanation, but the earl was already springing up the stairs toward his private sanctum, the famous scowl in full force.

Evelynne was beginning to have grave doubts about her plan, once she was embarked upon its execution. She thought how vexing it was that a scheme hatched inside one's head could seem quite prudent, but then, once it was set in motion, it suddenly felt rash and even downright foolhardy.

As she racketed across the city in her cab, she squelched the hoptoads of doubt that descended on her. She stroked the earl's card absently, taking strength from the knowledge that if he was as good a man as Edgar and Gilbert thought him, her mission could not fail. She was committed to her course, if only in that she had no return cab fare. If she was going to walk home, half across London in the dark, it would only be after she accomplished her aim.

The cabman deposited her at the entrance to the Monteith's town house. As she turned to the box to pay him, Gilly sprang silently from his perch and disappeared into a narrow recess between the town house and its neighbor.

Evelynne gazed up at the imposing stone facade of the town house, a cool, pale blue in the moonlight. Geometrically placed windows with white lintels and a graceful fanlight over the door gave it a classical aspect that was both pleasing and precise.

"What must it be like to live in such a beautiful house?" she sighed. Her family's rambling farmhouse, though large and well built, had been not nearly as elegant as this. But it had been a good home, a happy home, even if it was now lost forever.

"All right, my girl," she chided herself. "No use mourning over what's in the past. Stop gawking and get on with it."

She marched resolutely up to the front door and gave a firm rap with the lion's head knocker. She could see through the fanlight over her head that the hallway was brightly lit, and it never occurred to her that a gentleman could be away from home, and yet leave all the lights blazing within.

So when Wenders opened the door, she was so stunned by the magnificence of his honey-colored velvet livery and his powdered bag wig, she thought for an instant that this must be the earl himself. But Gilly had referred to him as a tall gentleman, and his athletic rescue implied that he was most likely a young one as well. No, this must be a very high-class servant.

"Yes . . ." Wenders hissed regally.

"The Earl of Monteith, if you please, sir." Her voice came out in a husky whisper.

"His lordship is not at home." Wenders was already closing the door when Evelynne caught at its edge. Rather than engage in a wrestling match with this unkempt youngster, Wenders took a tiny step back.

"Please, sir," she entreated him with her eyes. "Lord Monteith did me a great service this morning, and I have come here to thank him in person."

"I will tender your thanks." He nudged the door an inch closer to its frame.

"In person," Evelynne insisted. She pulled the tattered card from her pocket and held it out so he could read it.

"Yes, well, *morning* is the proper time for thank-you calls."

She laid a hand upon his burnished sleeve. There was something melting about the solemn gray eyes that gazed into his, something Wenders was not quite proof against.

"Very well," he capitulated, pulling the door wide. "You may wait in the back parlor. But I cannot say when his lordship will return." He ushered her through an elegant hallway, embellished with classical statuary and delicate marquetry tables, to a small, dimly lit parlor. There was no fire in the low hearth, and the room was distinctly chilly. Evelynne shivered a little and went to sit on a straight-backed chair, folding her hands neatly in her lap.

"Thank you. I won't mind waiting." She looked up at him and gave a slight smile.

At that moment Wenders knew what it was that was so per-

plexing about his lordship's visitor, aside from such an unorthodox time of arrival. This young person was dressed as a
lad and, indeed, spoke as one, but now sat here in the back parlor as prim and proper as his Great Aunt Augusta waiting to receive Sunday guests. This wasn't a lad at all!

Wenders knew his master, though hardly a monk, was definitely not in the petticoat line. Wenders detected a mystery. And
like all servants, he quite loved a mystery, especially one in
which he could play an integral part. This would give him great
prestige at the downstairs dining table, perhaps even enough to
put his lordship's smug French chef, Emile, out of twig.

"Uh-hum." He cleared his throat. Evelynne looked up, startled. She was so preoccupied by her upcoming interview with
the earl that she hadn't realized the man was even still in the
room.

"It might be warmer in the library. His lordship keeps a fire
in there day and night. If I might show you up, Miss . . . that is,
Mr. . . . ?"

"Marriott," Evelynne stated. "Ethan Marriott, though I daresay his lordship won't know the name. I don't have a calling
card." She plucked at her pockets and gave an awkward shrug.

"The library?" Wenders coaxed.

"Oh." She jumped to her feet. "Yes, please, if it's warmer."

Evelynne followed him up the sleekly curved staircase to the
Earl of Monteith's holy of holies.

"Because," Wenders explained the next day to his eager audience in the kitchen, "I'd no intention of letting a young lady,
no matter how oddly dressed, sit forever in that damp parlor."

Unfortunately, he hadn't had time to voice those sentiments
to his master, who now threw open the library door with such
force that Evelynne dropped the book she was holding. She
spun away from the mahogany stacks, staring wide-eyed at the
tall figure striding into the room. *Dark as the devil.* Her
brother's words leapt into her brain as the man bore down on
her. *Can wither a subaltern with a glance.* God it was true! And
she was a fool!

The Monteith stopped only a few feet from her, his barely
suppressed rage almost shimmering in the air between them.
Evelynne had no way of knowing that she was not the cause of
the earl's displeasure. She felt light-headed and almost cried out
in alarm. He was more than intimidating, standing there before

her in his severe black evening clothes and brilliant white cravat, his hair and eyes darker than Hades.

"Pick it up." He spoke slowly, as if to a half-wit. Evelynne closed her mouth, swallowed, and bent to pick up the volume. It was a new edition, one of Mr. Scott's adventure stories, one she would have loved to read to her brothers. She smoothed the pages—the book had fallen open, but fortunately the pages were not bent—and handed it to the earl. He was immensely tall; Edgar had always called her a "Long Meg," and yet she barely topped the Monteith's shoulders.

"I'm very sorry," she said in a low voice, resisting the urge to curtsy. Instead, she gave a small, stiff bow. "You startled me, charging in here like that."

The earl didn't reply. She looked up at his glowering face and thought how odd it was that a man could wear such a horrid expression and still be so breath-catchingly attractive. His hooded eyes—gray or brown, she couldn't be sure—glared down at her, and his cheeks and lips were taut with displeasure. It was not unlike the expression her youngest brother displayed just prior to one of his infrequent but very provoking tantrums.

"I've obviously made a mistake, my lord." She lowered her head. "I'll not trouble you any further." He didn't move an inch as she went cautiously past him. She stopped in the doorway. "But I should warn you—it's no use throwing a tantrum if there's no one here to see it."

She wasn't quite into the hallway when he demanded, "What did you say?" in a voice like ice.

A fleeting grimace of victory crossed her face before she turned back to the earl. He wasn't through with her yet.

She walked back into the room, and he closed the door behind her. He went to a walnut sideboard and poured himself a large brandy. He looked a bit calmer as he raised one eyebrow and inquired, "A tantrum?"

"I know that look, you see," she explained. "I have three younger brothers."

"The devil you do!" He swung away from the sideboard. "And what's that to me?"

"Well, that's particularly why I'm here." Her eyes darted about the room, wanting to rest anywhere but on that scornful, strangely engaging face. She wished her carefully worded speech hadn't fled completely from her mind.

"It's about one of my brothers . . . I've come here on some unfinished business—"

He cut her off abruptly. "I don't do business in the middle of the night. Especially with havey-cavey fellows who cajole their way into my private rooms."

"I didn't cajole anyone!" she sputtered furiously, incensed by the unfairness of his accusation. "The man in the hall brought me up here."

The earl gazed at his visitor with bemused detachment. He had wished only that evening for something to shake up the boring sameness of his days. Now before him stood an infuriating ragamuffin in a ridiculously old-fashioned jacket, who had clearly cozened his toplofty butler, and who was somehow making inroads at coaxing him from his own foul humor.

"The man in the hall, indeed!" he mocked. Evelynne noted that his voice had taken on the hint of a Scots burr. "And in what distant kingdom were you raised, that you don't recognize a butler?"

"I was country bred." There was pride in Evelynne's voice. "We didn't need anyone to fetch and carry for us. We looked after ourselves."

"Oh, I see," he drawled. "You and your three brothers."

"Yes, that's right." She stood upright before him, clenching and unclenching her hands. "And though I may not come from a great city, I know poor manners when I see them. And I'm glad my brothers aren't here to witness how a titled lord treats his visitors."

She strode determinedly toward the door, and he was surprised and intrigued by the strength and resolve he saw in that angular face. His anger had all fled and was now replaced by an implacable curiosity.

"Softly, softly, halfling." He put his back to the door and held up a hand. "I'm country-bred myself, but my manners have always lacked, in spite of repeated beatings. I'm a Highland Scot with an uncertain temperament—which is almost a redundancy, you know. However, I don't make a habit of aiming my wrath at defenseless young lads."

"I'm not defenseless." Evelynne put up her chin. "And not so very young."

"No." The earl leaned toward her and studied her face with narrow-eyed intensity. "Nor yet a lad, I think."

Evelynne shut her eyes. The entire day had been a disaster,

culminating with the present indignity of being found out by the earl. She would burn her breeches the instant she got back to Camden Town.

"My manner of dress is my own business," she said at last, with as much composure as she could muster. "It serves my own purposes and implies nothing underhanded. I did not come here intending to mislead you."

He eyed her speculatively. "Oh, I assure you, I wasn't misled for long. You have a charming habit of looking up through your lashes. A trick few lads have ever cultivated. It's a dead give-away, I'm afraid."

"It's because you're quite tall," she explained a little lamely. "I expect most people have to look up at you."

He laughed. "Not through their lashes, they don't." The Monteith reached out and tipped her face back. "You might want to trim them if you need to keep up this impersonation 'for your own purposes.' " He ran the ball of his thumb gently along her eyelid. "They're very long and thick, these lashes, and not boyish at all, you know."

Evelynne felt a strange shivering that started somewhere at the base of her spine. The earl's hand lingered an instant on her brow. "Though you probably don't know. I gather you rarely look in the mirror, if the state of your hair is any indication."

Evelynne drew a hand through her tangle of curls to disguise her unease. The earl's whispering touch on her face had greatly disturbed her, and she was suddenly apprehensive.

"I think I was misguided to come here." She eyed the closed door longingly. "I regret the interruption, the lateness of the hour . . ."

The Monteith would not let her pass. He crossed his arms over his wide chest and grinned down at her.

"What, crying craven? I thought you were made of sterner stuff. We got off to a bad start, you and I. I've political foes who are seeking to discredit me. I was warned, even tonight, that such plots are afoot, and I'm afraid I mistook you for one of my enemy's little minions."

"Me? How could I imperil you?" Evelynne was surprised when he laughed outright.

"My dear, naive country mouse. Planting ladies in gentle-men's bedchambers to create scandal is a rather ancient ploy."

"And you thought that's why I'd come here?"

"Well, your disguise did gain you access to my private rooms."

"Yes, but this is your library, not your bedchamber." She felt herself blushing. "Well, anyway, it's hardly the setting for intrigue."

"My private study lies through that door." He motioned to a paneled portion of the far wall. "Any my bedchamber lies beyond that. So whether you were here to steal my papers or compromise my good name, you found the perfect location."

"You, sir, are starting at phantoms!" she said tartly. "How would I know where any of the doors in this house led to?"

"Well, if your accomplices had done their research—"

"My accomplices! Do I strike you as that sort of woman?" Evelynne's hands were at her waist. "Well, do I?"

Standing before him in her mismatched boy's clothing, slim and straight, with fire in her eyes and the bright stain of outrage on her cheeks, she looked the very antithesis of 'that sort of woman.' But the earl just smiled languidly and said, "It's rather too soon to tell."

He was rewarded for his taunting when she colored up even more. *How delightful!*

Evelynne tried to disregard the appreciative gleam in the earl's eyes as he reveled in her discomposure. The man was baiting her, and she had learned early in life, as the frequent victim of her brothers' jests, that the only way to deflect teasing comments was to ignore them.

"My lord," she began in what she hoped was a reasonably controlled voice, "it's true we have been at cross purposes since you came into the room. If we could just sit and speak calmly, I promise I will take up only a little more of your time."

Before the earl could respond, there was the sound of a great commotion in the downstairs hall.

"Evelynne! Eve!" It was Gilly's voice.

"What the devil!" The Monteith turned to the door as Evelynne flew past him and out onto the landing.

In the foyer below, Wenders and a rather willowy young footman were trying to restrain Gilly from racing up the stairs.

"She's my sister!" he gasped, twisting in their clutches. "I tell you I saw her come in here!" He strained against his captors, calling "Evelynne!" once more up the stairs. Then, seeing her pale face leaning over the polished banister, he stopped his thrashing about.

"Gil!" she cried out in dismay. "What ever are you doing here?"

"Rescuing you." His wide grin carried up to the second floor. Then his face grew serious as he recognized the tall man who had come to stand behind his sister. The gleam of battle faded from his eyes, to be replaced by an expression of solemn devotion.

"Oh, it's you, sir," he breathed, and then added, "sorry for all the racket."

The Monteith gazed down at the lanky boy in the ragged jacket, and then looked at the tall, slim girl in the worn coat who stood at his shoulder.

"Ah, it begins to make sense now." He beckoned Gilly up to the landing with a crook of his index finger. "Oh, it's all right," the earl called down to Wenders, who had started to accompany the boy up the stairs. "I believe I can handle the two of them myself."

"I will be waiting in the hall," Wenders muttered, straightening his wig and tugging at his disarranged livery.

"I am greatly relieved," the Monteith said dryly, and then ushered his two guests into the library.

He watched them in silence for some moments, hands clasped behind him like a stern schoolmaster. They stood before him shoulder to shoulder, one dark and one fair, but of a marked resemblance, nonetheless—the same angular faces, the same straight noses, an identical expression of watchful expectation in their eyes. And they were clad in similarly out-of-date clothing.

"I observe you both have the same tailor," he remarked, before returning to his brandy. "And to what do I owe this familial visitation?" He turned to Evelynne. "I presume this scamp, whom I rescued from a somewhat hazardous situation this morning, is one of your well-mannered brothers."

Evelynne was holding tight to Gilly's arm to keep from boxing his ears. This latest development had nearly overset her, and her breath was coming in shortened gasps. The thought that her brother had followed her through London's darkened streets was not to be borne. But she would deal with *him* when they were alone.

"Yes, my lord," she responded through clenched teeth. "This is my brother, Gilbert Marriott." Gilly gave a slight bow in the earl's direction.

"And are there any more of your numerous brethren lurking about my front door?"

"No," Gilly replied. "Only me. My sister didn't know I was out there; I followed her from our lodgings."

"So you knew she was coming here?"

"No, I jumped onto the back of her cab. It's a great trick—" He smothered a cry, as Evelynne pinched his arm in vexation. "Well, I do it all the time."

"Yes, I expect you do." Monteith tried to suppress his amusement, before addressing the sister. "And you, Miss Country Mouse, came here, I now gather, to thank me for my timely intervention on behalf of your brother."

Evelynne nodded. She finally had the opportunity to speak her piece, then discovered that she had lost her voice. Her throat was dry as tinder, and she couldn't quite catch her breath. The earl must think her a looby.

"And was that *all* you came here to say?" His brows rose together as he lowered his head.

"No." Her voice came out breathless. "That wasn't all." Her eyes beseeched him not to misunderstand.

The earl turned abruptly away from her, with a tight smile. "I thought not." He ran one hand idly along the back of a horsehair sofa. She had seen him earlier in the throes of a black Scottish rage, but his expression then hadn't frightened her as thoroughly as the cold, sardonic mask he now wore. He turned back to her, his dark eyes spearing her.

"Let me guess. You would have thanked me prettily for your brother's life, with a tear trembling on those wondrous lashes . . ." His voice was mockery itself, as he added, "Next time, Mouse, I'd suggest a gown and bonnet—men are much more susceptible to women in their *own* clothing. Hmm, let's see . . . then you would have hinted, just a tiny hint, mind you, that your family was in some financial distress. Does this scenario sound familiar? Does it?"

Evelynne gave a strangled mew. Gilly glared at his hero. "She needs something to drink, sir."

The earl flung a hand toward the tray of decanters on the sideboard. Unsure of which bottles held spirits, and which might hold water, Gilly poured two clear liquids together into a thin-stemmed glass, and returned with it to his sister.

As Evelynne choked down the fiery concoction, Gilly stood

foursquare before the earl and said, "I think it's fair to warn you, sir, she only gets like this when she's really, really vexed."

Before the earl could couch a reply, Evelynne stepped past her brother. The temporary vocal paralysis, brought on by Gilly's abrupt and unexpected appearance, had subsided. And, as the earl had earlier lashed out at Evelynne because he dared not free his hand with Skelton, she in turn now took him to task, venting her anger at Gilly, at Ollie Hooper, and at the whole tangled mess her life had become.

"You, sir, are mistaken in your arrogant presumption that I have come here to importune you. When my brother spoke of you today, I thought, this must be the most selfless of men, to risk his life for a stranger. But now, now that I have had the opportunity of meeting you in person, why . . . I take leave to tell you that you are the most ill-tempered, puffed-up, and suspicious man I have ever met!" She paused for breath, noting with satisfaction that the earl's cheeks were taut with anger. She took another swallow from her glass, and then laid it with a sharp snick on a side table.

"You have this night accused me of political intrigue, moral pandering, and now, you dare imply that I have come to your home to petition you for money!" She dragged his card from her coat pocket and with three vicious swipes tore it into bits. She cast the pieces at his feet. "So much for Major Robert MacIntyre!" she cried bitterly. Gilly stood white-faced, and still the earl said nothing.

"I had a gift for *you*." Evelynne's voice was low, but her words were crystal clear in the tense silence of the room. "A rather valuable one, in my estimation. Now, I don't believe you even deserve my thanks." She swung around to her brother. "Come, Gilbert, it's time we were home."

They went as one out onto the landing, and so didn't see the look of sudden awareness that crossed the earl's face as he murmured the name "Marriott." He tapped one finger against his lips as he gazed down at the scattered pieces of the calling card that littered the Aubusson carpet.

They swept down the staircase, Evelynne, head held high, and Gilly craning around to get a last glimpse of his idol, who had emerged from his library onto the upper landing. The earl regarded their departure with a curiously pensive expression in his eyes.

They passed the flabbergasted Wenders without a glance and

went through the elegant front door and out into Cavendish Square.

Gilly bided his time as they walked rapidly away from the Monteith's town house. He'd never seen his sister in such a rare temper, and he knew it was only a matter of time before she turned her anger upon him. Not but what he deserved a tongue lashing for following after her. Their relationship had always been based on trust. He should have insisted on traveling with her, rather than sneaking along in her wake.

It wasn't until they reached the corner of the square that Evelynne released her hold on his arm. He rubbed his elbow with a circular motion. She had a devilish strong grip for a girl.

"I don't suppose saying I'm sorry will wash." He cocked his head hopefully. "I was worried about you. Knew you were in a dither after work today. And then you went running off after supper without any explanation. I know I should have stayed outside the house, but when the earl returned home—well, I didn't know he was the earl just then—I waited some more, and you didn't come out . . . well . . . I thought that . . . you know."

"What?" Evelynne snapped. "That he was having his way with me? Oh, odious boy! Oh, odious man!" She shook her fist at the graceful town house. "That man wanted nothing from me but a target for his ill-humor. And now my head aches so." The alcohol she had drunk was just beginning to make inroads on her senses. Her pulse raced with anger, and yet she felt somehow fuzzy and slow, as well.

Gilly put his hand on her brow. "Steady, Eve, it's all right. I expect you're just not used to spirits."

She started to reply, when Gilly grew rigid and drew her quickly into the shadows of the square's elaborate wrought-iron fence. "Hsst," he cautioned, a finger to his lips. "It's that coach again."

"What coach?" She craned her head to look around him.

"While I was waiting for you, before his lordship got home, it was waiting opposite his door, with two men on the box. As soon as the earl's coach appeared in the square, they drove away. And now they've come back."

"Perhaps it's merely an acquaintance of the earl's?" She could clearly make out the dark conveyance that was parked across from the town house.

"Then why leave just as he arrived?" Gilly's logic was

sound. "I think they were waiting to see when he turned up. And then they went off to report to someone."

Evelynne mulled this over. "He did say he had political ene-mies, and told me they were plotting to discredit him. Frankly, Gil, I thought him wits to let."

"Well, what are we going to do?"

"*We* are going to walk back to Camden Town," she said, urg-ing him around the corner and out of sight of the mysterious coach. Gilly lagged. "It should take all of two hours," she con-tinued. "And we will each dwell on our respective sins—I will grapple with my impulsive nature, and you will focus on your habit of always being where you don't belong."

While Evelynne was speaking, Gilly observed one of the coachmen had climbed from his perch and was speaking with a figure in the doorway, undoubtedly Wenders.

"Please, Eve," Gilly whispered urgently. "Can't we stay till we see what's toward? He did save my life this morning."

She grumbled slightly, but nevertheless crouched there with him in the shadows and watched the scene that unfolded down the street. The coachman gave the butler a note, and he with-drew into the house. Five minutes later, the earl himself ap-peared on the doorstep, caped and booted, no longer wearing his evening finery. He crossed over to the coach and spoke with the driver, who had not yet remounted the box. To Evelynne's horror, there was a sudden outcry as the second coachman came up behind the earl and struck him twice across the back of his head.

"Oh, my God!" she cried as the earl sagged against the side of the coach. "He's been hit!"

"It's an abduction!" Gilly whispered fiercely. "I'll go rouse his servants—you wait here." And before she could protest, he had slipped across the cobbled street, and, hugging the shadows of the row houses, he made his way toward the earl's front door.

"Be careful, Gil," she mouthed the words.

She watched in stunned disbelief as the two coachmen now thrust the earl's inert body into the coach and quickly shut the door.

"Hurry, *hurry!*" she urged. The two fellows swung up onto the box. Gilly had not yet reached the earl's door as they whipped up their team and clattered straight toward Evelynne's corner.

"Oh bother!" she cried as the coach came even with her. The

horses lost their footing as they rounded the corner, and the coach slewed sideways, losing almost all its momentum. Evelynne ran into the street and leapt upon the rounded back of the vehicle, hoping foolishly that her added weight would cause it to halt, or at least slow down. Once the horses regained their footing, though, the coach surged forward, and Evelynne had no choice but to drag herself into the tarp-covered baggage well. It was either that or leap off the speeding vehicle.

She wondered if there was some divinely inspired reason why she and Gilly were fated to have the same adventure on the same day. As she arranged her long legs in the narrow compartment, Evelynne fervently hoped her brother had seen her mad leap onto the coach. With any luck, the Monteith's men would quickly come in pursuit of them.

But as the coach rattled out of Cavendish Square, Evelynne had a chilling thought—what if the odious earl was dead? His body had appeared so lifeless when the two kidnappers dragged him into the coach. For some reason, that thought twisted her insides into a painful knot.

"Please, God," she whispered fiercely, "let him not be dead."

Chapter 3

༄

In spite of her determination to remain awake and alert, the combined effects of the alcohol she had drunk in the earl's library and the swaying motion of the coach soon lulled Evelynne into a dreamless sleep. It was only when the coach had ceased its forward motion that she at last awoke. She was curled in the stuffy, cramped dankness of the luggage boot, and for some moments after awakening she could not think how she had gotten there. It was all because of the infuriating Earl of Monteith, she recalled with chagrin. He had gotten himself kidnapped—hit on the head and tumbled into this very coach. She earnestly wished she had stayed awake, for she had no idea of how much time had passed, or where in the whole of England she might be.

She cautiously raised one edge of the tarp that concealed her. It was still full dark, and the coach seemed to be in an open shed beside a stable. She'd apparently slept quite soundly through the removal of the earl's person and the unhitching of the team. Some accomplice she'd make!

She peeped through the tarp once more to make sure the stable yard was empty, and then hoisted herself out of the boot. She slipped to the ground, staggering slightly, for one leg was all pins and needles. She was in the side yard of a country hostelry. It appeared quite run down; the roof sagged, and its Tudor-style walls were darkened with soot and age. One guttering lantern lit the front yard, and above the doorway a weathered sign read, EEL AND BARROW. No one seemed to be moving about, either inside or out, though several of the downstairs windows showed light.

As she had seen her brother do in Cavendish Square, she crouched down and scurried for the shadows at the side of the inn. She waited, panting, beside a tall sticker bush. No alarm was raised.

Behind her an ivy-covered trellis rose to the second story. She was contemplating whether it would support her weight when a light appeared in the window above her head. She jumped back directly into the stickers, and then prying herself loose with a most unladylike oath, she looked up. She'd swear it was one of the coachmen who stood near the window above her. He faced slightly into the room, speaking to someone. She decided to take her chances with the trellis.

Fortunately, the ivy was thick and well grown, and furnished many handholds. It wasn't much more difficult than climbing an apple tree on her farm. She reached the second story and pulled herself up beside the lit window. She perched there, wrapping a tough strand of ivy about one hand to anchor her, and pulled a spray of green leaves loose from the stucco to screen her face as she peered into the room.

Three men were within. The earl lay in tumbled disarray upon a narrow bed just to the right of the window. He still wore his caped greatcoat, and there was dried blood on the pristine whiteness of his neckcloth. He looked so pale and still that she feared he was beyond her help. The other two men conferred beside the bed. The one nearest the window, a tall, lanky fellow with ginger-colored hair, was indeed one of the kidnapper/coachmen.

The second man was clearly of the nobility, for his fine clothing and air of consequence were unmistakable. She would have guessed his age to be somewhere in his early fifties, but the deeply etched lines beside his mouth and the dark pouches beneath his eyes made him appear older. His wavy brown hair was pomaded into a high pompadour, and his profile, as he turned to his confederate, was aquiline in the extreme. He was well set up, and wore a nip-waisted coat of deep purple velvet and smallclothes of lavender silk laced with silver. Not the usual patron of the Eel and Barrow, she'd bet her bonnet on that.

Though the windowpanes were made of thick, uneven glass, they were poorly fitted, and she was able to hear most of their conversation.

"Aye, reckon he'll be out for another hour or so," Tall Coachman was saying. "Had to have at him again just outside of Basingstoke. Raising a proper racket, he was. Must've spit out his gag. Sorry about all the blood. Alfie was a little free with his cosh."

"He'll survive," the gentleman in purple drawled. "No one's got a harder head than Monteith. And when he does awaken, stick to our plan. You're to douse him with spirits and keep him in a drunken state for the next two days. The landlord's been well paid to turn a blind eye. In two days' time, once the hue and cry to locate his lordship has reached a peak, some very influential gentlemen will discover him here . . . in the arms of a rather notorious courtesan."

"But gentlemen always sport with lightskirts. Nothing so dicey about that." Tall Coachman sounded puzzled.

The man in purple gave a sneering chuckle. "Oh, but our dour Scot has a reputation beyond reproach. There's never been the breath of scandal attached to his name. But after this, his pious family will shun him, and his so-righteous political views will be seen as hypocrisy." Even through the wavy glass, Evelynne could detect the gloating expression on the gentleman's face.

"Just as you say, m'lord. We'll not let him outen our sight."

"See that you don't." He tapped the gold head of his walking stick upon the tall man's chest. "You wouldn't want to disappoint me."

They walked to the door, and Evelynne could no longer hear their words, though they spoke for several moments more. Then the gentleman left the room, and the coachman came to stand at the window. He leaned to peer out, and Evelynne almost lost her hold as she swung back away from the lighted square. She scrambled below the sill, hoping that he wouldn't swing open the casement and look down, for they would be quite nose to nose. She hung gamely on, fighting to gain a foothold in the vine.

Below her in the stable yard there was a clattering sound, and she watched over her shoulder as a pair of matched grays, harnessed to a smart racing curricle, were led from the stable by a short man who looked like he might be Alfie, the second coachman. The carriage passed directly below her perch, but fortunately her dark jacket and the thick sprigs of ivy helped to camouflage her against the side of the inn.

"Drat you, Gilbert," she breathed. "You should be having this adventure, not me. I should be home in my bed in Camden Passage, dreaming of our farm and of lovely gowns. I'd even settle for dreaming of the pin factory—anything not to be hanging here in midair against the wall of a hedge tavern, wondering how I am to rescue an unconscious earl." She blinked back her tears of frustration. This was no time to get weepy—she needed all her wits about her.

The question that kept spinning through her head as she clung there, unable for the moment to go up or down, was how she had even come to this pass. Was it because she somehow still felt obligated to the earl for rescuing her brother? But that feeling of obligation did not explain the blind sense of urgency that overcame her in Cavendish Square. What had compelled her to leap onto a moving coach? Nothing could explain that. And yet, it was by far the strongest impulse she had ever felt in her life.

And where were Gilbert and the reinforcements? Surely, her brother had roused the earl's people in time to send someone in pursuit. Had the coachmen eluded their pursuers? Until help arrived, she'd have to come up with a plan of her own.

There were indistinct voices at the front of the tavern, and she watched as the gentleman in purple tooled his carriage out of the stable yard. Alfie apparently didn't travel with him, for he drove off alone, most likely heading back to London, though Evelynne could only guess in which direction that city lay. So now she had both of the kidnappers to contend with.

The tall coachman's voice sounded above her head. "Well, his bleedin' lordship's gone at last. Now for a bit to eat an' a nice pint of ale." His shadow moved away from the window, and she waited a minute, then crept up for a look. He was gone.

Without regard for the consequences, she caught the window ledge and pulled the casement open. Thank God, it wasn't latched. With a little grunt she boosted herself up onto the sill. This was definitely Gilbert's adventure she was having!

She climbed in, pulled the window partially shut behind her, and went swiftly to the door. The key was still in the lock. Tall Coachman hadn't even bothered to secure his charge. She turned the key—that would at least give her a chance to escape if they returned any time soon.

The chamber was lit by a branch of tallow candles. She removed one and went to examine the Monteith. He lay unmoving, his face drawn and pale. She laid the back of her hand against his throat. His pulse was rapid, but strong. She probed his head for wounds. High on his left temple there was an ugly swelling, and his crown bore another lump, the size of a walnut. But it was a ragged tear over his right ear that was the source of all the blood on his neckcloth. At least it had stopped bleeding, for her fingers came away dry from the wound. It needed to be cleaned, though. A washstand with a fly-specked mirror stood against the opposite wall; it held a basin of water, but no face cloth or towel.

She studied the earl a moment, then gently lifted his head from the dingy pillow and carefully unwound his neckcloth. Two yards of fine Egyptian linen, a bit bloodstained, but it would do nicely. First she made a small tear in it with her teeth and rent it in two, forming one of the strips into a compress.

Holding the small basin in her lap, she sat beside him and dampened the linen pad. He drew a ragged breath as she applied it to the swelling on his temple, and he actually groaned when she started to clean the cut over his ear.

"Poor, grumpy Monteith," she chided him in a low singsong voice as she rinsed out the cloth and reapplied it. "Poor, rude, grumpy—"

"Enough!" A hand reached out and caught her wrist in a firm grip. His eyes were open, and he was gazing at her as if she were the Fiend Incarnate. His eyes were blue, she noted almost absently, so dark they looked like obsidian in the candlelight. "I was right," he rasped. "You were part of the conspiracy."

"Oh, fiddle!" Evelynne snapped. "If you start on that again, I'll go right back out the window and leave you to fend for yourself."

He winced as she applied the compress to the back of his head. "Then how do you explain being here? How do you—aah!"

"Hurts, doesn't it?" she said a little vengefully. "You're bleeding, and probably concussed, and there are two very nasty men close by who wouldn't mind adding another lump to your skull. So if you'll keep quiet for the moment, I'll explain everything when we get clear of here." *If we ever do.* She wrung out the compress one last time, and, folding it neatly into a square, she placed it over the ragged cut, then bound it in place with the dry strip of linen.

Suddenly, there was the sound of the doorknob turning. It jiggled harshly several times. An oath rang out from the other side of the door, and then heavy footsteps retreated down the hall.

"Unlock it," the earl whispered urgently. "And then get under the bed. They'll think the latch was just jammed. Do it!"

Without demur, Evelynne went quickly across to the door, unlocked it, and then after pushing the basin hastily onto the washstand, she scrambled under the low bed, refusing to imagine what sort of unwholesome creatures might lurk in such a place.

"What about your bandage?" she hissed up at him. "They'll know someone's been here."

"Don't worry. I'll cover it with the pillow." He paused and then chuckled weakly. "I'm a very restless sleeper. But you wouldn't know about that."

Dear God, she thought, the blows to his head must have addled him.

Fortunately, only one of the kidnappers returned—Alfie, she believed, for his voice had a higher pitch than Tall Coachman's.

"Still sleeping, my lord?" he quipped. "I thought you'd gone and locked me out. Had to fetch the passkey from below. But here you are, still snug in yer bed, and me with nothing to do but keep a watchful eye on you." He pulled a wooden chair up beside the bed, propped his feet on the edge of the mattress— Evelynne heard the bed frame creak—and within minutes was sawing wood, with great honking gusts.

The earl's hand appeared on the other side of the mattress, and he motioned her to come out. She pulled herself from under the low frame and sat up, rubbing the dusty feathers of cobwebs from her hair. The Monteith was certainly seeing her at all her best moments.

"Try to get out now," he whispered. "While he sleeps."

"Not without you." She shook her head.

"You can't help me alone—find a magistrate, a vicar—anyone." He closed his eyes, face pinched with pain, as though the effort of speaking was too much for him.

"No," she insisted. "I haven't a clue where we are, and it's hours yet till daylight. And you need looking after." She said more softly, "These men mean to harm you . . . oh, I can't go into it now. We need to get away from here."

"Where?" With a grimace, he propped himself up on one arm and leaned toward her; their faces were now only inches apart.

"The coach that brought you here—they'll never look for us in there."

"And do I go out the window, or down the stairs into my enemies' waiting arms?"

Evelynne knit her brows; even half-concussed, his lordship had a logical brain. "No, you're right. We can't leave this place till you're in better fettle. I'll see if there's some place in the inn where these scoundrels won't find us. We can wait until tomorrow night and slip out after dark—"

Alfie mumbled something in his sleep, gave a few staccato snores, and shifted in his chair. The Monteith's hand was instantly on Evelynne's mouth, his eyes locked with hers in alarm. They waited unmoving for several minutes, but Alfie didn't stir again. The earl drew his hand slowly from her mouth; it felt almost like a caress. Her heart was thudding, and she prayed it was Alfie's restless sleep, and not the earl's touch that made it pound so.

"Go, then." He fell back against the pillow. "I'm damned if I can make you see reason."

With a stealth that would have done Gilly proud, she glided to the door, opened it without a sound, and slipped into the hall. She had a momentary fear that Tall Coachman might be camped out in front of the door, but the hall appeared quite empty. A front window on the stair landing shed some milky light into the corridor. Evelynne tried to recall the layout of the inn from her sojourn outside, and she remembered there were three windows along the second story. Three windows outside, and yet four doors inside along the hall. She tiptoed to the farthest door in the row. She detected the faint odors of camphor, lye soap, and starch. She held her breath as she turned the knob—the door opened easily into a long narrow space.

In the inn's heyday, it had no doubt been used solely as a linen closet; a large press banked one wall, but it had since become a catchall for brooms, mops, carpet beaters, and pails—which suited her needs to perfection.

It the semidarkness, she carefully cleared a path to the rear of the closet, and there she made a space for the earl to lie down. She pulled some sheets and a blanket from the shelves beside her, making a pallet along the back wall. Then she took one more sheet, threadbare like the others, easily tore it into strips, and swiftly tied them together.

Carrying her makeshift rope over one shoulder, she sidled back to the earl's room, praying that Alfie slept on. He was tipped back precariously on his chair, but the regular, guttural snores attested to his continued cooperation.

The Monteith saw her affirmative nod and tried to sit up. She moved quickly to his side. "Stay a minute." She settled him back against his pillow. With cautious haste she attached one end of her sheet-rope to the back leg of the bed, and then stepping carefully around the sleeping Alfie, she snaked the other end out the open window.

"You're not the only person with a brain, Mr. Robert MacIntyre," she congratulated herself. And now to get the earl away from this room.

He had managed to sit up and swing his legs over the side of the bed. But it was clear he would be unable to rise without her assistance. She knelt beside him.

"Let me help you," she whispered against his ear. "I'm very strong, and it's not far, just down the hall."

"If I fall, he'll wake up . . ." The Monteith's voice was strained.

"If he wakes up, I'll strangle him with that rope." She grinned at her own ruthlessness and at his surprised expression. Placing her shoulder beneath his arm and, holding tight to his waist, she levered him off the bed. She felt him stagger, and then regain his balance. Then they were miraculously across the room. She'd left the door unlatched; they went through it and out into the hall. She paused a minute, shifting the earl's weight a little against the wall as she silently turned and shut the door. He watched her with bright, fevered eyes, noting how gracefully she moved in the semidarkness, amazed at how capable and sure she was.

"Who are you?" he breathed as she slipped beneath his arm and coaxed him along the hall.

"I'm not sure anymore," she said truthfully as she guided him into their new sanctuary.

Evelynne settled him on the makeshift pallet and pulled a blanket over his inert form. "Are you comfortable, my lord?" She waited a moment, but there was no reply, only the sound of his even breathing.

He'll do, she thought, at least for the time being. Now it was time to do some foraging in the kitchen, before the chambermaids were about.

The servants' staircase was just opposite their closet. It was a narrow sidewinder with rickety stairs. Evelynne followed it

down, missing the last three steps in the darkness, and pitching
onto the slate floor of the kitchen. She picked herself up and
thanked God she hadn't broken or sprained anything in her
headlong tumble. All she needed was to get injured, and then
they'd really be in the basket.

She didn't dare light a candle for fear of rousing anyone, but
the banked fires from the hearth shed a sufficient light for her
to examine her surroundings. It was remarkable how acute her
night vision had become in the last hour.

The kitchen table was empty, except for a large breadboard,
but there were several doors leading off the room, and she suspected that behind more than one of them there was food.

She found a rush basket on a sideboard and soon had it filled.
She took a loaf of dark bread and a round of cheese from the
larder, a jar of preserved peaches from the keeping room, and a
small jug of what she hoped was cider from the earth cellar. She
also pulled a pair of tallow candles off the rafter hook where
they hung, and added a small tinderbox, one of several on the
hearth mantel, to her collection.

She climbed back up the stairs with extra caution and
checked the corridor thoroughly before entering the utility
closet. Once inside, she placed a rolled sheet at the base of the
door to prevent any light from spilling out, and lit one of her
candles. The Monteith was sound asleep, sprawled along the far
wall, his blanket tossed half off. Once the maids started moving
about they would have to stay tucked at the back of the space,
behind a barrier of mops and brooms, but for now he could
sleep comfortably stretched out.

Evelynne slid down beside him, laying the basket at her feet.
Resting her chin on one hand, she gazed down at her charge. In
the flickering candlelight, she could see a few strands of white
hair at his temples sprinkled in with the black. If anything it
made him look even more attractive. She tucked the tangled
blanket under his chin and sighed, noting the fine planes of his
pale face, and the high Celtic cheekbones, which were now a
little flushed with fever. In repose, his face had an almost austere beauty. She'd never been this close to such a strikingly
handsome man before. It was quite unsettling.

His lips were slightly parted, and she heard each swift intake
of breath, followed by a long, even exhalation. Jemmy breathed
just like that when he was in a totally relaxed sleep. *Jemmy*. His
image came to her with a sharp pang. *And Josh and Mrs. Coop*.

It seemed as though a lifetime had gone by since she left them in their cozy parlor. And Gilly—was he dancing with his usual impatience, anxious that his sister hadn't yet been found? Had he vexed the earl's butler quite to distraction? Had he even gotten into the earl's town house?

No, Eve, don't think like that, she cautioned herself. *He's an important man. Someone must be looking for him.*

She broke off a bit of bread and cheese and nibbled them to distract herself from such self-defeating thoughts. She swallowed a measure of cider from the jug—it was good home-brew—and wondered how long it would be before the chambermaids began their morning rounds.

Perhaps half an hour had passed when she heard the raucous crowing of the stable rooster.

"My lord?" Evelynne shook the earl gently by the shoulder. "My lord, you must wake up."

He stirred a little under her hand, and then his eyes opened. He regarded her with a bemused expression.

"Still here?" he asked hoarsely.

"Of course we're still here," she said, putting her food back into the basket. "Where else would we be?"

"No," he said. "I meant *you're* still here. Not gone for help."

"No, and I don't intend to. You're in no state to be left alone."

He gazed up at her and said ruefully, "I'm glad my officers on the Peninsula were better at following my orders than you are."

"Well, no doubt you were in better shape to be giving orders," she retorted.

"So you're taking advantage of my feeble state?"

"You may think what you like, my lord," she sniffed, and started piling brooms and mops in a haphazard jumble, which would, with any luck, keep them hidden from sight.

"Now, you'll have to rearrange yourself." She moved the food basket aside. "We both have to fit back here if this hiding place is to prove any good. Can you sit up?"

She crouched beside him and helped shift him into a sitting position. He groaned as her fingers gripped his right shoulder. She snatched her hand away. "Oh, I'm sorry. Did they hurt you there as well?"

He winced slightly, leaning back against the wall. "No, that's an *old* wound."

"Good heavens, you are in a state!" She shook her head disparagingly, but then grinned across at him. "I'd no idea what I was taking on."

"I'm grateful for all compliments," he drawled, grinning back at her. "I see you've done some foraging." He motioned to the basket; she held it up for his inspection. "Not bad. Not bad at all. Perhaps you might not have been such a liability on the Peninsula, after all."

"And I'm also grateful for all compliments." She gave a little bow with her head, partly to hide her blush, for the earl's idly spoken compliment had pleased her greatly. "Would you like something to eat before I put out the candle?"

"Just something to drink." He took the jug from her hand and raising it to his lips, he took several swallows. "God, my head feels like blazes." As he spoke, he rubbed at his bandage with the palm of his hand.

"I know," she said gently. "But you can go back to sleep, once we get ourselves arranged. Can you tuck your legs up—it's a pity they're so long." She watched with amused exasperation as he tried with little success to reduce the amount of space he took up. "I fear our hiding place was meant for a man of normal height."

"In faith," he said, with a dry chuckle, "you're the first woman to complain of my size."

She disregarded his comment and critically observed the layout of the small space. "If you put your legs beneath the lower shelf . . . and slide forward." He did as she suggested, swinging around so he was parallel to the back wall, tucking his booted feet under the linen press.

His back was a foot or so from the side wall, and he turned to her with a frown. "Damn, I'm afraid I can't stay like this for very long. It's hellish not being able to lay my head down."

"It's all right," she said softly as she slipped into the space behind him and turned slightly so that she rested against the side wall. "Here." With gentle hands, she guided him back until his head was pillowed against her shoulder. "Better?"

"Mmm," he sighed. "Much better."

"Do you need anything else before I put out the light?"

"Sleep," he murmured, shifting against her. "Just some sleep . . ."

Evelynne snuffed the candle and set it beside her. She pulled a dark blanket over their heads, the better to conceal them in the shadows.

"Not going to suffocate, are we?" His voice, muffled against her jacket, sounded almost peevish.

"I expect we'll survive," she assured him dryly, then added, "but I must say I find it incredible, my lord, that they ever let you into the army, and that having done so, that they won any battles at all!"

He made no reply, but she felt the laughter rumbling deep in his chest. Oh, he was a trial, all right!

Evelynne slept for the second time that long and arduous night with the Earl of Monteith against her side, his head heavy upon her shoulder, his upper body wedging her into the corner. Yet she slept soundly, deeply, having dozed off with an inexplicable sense of contentment and security. It was not unlike the feeling she had when she was safe at home with her three brothers.

But when she awoke perhaps an hour later, with the earl's head lying now upon her breast, and her hand curled against his cheek, she realized the feelings this man aroused in her were anything but sisterly.

He was arrogant and moody, short-tempered and suspicious, too tall, too dark, and too good-looking by half. But when his eyes gleamed in humor, or he offered up his rare smile, why, she imagined, she too might follow him to hell and back.

And while he might now be injured and weak as a kitten, it did not alter the realization that it was the supple, muscular body of a soldier that lay in her arms. And when he was feeling more himself—by that very evening she hoped—he would be a man to be reckoned with.

She felt his brow with her hand. It was quite warm, but that might only be because of the blanket above their heads. She hoped he wouldn't turn feverish, for if he started to cry out, they would surely be discovered.

She wondered what was happening with his two kidnappers. They had most certainly discovered his escape by now. But she had heard no outcry or alarm raised—no sounds of anyone searching the rooms. She hoped her subterfuge with the sheet rope had fooled them into thinking his lordship had gone out the window, and would keep them from searching inside the inn.

The fate of the two coachmen was revealed to her quite soon. There was the sound of a door opening, followed by the chattering voices of two chambermaids as they collected their cleaning tools.

"Oh, Polly, ye missed all the fuss this mornin'. Them two Lunnon fellows mislaid their gentleman friend last night, ye know the one they was supposed to be watchin' over? He scarpered while the little fellow was asleep. Went out the window, 'e did, on a bedsheet!"

Unsure if the earl was awake or not, Evelynne covered his mouth with her hand, lest he make a noise in his sleep. At least the blanket seemed to be an effective camouflage, for the maids continued their gossip, completely unaware that they had a most interested audience.

"Went out the window, did 'e?" Polly chortled. "Lucky 'e din't land on his noggin, he were that drunk last night. Couldn't barely stand."

"And don't *I* know it! I helped the tall, redheaded fellow get 'im up the stairs and into 'is room. 'E were that grateful, I can tell you."

Polly gave a sly titter. " 'Ow grateful were he? And why wasn't you in your bed last night, my girl?"

Her companion sniffed. "Not that it's anybody's business, but we did have us a little visit in that great, empty coach he come in—shared a pint o 'ale wiv me, 'e did, till the little fellow came to fetch 'im."

"Shared a pint o' ale, eh? Oh, Angie, you're a rare'un. I ain't never heard it called *that* before!"

With a clatter of pails and a burst of raucous giggling, the two maids moved on to their chores, shutting the door firmly behind them.

The earl pried Evelynne's fingers from his face and said languidly in the dark, "You probably shouldn't have heard that. In spite of your unorthodox manner of dress, I suspect you were gently reared."

"Oh, pooh." Evelynne was dismissive. "Our maids were forever saying bawdy things to each other. I'm not some little milk-and-water miss, you know."

"Yes, I don't know how I keep forgetting," he said, settling himself a little more against her, as if he were totally unaware that he was now lying in her arms. "You are country-bred, I recall. I also recall you saying that you had 'no servants to fetch and carry for you' and that you looked after yourselves."

"I may have exaggerated," she said hesitantly. "We did, of course, have dairy maids, farm lads, and such . . ."

"And such?"

"But no butler," she assured him.

"Well, that's all right then." He craned his head up, as if seeking her face in the dark. "Speaking of butlers, do you think you could tell me what transpired since Wenders had the bad sense to bring me that redheaded fellow's note?"

"Are you feeling well enough, my lord? It's a rather confusing business. If you're headachey or anything, it might make you worse."

"Of course I'm headachey," he growled. "I've been hit on the head three times at last count. And what's making it worse is not knowing who is responsible. So if you'd get on with telling me, instead of behaving like a damned coddling female . . ."

He felt her tense beneath him and was instantly contrite.

"Gad, I'm sorry. My sergeant always said I was the worst patient."

"We'll have to trade stories, he and I," she said tartly. "But you're no crankier than my brothers when they're ill, so I expect I'm proof against the worst crochits."

"We'll see," he murmured. "Perhaps some food might help."

"Well then, you'd better sit up." She shifted under his not-inconsiderable weight.

Regretfully, he raised his head from the soft cushion where it had lain, wondering how such a slim-looking girl could have such a delightful bosom. He shrugged off the camouflage blanket as she lit the candle. Sitting upright against the wall, the earl proceeded to attack Evelynne's store of food. She sat shoulder to shoulder with him, watching with satisfaction as he ate. A man who could muster such a hearty appetite had to be on the mend.

She told him all she knew of his abduction and the conversation she had overheard between the gentleman in purple and Tall Coachman.

"A man in his middle years, you say, with a beak of a nose, and ridiculous high hair?" he asked, breaking off a piece of cheese. She nodded. "Did you see the crest on his carriage?"

"No. But he was driving a racing curricle, with matched grays, a pair, not a team."

"Ah, you truly are your brother's sister," he pronounced. "Most females wouldn't know a curricle from a coal wagon. But it's Skelton, as I feared."

"Who?" She reached over his arm for a slice of peach.

"Randall Skelton. Baron Skelton, actually. He's a rather dissolute member of the prime minister's set. Came into a deal of Scottish land through his mother, and now he's become one of my chief opponents in Parliament. He warned me only last night that I'd incurred his anger."

He sampled a peach and then held the glass jar up before him. "These are really quite tasty. You, my girl, are a great little forager."

She bent her hand to lick the sticky peach juice from her fingers and to hide her embarrassment. It was most peculiar that when the earl railed at her, or even when he was rudely sarcastic, she never lost her footing, but let one kind word pass his lips, and she blushed like a schoolroom chit. It was most confounding.

"Do you think the kidnappers have sent word to him that his quarry's gone to ground?" she asked.

He thought a moment. "If they know what's good for them, they'll keep Skelton abreast of every development. He's got a long reach and a longer memory. Better to confront him with their failure than to run from a botched job."

"That doesn't bode well for us," she observed. "If they've notified Skelton, that means we'll have another man to deal with."

"At least one more," the earl concurred. "Skelton may bring in other reinforcements, Alfie and Company having proved rather unreliable."

"Then there may be a small army on your trail," she said with dismay.

"Yes," he said, taking her hand in his. "But because of your clever plan of misleading them with the bedsheet, we haven't left any trail."

"My clever plan, indeed!" Evelynne grumbled, snatching her hand back from the earl. "If you'd followed my first plan, we'd have been hiding in the job coach when the coachman and his obliging chambermaid came along."

"I'm sure there was room for four." The earl stifled a laugh as she pinched his arm. "But in truth, we owe that young woman a debt of gratitude—if she hadn't distracted the redheaded fellow, we'd have had to deal with him, as well as the slumberous Alfie."

"I suppose," she agreed dubiously. "But it all seems very precarious to me. I'd no idea luck played such an important part in outwitting one's enemies."

He put his head back against the wall. "Wellington used to say, 'A wise man makes his own luck.' " He chuckled. "Or a wise woman, as the case may be." His voice grew serious as he searched her face. "Miss Marriott . . . I don't even know how you are called."

"My name is Evelynne," she said, unable to look away. His eyes, so dark in anger, were now the color of gentians.

"Evelynne, then, if I have your leave to use that name. I was horridly rude to you last night. I misread your gratitude, like the uncouth Scot I am. But before God, there's not a woman I know, nor yet I think, a man, who would have done for me all that you have. You may toss my gratitude back in my face, as I did to you last night, and I wouldn't blame you, but you have it nonetheless." His eyes held hers. "Evelynne, I'm beginning to think that *you* are my luck!"

Oh, this is dreadful, she thought as tears welled up in her eyes. She dashed them away with the sleeve of her jacket and said in what she hoped was an even tone, "I accept your apology, my lord. That was very nicely said." And then she added, "Especially coming from a man who is an uncouth Scot—"

"And headachey," he pointed out, his eyes alight.

She laughed. "Yes, that too. Only I wonder you can joke at such a time, my lord."

"Robbie," he said. "My friends call me that. Can I count you my friend, Evelynne?"

"Yes, my lord . . . Robbie." It felt very dangerous to be using his given name; somehow it lessened the vast distance between them. "But you haven't answered my question."

"What? How I can joke? It's a soldier's trick. My men were positively boisterous on the Peninsula. It helped them get past the strain of being in constant danger. But as for me, I'm usually much too serious—they call me the 'dour Scot' in London, you know. But you probably don't know, not being part of that rackety bunch of do-nothings called the *ton*."

"No," Evelynne said with a small sigh. "I'm certainly not part of the *ton*."

The early took her hand between his two. "And a good thing,

too. Society misses are particularly bad at leaping onto moving coaches, climbing in windows, and foraging for food. In fact, they're good for very little."

She disregarded his caustic remarks, for she knew beyond a doubt that belittle them as he might it was precisely one of those society misses he would wed someday. And by then the farm-bred factory girl who had rescued him would have long faded from his memory. She gave another small sigh and gently slid her hand from his grasp.

"We'd best put out the candle before the maids come back with their mops. And we should rest—I suspect we may have quite a distance to cover tonight before we find any assistance—this area appears quite remote."

Sensing her change of mood, the earl didn't consider resuming their former sleeping positions. Instead, he shrugged himself into the corner beside the linen press, opposite where Evelynne sat. She snuffed the candle and pulled he blanket once more over their heads.

The Monteith tried to sleep. However, his persistent headache and the closeness of the air beneath the blanket kept sleep at bay. His neck was at an awkward angle, and he had a cramp in one leg. He thought longingly of how he had awoken with the gentle swell of Evelynne's breast beneath his head. Of how her soft hand curved along his cheek. Of how comforting it felt to lie in her arms.

He checked his thoughts. The blows to his head must have unsettled his brain.

Well, if he couldn't sleep, he could at least pass the time trying to formulate a plan of escape. First thing, they needed to find out where they were. They couldn't have traveled more than thirty or forty miles out of London, at the most . . .

. . . *She really is quite lovely, though I doubt she even knows it. I've never met a woman who is less self-conscious. But why the devil is she dressed like a boy? I'd meant to ask her that— and about her connection to Edgar Marriott as well.*

He shook himself out of his reverie. They'd need to get to the nearest town, find a magistrate or a lawyer. Unless by some miracle Evelynne's brother and Wenders showed up with a rescue party. . . .

. . . *Her eyes are so beautiful, like the color of sea and sky on a stormy day.*

Sitting there in the darkness, he pictured Evelynne's gray

eyes, recalling how they reflected each of her moods—shining and clear when she laughed, smoky and dark when she was vexed, glistening when she cried, as she had done when he tried to thank her, and finally, clouded and opaque when she was sad. And she had grown sad when he spoke of the *ton*. He'd seen how the bright light faded from those fine eyes.

No, she wasn't part of his world, this Country Mouse, but he needn't have brought the point home to her quite so strongly. She wasn't a society miss, but she had breeding, and heart, and a damned clever head on her shoulders. There wasn't much the *ton* could offer to top that.

"Devil take them all!" he grumbled, shifting his position and rapping the lump on his crown against the wall in the process. "Aoww . . ." he groaned, rubbing the spot gingerly. This was not his finest hour.

But then, as in a dream, Evelynne's arms reached out to him. Gently clasping the back of his head, she enfolded him and drew him down to rest once more against her side. "You must sleep, Robbie," she breathed against his ear. "You must get well."

But there was no response. The Earl of Monteith was lost to the conscious world, and as he slept, he smiled.

Chapter 4

❧

Gilly watched in stunned disbelief as his sister scrambled onto the back of the lurching coach. He started into the street, as if to pursue the vehicle, but once it cleared the corner of the square, it moved rapidly away.

His heart was pounding, and he was trembling with shock as he ran back to the Monteith's front door and hammered urgently with the knocker.

Wenders, unlike many society butlers, preferred to answer the master's door himself. He did not want to leave such matters of delicate protocol as greeting high-ranking government officials in the hands of a mere footman. This evening, however, his patience was beginning to wear a bit thin, what with the continual comings and goings of an ill-assorted group of individuals.

And now, once again, there was an infernal rapping at the front door. He looked up from the newspaper he was reading as he sat in a padded chair at the far end of the hall. It was really altogether too much.

"Cummings," he called to the languid footman, who was preening in front of the hall mirror. "Would you see who is at the door? And if it is anyone of less importance than the Prince Regent himself, we are not at home."

Cummings begrudgingly left off inspecting his creamy complexion and sauntered to the front door. The rapping had grown to a crescendo, and there was now the muffled thud of fists pounding against the wood. Cummings halted.

"Sir?" he said tentatively. Wenders looked up unsmiling. "It appears there is a very agitated person out there."

"And . . ." Wenders raised an ominous brow.

"Perhaps it might be a good idea to get Tomkins or Sharkey

up here. It sounds like a rough character—and you know I'm not very robust."

Wenders closed his eyes and shook his head slowly. When he spoke at last, it was with the measured voice of someone whose tolerance was at last depleted.

"Cummings," he intoned, "you mincing featherweight. I am not ordering you to repel an invasion of the French. I am merely asking you to answer the door."

With great trepidation the footman drew open the portal, and then fell back with an abrupt shriek of fright as Gilly tumbled through the doorway and pounced on him. Cummings had already tangled with this fire-eater once tonight and come away the loser.

"Your master! He's been taken!" Gilly cried, fastening his hands on the hapless footman's lapels. "What took you so long to answer the door? It's too late now—my God!—What's to become of my sister?"

He threw off the wilting footman when his frantic eyes beheld Wenders rising magisterially from his chair.

"Sir! Sir!" There was a sob in the boy's voice now. "They've abducted the earl, and my sister's gone, too. Gone with the earl. We must follow. Oh, isn't there anyone here who can help me?"

Wenders shot the footman a look of reproach. "Dolt!" he uttered. "Pray your dawdling hasn't cost the earl his life." He turned to Gilly. "Easy, lad, easy. Come up to the library. We can speak there."

"But they're getting away!"

"Shhh. By the time I ordered up a carriage, they'd be clear outside London. There are other ways, lad. Other ways." Wenders spoke calmly as he drew Gilly, resisting, up the stairs to the warmth of the library.

"Come, boy, sit here." He ensconced Gilly in a cushioned chair. "We don't want to be precipitate. Who goes slowly goes safely."

He fetched the boy a small glass of cordial. "Sip it, there's a good boy. You look like you could do with a drop."

Gilly gazed up at the broad magnificence of Wenders in his honey-colored livery. The butler was clearly a person of importance in this household, but he could hardly be called a man of action. They would need to find assistance.

"Help," Gilly stated baldly. "We need help."

"Yes, and we shall have it, if your story bears scrutiny. Why do you claim my master was abducted? He was called away only moments ago to Sir Robert's Poole's home outside of London."

"No," Gilly insisted. "I tell you they abducted him. Eve and I saw the earl speak with one coachman in the street, and then the second one coshed him. They pushed him into the coach and drove off. And my sister threw herself onto the coach as it was leaving."

"A most unorthodox female, your sister," Wenders commented, almost approvingly. "But I saw the note from Sir Robert myself. It was in his own hand."

"A forgery!" the boy cried. Could this fellow know so little of criminal methods? "The earl told my sister someone was plotting against him. Oh, God! it's getting later all the time. Can you not call someone to aid us?" Gilly was beginning to feel hopeless.

Observing the lad, Wenders stroked his chin, then went to a desk and penned a quick note.

"Cummings, get up here," he called from the library doorway.

The breathless footman appeared on the landing.

"Here, give this to Sharkey. Tell him to ride posthaste to Sir Robert's home. And I want you to go by cab to all of Sir Robert's clubs here in town. I suspect he may be in the city this evening. If you return here before you have completed this task, you will wish your mother had never had the bad luck to meet your father. Do I make myself clear?"

Cummings muttered and stuttered, took the note, and hastily departed.

"We'll get to the bottom of this, lad, never fear," the butler assured Gilly. "The earl is a dangerous man to cross—with powerful friends."

"And powerful enemies, too," the boy added. "Besides, what good are powerful friends when the earl is alone, and most likely injured?"

"Hmm?" Wenders looked a little concerned. "Well, we will just have to hope that your sister is as resourceful as she is impetuous."

Sir Robert Poole appeared in three-quarters of an hour. He had fortunately been at White's, where Cummings discovered him, dining with some political cronies.

He was not a tall man, but his head of thick white hair, and his imposing physique—broad shoulders and barrel chest—gave him an aura of great power. His face was handsome, in a florid way, and he carried his fifty-odd years with robust ease.

Gilly's first impression, as Sir Robert came striding into the earl's library, was a feeling of enormous relief. Here at last was a man of action. Even in elegant dinner clothes, Sir Robert had the look of a caged tiger.

"What's this I hear about an abduction?" His voice, noted in Parliament for its ability to keep even the most bored attendees awake and alert, boomed through the paneled room.

Wenders bowed. "Sir Robert, this young gentleman witnessed the earl being forced into a coach. My master had been called from the house by a note from you, sir."

"I sent Monteith no messages. Gad, this is as I feared. You, lad," he barked at Gilly. "Tell me what you saw."

Quite unafraid, Gilly recounted what had transpired outside the earl's town house, and then gazed at Sir Robert expectantly.

The man thought for a few moments, his hand upon his cleft chin. He went to the door and called down to the hall, "Mr. Fletch, I think we need you up here."

A reedy little man appeared, a wizen-faced fellow, with the brightest eyes Gilly had ever seen. He wore a corded topcoat and moleskin breeches—a very odd sort of companion for the dapper Sir Robert.

"Aye, sir." He sketched a salute to the white-haired gentleman, who gave him the details of the earl's abduction.

"Mr. Fletch is my, er, aide-de-camp," Sir Robert explained to Gilly, seeing the boy's puzzled expression. "He assists me in some of my investigations. Now, lad, tell us everything you remember about the coach and its drivers. If we're to track down these scoundrels, we need to identify them."

Gilly wasn't sure how much he could tell them. He had watched the coach idly when it first waited before the earl's door, but it had been on the shadowed side of the street. Afterward, when the earl had been kidnapped, he had been more concerned with getting help than in observing the abductors.

"The first coachman was quite tall," he began, "with gingery hair curling below his hat. The other fellow was rabbity-looking, short and wiry. They both wore gray driving coats and were clean-shaven. The coach? . . . Hmm, let me think. It was a black job coach with yellow wheels, in decent repair, although it was a bit scuffed on the left door. There was no crest on it, or writing anywhere. There were four horses, lightweight coach horses, two chestnut and two dark bay. One of the chestnuts had a blue eye and a wide white blaze. I'm sorry, but that's really all I can tell you." Gilly looked down at his scuffed shoes.

Sir Robert and Mr. Fletch exchanged meaningful glances, and then Sir Robert went to Gilly and raised his downcast chin with his forefinger. "What's your name, lad?"

"Gilbert Marriott, sir." He looked despondently up at the white-haired man.

"You've got a gift, Gilbert Marriott. There are trained men who couldn't have told me all that you have. Well done, my boy, well done, indeed."

Gilly's face lit up.

"Sounds like Taff and Alfie, if you ask me," Mr. Fletch remarked. "They've done Skelton's dirty work before this. I'll get my men onto the job stables here in town, see if we can discover which one rents out a rig and team like the lad described. One blue eye, indeed . . ." His face crinkled merrily. "I'll take the lad with me, Sir Robert, if you like. I can always use an observant youngster when following a trail."

"He's probably ready for his bed." Sir Robert touched the back of Gilly's fair hair.

"No, sir, please, sir. May I go? I couldn't sleep a wink, not with my sister taken off to God knows where. Let me help."

"You're sure?"

Gilly nodded enthusiastically in reply.

"We'll find the earl and your sister. And the man who is behind this, as well. Run along now, and see how you like being an investigator."

Gilly wrote a brief note for Mrs. Coop, explaining that he and Evelynne were unable to return home just yet.

"My landlady will be in the devil of a pelter, there's no getting around it," he said over his shoulder to Sir Robert as he handed the note to the butler.

"Yes, well, females are renowned for their excess of sensibility," Sir Robert pronounced. "We must forgive them their delicate natures."

"Ho!" Gilly crowed as he headed out of the library beside Mr. Fletch. "You haven't met my sister!"

"A most unorthodox family, sir." Wenders shook his head at Sir Robert, then quirked his mouth into the semblance of a grin. "Most unorthodox."

Chapter 5

〜

When the Monteith awoke, he was alone. He lay sprawled under the blanket, a stack of sheets beneath his head. His headache had subsided almost completely. He was hungry and thirsty, and was painfully aware that it was some time since he had answered the call of nature. His redoubtable caretaker had forgotten that little necessity.

He drew himself to his knees and, using the edge of the linen press for balance, hoisted himself to his feet. He stood, reeling slightly in the dark, and waited for his head to stop spinning. God, he despised being ill! He had survived a French sniper's bullet to his head and the battle wound that had damaged his shoulder. He would survive this, as well. It was absurd that a very managing young woman had been controlling his fate. It was time he took matters back into his own hands.

He opened the closet door and peered out. The savory smells of the supper house assailed him, wafting up the back stairs from the kitchen below. His stomach rumbled audibly.

Down the corridor a door opened abruptly, and a rotund fellow in a bottle green jacket stepped into the hall. He patted his ample girth. "Make haste, m'dear," he called into the room. "Your gal's gone down already to make sure we're not disappointed in our meal. Ah, how delightful you look, Mrs. Potter."

A bewigged and highly rouged lady, also of an abundant circumference, joined the man in the hall. She tapped him playfully with her fan. "La, Mr. Potter, I vow I could eat a horse!"

Looks like she already has, the Monteith muttered to himself.

As the couple made their way, arm in arm, but not quite side by side, down the front stairs, the earl slipped from his hiding place and, with a slightly unsteady gait, approached their room.

"Ah, so eager for your dinner, you neglected to lock up." He eased himself through the doorway. The chamber was similar to the one he had been held captive in, with a few more concessions to comfort. A small fire burned in the hearth, and the rope bed bore a woven coverlet.

He made use of the chamber pot, discreetly placed behind a faded screen, and then investigated the contents of a wall cupboard. The sight of the man's dented but serviceable beaver hat and his long gray muffler hanging on a peg gave the earl an idea. He snatched up the items and felt in his waistcoat pocket for his purse. He wouldn't be reduced to thieving. His purse was gone. *Damn!* The kidnappers must have taken it. Clearly, they had no scruples about theft. He found a few bob in his greatcoat pocket, which he tossed on the dresser before he left the room.

The corridor was still empty, as was the utility closet, much to his chagrin.

"Drat the girl!" he muttered. "I've an itch to be away from this place before Skelton returns with his men."

He lit a candle in defiance of Evelynne's dictum that they remain in darkness as long as people were moving about, and sat down with the basket of food in his lap. He divided what little remained of the bread and cheese in half, and ate his portion with slow, thoughtful bites.

He gazed at the beaver hat and muffler lying beside him. With some padding under his greatcoat, the hat brim pulled low over his eyes, and the muffler around his lower face, he hoped he could somehow alter his appearance enough to leave the inn without being recognized. Perhaps they could pass unremarked through the kitchen, where there was bound to be a bustle of activity this time of evening.

He knew he could do it alone—he was surprisingly steady on his feet, all things considered, but what would Evelynne think if she returned and he was gone. But where the devil was she off to?

He took a pull from the cider jug. *What if she doesn't return?* a small niggling voice inside his head queried. *Suppose she's gotten tired of being cooped up here with a stranger? Who'd blame her for leaving? She owes you nothing.* He crumbled a bit of cheese between his fingers.

She could walk out of this place as free as a bird. There's no one to tie her to you or the abduction. She could be halfway back to London by now. The idea, once planted in his brain, wouldn't let go. He grappled with it for several uncomfortable minutes.

Well, what if she is gone? he addressed the voice. *I'll get by just fine on my own.*

The earl was sopping up the last bit of peach juice with the last crust of bread when Evelynne slid through the door. He didn't look up.

"Oh good, you're awake. I hope you weren't worried." She climbed over the barrier of brooms and mops, and crouched before him. "I slipped outside through the back kitchen door. They barely noticed me. I had a talk with the ostler, told him I was looking for work hereabouts, and wondered what sort of people stayed at the inn.

"He chewed my ear off on the subject of Randall Skelton. It seems the ostler's son is a little slow in the head, and Alfie cuffed him several times for being clumsy with his lordship's rig. I think he might help us, Robbie, for he's not at all in charity with Lord Skelton or his men."

The earl still said nothing.

Evelynne observed him, leaning forward a little. "Are you feeling all right? I didn't mean to rattle on like that, but I thought you'd want to know. How is your head?" She reached a hand to feel his brow.

He pulled back from her touch and growled, "It's just fine."

"Well—" She sat back on her heels. "Your head may be fine, but your temper certainly hasn't improved." She noted with exasperation that nothing remained of their provisions. "And I see you've eaten all our food."

He protested, "I saved you half," then realized, looking down at the empty basket, that during his distracted revery he had consumed every morsel.

"I was thinking of ways to get us out of this accursed place," he explained. "And I just kept eating, I guess." He tried to muster a sheepish expression, hard work for a highly bred earl.

"No mind," she said, trying not to sound testy. Her trip through the kitchen had whetted her appetite. "We can buy something once we reach a village."

He winced. "I've no money, Evelynne. The kidnappers took my purse."

"Nothing?" She looked at him in disbelief.

"Only a few coins, and I just spent those."

She was incredulous. "Spent them? Where? On what?" She

had a momentary fear that perhaps she was dealing with a mad-man—blows to the head often had unpredictable results. She recalled how one of their farm lads had fallen from a hayloft and thought he was Dick Whittington's cat for the better part of a week. The earl was moody to be sure, but now he sounded almost delusional.

"No, I'm not wits to let," he reassured her, noting the dubious way she was gazing at him. "I left the money behind for the owner of these." He held up his booty. She regarded the rather dented hat and the pilled muffler with annoyance.

"How nice that you found a haberdashery down the hall," she said with great sarcasm, crossing her arms over her chest. Her temper was starting to rise in direct proportion to her hunger. "I sneak downstairs and actually do something useful, and you stroll about up here and *shop*?"

He watched her with veiled amusement. The candlelight threw her face into strong relief—she looked like an angry faun, with her bright eyes and short, tangled curls. Did the girl never comb her hair?

"They're to use as a disguise," he explained patiently. "With some padding under my waistcoat and these covering my head and throat, I think I could get out of the inn undetected."

She rolled her eyes at him doubtfully, but then picked up the beaver hat and placed it tentatively on his head. It settled just below his dark brows, obscuring all traces of the bandage and most of his eyes.

"What a capital idea," she said, approving of the effect. "It appears you were doing something useful, after all."

He pulled a face at her. "I accept your apology. But I don't blame you for being cross. You must have caught it from me, for I've never felt more out of sorts."

"Are you still feeling unwell?"

"No, it's not that. My head is actually behaving itself. But it's this enforced inaction." He clenched his hand into a fist. "I feel a great need to be away from here. I wanted to leave earlier—my dizziness wasn't so bad, but you were gone."

"I'm here now. We can leave as soon as you're fitted out in this clever disguise."

"I thought you'd gone away for good." He looked intently at her, strangely reassured by her capable presence. "Not that I'd blame you if you had. I'd give St. Francis himself the megrims."

Evelynne hid her smile. "Then it's a good thing it's me, and not him who's looking after you." She began wrapping the muffler about his neck, making sure the folds rose above his chin. "It's a pity this driving coat of yours is so stylish. It doesn't fit somehow, with the shabby hat. Perhaps it would be better if I carried it down."

He stood in the narrow room and tugged off the offending garment. Beneath the long coat he wore a dark blue jacket and gray buckskins. His cambric shirt, without its neckcloth, opened to a V at his throat. Evelynne arranged the ends of the muffler so that the bared expanse of his chest was hidden, feeling her fingers grow warm where they touched his skin.

"Should I look a bit stouter, do you think?" He patted his lean midsection with one hand, thinking of the rotund Mr. Potter. It occurred to Evelynne that he looked quite strapping enough for her taste, but she kept the thought to herself.

"Perhaps a pillow under your waistcoat." She could find no pillow on the shelves, so she bundled some sheets into a plump roll. "Here, try this."

He wedged it under his waistcoat with a most satisfactory result. "Well?" He dug his hands into his jacket pockets and affected a slouch. With the beaver hat pulled below his ears, and the ends of the shabby muffler dangling down over his now paunchy stomach, he looked almost seedy.

"Most effective, my lord." She tried not to laugh, but the earl saw the spark of humor in her eyes.

"I expect you'll be blackmailing me over this at some point."

"I'll be a rich woman, then." She chuckled. "It should be worth a small fortune to keep this from the ears of the *ton*."

"Or from the ears of my valet, at any rate."

"Are we ready?" She bent to pick up his driving coat and draped it over her arm. He looked about their small haven, suddenly loathe to leave its narrow confines. He stalled for time, collecting their bedding, and the basket and jug. He rolled them together and tossed the bundle onto the highest shelf.

"Don't want to leave any evidence behind." He picked up the lit candle and stood beside Evelynne at the threshold. "You go down first—act casual—as though you're on an errand for one of the inn's customers. I'll wait on the stairs above you. If the landlord or one of our kidnappers is about, say something to warn me . . . say, 'I hear the London coach was held up again,' and then leave. I mean it, Evelynne, one of us has to get away from here."

She looked up at him with dismay. "But what will I do?" Her hands were on the lapels of his jacket. "I'll be all alone. It's night, and there are fearful things out there——"

He took her chin in his hand. "Don't gammon me, Eve. I don't think there's a Marriott born who knows the first thing about fear. But if you're so concerned about leaving me on my own, then wait behind the stable, and I'll come out when the coast is clear."

"You'd better!" She tugged on his jacket for emphasis. "Remember, I swore I wouldn't leave without you."

"I remember a lot of things, Evelynne." He bent his dark head and swiftly kissed her cheek. "My luck," he whispered, then blowing out the candle, he propelled her through the door.

A small party of men and women were gathered on the front landing, but they didn't even turn as Evelynne and the earl crossed to the back staircase.

Evelynne was trembling as they went down toward the kitchen. Wasn't it just like the man to discompose her when she most needed to think clearly.

He halted before the last turning of the stairs. "You'll do fine." He smiled and gave her a little nudge. She smiled back grimly and went slowly down the remaining steps.

The kitchen was less busy than it had been when she'd passed through earlier. It was now past the peak of the supper hour. The fire no longer blazed so high in the hearth, and the two serving maids were now scrubbing dishes at the sink. The cook and a young man seated beside her at the food-laden table were sorting through a tray of cooked meat. As Evelynne passed by, she glanced longingly at a fine roast turkey.

"Still about then, lad?" The cook looked up from her wide table.

"Aye, ma'am." Evelynne touched the coat she carried over her arm. "The guvnor wants this brushed out."

"Well, then, best take it into the yard." She motioned to the stout iron-hinged door behind her. Evelynne nodded and with an inward sigh of relief headed for the exit.

"Hold on a moment," the cook called out. "Can you give our Kenny a hand? He's taking a supper tray to his dad in the stable, and he can't manage both the tray and the doors, poor lamb." She put her hand fondly on the young man's head, and as he looked up at Evelynne, she saw an amiable, but vacant expression in his pale blue eyes. This must be the ostler's simple-minded son.

"Y-yes . . ." she stuttered. "I'll wait."

"Won't be a minute, lad." She bustled off in the direction of the taproom. "I'll just fetch him a nice pint of ale."

From the front rooms of the inn, Evelynne could hear the raucous cadences of a crowd. The Eel and Barrow certainly seemed to be overflowing with patrons this evening.

The Earl of Monteith made his appearance just as the cook returned with her brimming mug. In fact, they nearly collided. "Oh, my, ain't you the big one," she tittered, neatly skirting the earl as he stepped down from the stairwell and into her path.

"Sure, an' I'll be beggin' yer pardon, mum," he said with a fine Irish lilt as he touched his hat to her. "And haven't I just come down to see about the lad who's made off with me' coat."

"Well, he's right over there." She motioned to Evelynne, who was standing in the shadows by the back door. "He's waiting to help our Kenny bring over his da's supper."

"Don't hang about, lad, be off wi' ye, then, and mind ye get me coat clean this time."

"But—" Evelynne protested as the earl opened the door and shoved her out. "Kenny—"

"I'll gi' the lad a hand." Evelynne stood in the doorway and watched openmouthed as the earl, under the guise of helping to lift the ostler's tray, slipped a fat currant cake under his padded jacket.

She was waiting on the path behind the inn, under a full moon and a sky empty of clouds, when the earl and Kenny came through the doorway. The earl carried the supper tray, and the lumbering young man juggled the mug of ale.

"My da works in the stable," Kenny was saying. "He looks after all the horses."

"Do you like horses?" the earl asked, as Evelynne fell in step beside them.

"I likes all the horses. 'Specially the brown ones. Not the gray ones, though, don't like the gray ones, a'tall!" He turned to Evelynne with a wide-eyed pronouncement. "Nasty people owns gray horses, you know. Nasty hitting people."

"Yes, we do know, Kenny," she said soothingly. "But the nasty hitting people are gone now."

He shook his head at her. "No, they're gone, and they're come back. Like a bad penny, my da says."

"Come back?" The earl shifted the tray into one hand and opened the door to the stable's back rooms.

"Aye." Kenny nodded his head several times for emphasis. "Come back with more hitting people. My da, he kept me in my room, but I saw them through the window. Five, six, maybe ten."

"Damn," the earl muttered as they passed through the tack room and into the ostler's small apartment. The ostler, sitting with his pipe by the fire, smiled when he saw Evelynne come in with his son; he'd thought her a friendly lad when they'd talked earlier in the evening. But his smile of welcome turned to a frown of puzzlement when the earl stepped into his parlor. He laid aside his pipe and stood up.

"Put it here on my da's table." Kenny showed the earl exactly where to lay the tray. He turned to his father. "These are my friends, Da. They doesn't much like the nasty hitting people."

"I'm sorry." The earl addressed the ostler, "We don't mean to intrude . . ."

The ostler hadn't always worked in a rundown hedge tavern; in his youth he had served in the stables of a great lord. He could spot quality, even under a dented beaver hat.

"You're the gent they're all looking for," the ostler exclaimed with wonder, rubbing the back of his balding head. "If that don't beat the Dutch . . . them searching the county high and low, and you here all the time!"

Evelynne cast a look of apprehension at the earl, but he seemed quite at his ease. He stepped forward and bowed slightly. "I am Monteith, at your service, sir."

"Pleased to meet your lordship. Lemuel Smits is how I'm called." He wiped his weathered hand upon his breeches, then held it out to the earl, who shook it most cordially. "Then this here young fellow's your lad?" He beamed at Evelynne.

"No, he's not my lad in the normal way of things. But he's a good lad, don't you think?" The earl avoided Evelynne's stormy glance.

"Aye." Smits nodded jovially. "If he helped you get away from those ruffians, he's a very good lad."

Kenny seemed oblivious to the conversation going on around him. "Don't you want your supper, Da? I've brought your ale, an' all."

"Please." The earl gestured to the table. "Don't let us keep you from your meal."

"Don't know as how I could sit and eat with a lord in my parlor." Smits looked a bit doubtful.

The earl promptly pulled out a chair and sat down opposite the ostler's tray. He tugged the rolled-up sheet from under his waistcoat and tossed it onto a nearby settle, then placing his elbows firmly on the table, said, "See, I'm just plain Robbie MacIntyre now, Mr. Smits. An ordinary fellow come inside for a chat. And while you eat, perhaps you could answer a few of my questions."

Evelynne stood behind the earl's chair, watching with hungry eyes as the ostler made short work of his meal. He answered all of Robbie's questions between bites, and she was sure Robbie was not happy with what he heard, for more than once his fingers clenched upon the tablecloth.

"So we're somewhere between London and Southampton?"

"Closer to Southampton. When the wind is from the south, you can smell the sea." Smits wiped some gravy from his chin, and Evelynne licked her lips. "Mowbry's the nearest town, but I wouldn't go looking for help there. Your lofty friend Skelton's put the word about that you're a runaway lunatic and dangerous, to boot. He's got his bullies stirring things up; the townspeople won't want to cross them."

"But surely there's a magistrate or a squire, someone who won't be intimidated by Skelton's men."

Smits shook his head. "Those are the first places Skelton would expect you to go. He's sure to have his ruffians keeping watch. It's a pity you don't know anyone hereabouts."

The earl thought a moment. "Well, as a matter of fact I do. How far are we from Levelands?"

"Mitford's place?" Smits whistled and looked impressed. "That's a dandy spot to hide out. Levelands must have sixty rooms, if it has one. But it's a day's journey from here if you're traveling on foot. I'd offer you horses from the stable, but it'd be worth my job if the landlord found out. He's been hand-in-glove with Skelton for quite some time now. All kinds of goings on late at night. You're not the first mysterious visitor we've had here, my lord."

Evelynne laid her hand on the earl's shoulder. "I don't mind walking. We can keep to the country lanes, and, with any luck, we won't run into Skelton's men."

"He's got a passel of fellows after you," Smits said to the earl. "Half his crew's inside having supper now, but the rest are scouring all the surrounding towns. But mayhap he's concentrating on the roads to London. It might not occur to him that you'd go west."

Kenny, who had been drawing in chalk upon a large slate while his father ate, piped in. "I could take 'em to the chapel, Da. The road to Pegeen's house. No hitting people on that road, I bet."

Lemuel Smits looked dubious.

"It's worth a try," the earl said, rising. He pulled on his long driving coat. "Your lad can take us as far as the chapel, and we'll make our own way from there."

"Just keep on to the west. Can you follow the stars?"

"I've done a bit of navigating by the sky. In Spain."

"Well, I do believe they've got the same sky above them as we do. I'll draw you a map with some landmarks to watch for." Smits took a small pad from his vest pocket. He scratched some lines with a nubbin pencil and handed it to the earl. "I'd take you myself, but I need to stay here. Those rogues will be calling for their horses any time now, and Kenny's best kept outen their way."

Smits walked with Monteith and Evelynne to the door. "Kenny, lad, go see that there's no one about outside. Whistle if it's clear." Kenny slipped past them, a look of delighted expectation in his eyes. Evelynne guessed he was rarely given such responsibility.

The earl put his hand on the ostler's shoulder. "You're a good man, Lemuel Smits, and I never forget a favor. When this business is over, I'll see that you and the boy will profit from your kindness."

Smits grinned. "Just get away safe, my lord, and I'll have my reward."

There was a low, clear whistle from the stable yard.

"Best be off now, and, mind, keep this good lad close by you." Smits tugged gently on Evelynne's hair.

"Oh, I intend to." The earl's eyes gleamed down at her. "He's quite the rarest lad I've ever met."

The stable yard was quiet as the two of them made their way to Kenny, who stood in the shadows of the large barn. With a finger to his lips, he led them behind the stable building, through a weedy garden, to a ramshackle chicken coop.

"Wait right here," he whispered, and disappeared back in the direction of the inn. They waited some minutes in silence, and then Evelynne turned to the earl with a look of dismay.

"I hope he hasn't lost heart. This is probably rather more Ethan he's ever taken on before."

"Oh, he'll do." The earl leaned back against the rickety coop. "If there's one thing I've learned to have faith in, it's the backbone of the British yeoman."

"Well, Kenny's not exactly your regulation yeoman."

The earl played with the fringes of his muffler and regarded her from under the low brim of his hat. "You're just getting starchy because someone else is in charge now."

Evelynne opened her mouth to deny such an arrantly ridiculous accusation, and the earl leaned forward and kissed her. He didn't touch her with his hands at first, just let his mouth play over hers, feeling the inward rush of her breath and savoring the warm, sweet taste of her lips.

She didn't back away, but said, "Robbie . . . no . . . I . . ." He reached out then and caught her firmly in the crux of his arm, his hand cupping the back of her dark head.

"Hush," he murmured against her cheek. "It's time you learned to lean on me."

"But you can't—" He kissed her again, harder this time, capturing her tender mouth, stilling her protests. She wasn't kissing him back—it was too much to hope for—but neither was she fighting him to get away. With a flex of muscle he curved her slim body against his chest.

"See, Evelynne, it's very easy to lean on me." He pulled back a little to watch her face. His gallant girl looked like a rabbit in a death snare. He'd apparently just discovered *something* that frightened Evelynne Marriott. *Damn!*

He dropped his arms immediately. "Ach, Evelynne, don't look at me like that. It's over. Just a momentary lapse. I won't say I'm sorry, however. I'm not. I've wanted to do that for the last twelve hours."

"Yes," she snapped, "and I've wanted to box your ears more than once, and never gave in to the impulse."

She turned from him and wandered a bit beyond the coop. "And where is that Kenny? I seem to be the only person here who's at all concerned with our escape."

"God save me from single-minded females!" the earl muttered.

Evelynne spun to him and almost forgot to keep her voice lowered. "And God save me from men who think that every woman is theirs for the taking! You're no better than that red-headed coachman."

"Has he been trying to kiss you, too?" He looked at her with wide-eyed speculation.

"No . . . of course not!" She crossed her arms huffily. "Oh, I see. You're having a joke at my expense. I'm glad your lordship finds me laughable."

"His lordship finds you to be many things, Eve. . . ." The earl's voice was soft and deep. "But never, ever, laughable."

Kenny appeared around the corner, just then, and Evelynne bit back her retort. The boy was carrying a round cloth-bound parcel under his arm.

"Is anything amiss?" the earl asked.

"Right as rain," Kenny said with an encouraging look at Evelynne, who was still frowning. "Follow me. I do know the way to the chapel just fine." He turned and headed for the open field behind the inn.

The earl strode off after Kenny without a backward glance. Evelynne hesitated, watching the two dark shapes move away from her—the shambling form of the ostler's son and the lean silhouette of the earl, his long-skirted greatcoat rippling out like a sail. She knew with a deep-seated certainty that the danger that lay behind her at the inn was a pale phantom to the peril she would encounter once she was on the road alone with the Monteith. She'd need more than her quick wits to stay safe; she'd need to lock her heart in the very deepest recess of her soul and pray that it stayed there until this adventure was done.

"God protect the weary traveler," she said aloud to the scattering of stars above her head, and then scurried to catch up with her companions, who awaited her at the edge of the field.

Kenny led them across several farmsteads, and along a woodland path, thick with untrimmed bracken, where the light of the moon was obscured by towering oaks. They forded a narrow stream and came at last to a small village, where a stone church sat at one end of an open green.

"We do come here on Sundays," Kenny explained as they stood in the shadow of the flint chapel. "We sing, and all, me and my da. I sleep sometimes. Da says it's the silent prayer." He chuckled.

The earl peered down the length of the green. The village seemed quite deserted. If Skelton's men were patrolling, they were not making it public knowledge.

He looked at Evelynne. She was standing, shoulders hunched, with her hands in her pockets, gazing at the ground. She hadn't said a word since they'd left the Eel and Barrow, just tramped along in his wake like a proper little soldier. She looked cold and tired, and she must be very hungry. It would be a kindness to send her back to the inn with Kenny. Smits could keep her hidden. Once he got to Levelands, he'd send one of Mitford's coaches to take her back to London.

"Mouse," he said softly. She looked up. "I want you to go back."

She shook her head and dug her chin deeper into her collar.

"I can travel faster alone," he explained. "And you look just about done in."

She glared at him and shook her head again.

"I expect she's cold," Kenny stated, and proceeded to pull the knit scarf from his own throat. He held it out to Evelynne.

"Thank you," she said, taking it and tucking it inside her jacket collar. "How did you know?"

"Saw you shiverin'," Kenny answered.

"No." The earl was smiling. "She meant how did you know she was a girl."

"My sister Pegeen's a girl," he said cryptically, and then added, "lives down this here road. Married last year in the chapel, she were."

"And . . ." the earl coaxed.

"Her husband, Davey, he says to me that a man looks at a woman a funny way. But a good way." Kenny continued, "Sometimes Davey looks at Pegeen something powerful."

"And who has been looking at this girl 'something powerful'?" the earl asked softly.

Kenny said simply, "Why, you have, sir."

The earl sighed. Out of the mouths of babes, practically.

"So, you don't think she can pass for a lad?"

"Oh, yeah," Kenny concurred. "Fooled me da, I do think. But not Kenny. Kenny sees things, he does."

Evelynne shuffled her feet. "If the two of you are finished discussing my lamentable disguise, I believe we should get on."

The earl looked concerned. "I really think you—"

"I don't care what you think." Her eyes flashed as she leaned toward him. "I'm traveling west to Levelands, wherever that may be, and you, my lord, can't stop me."

The Monteith rolled his eyes at Kenny. "She's not only female, she's a shrew, besides."

"Oh, aye!" Kenny hooted. "Pegeen's got a tongue on her what could flay an ox!" He turned to Evelynne. "But here's summat to cure your temper, miss." He handed her the cloth-covered parcel. "I knowed you was both hungry—I seen the gentleman take the cake from Cook's table. So in I goes, back to the kitchen, and gets you this turkey."

Evelynne's knees almost buckled. "The whole turkey?"

He grinned. "Saw you lookin' at it."

The earl took the wrapped bird from Evelynne—it required only a slight tug—and tucked it under his arm.

"Kenny," he pronounced, "you are a brick. I'll be back here one day soon, and then you and your da can come work for me. Would you like that?"

"With horses?" Kenny's eyes lit up.

The earl nodded. "But no gray horses and no nasty people. And now we'd better be on our way, my stubborn shrew and I." He shook Kenny's hand. "I thank you, my friend, for all your help."

Evelynne touched Kenny's sleeve. "I'm glad we met you and your father, Kenny. It's been the only nice part of our adventure." She leaned forward and whispered, "And thank you for the turkey. I was *famished*!"

Kenny watched them skirt the edge of the town, heading west, just as his da had instructed. Even when they'd passed from his sight, he stood gazing after them, wondering when the gentleman would notice that the girl also looked at *him* something powerful.

Because he saw things, Kenny did.

They strode along in silence for quite a while. Every so often the earl would tear off a piece of turkey and hand it wordlessly to Evelynne. She munched and walked, walked and munched. Once she stumbled in the darkness on a root or a rock, and the earl steadied her with a hand on her arm. She pulled abruptly away from him, started to say something, and then thought better of it. She walked on.

He watched her marching resolutely ahead of him, long legs swinging along the night-shadowed lane. She was making every effort, he knew, to prove that she wouldn't slow him down. He was having trouble just keeping up with her. And unless she paced herself, she was going to use up what little store of energy she had left before the night was even half over. All for the sake of pride.

"Could we proceed a little more sedately, Miss Marriott?" he called from a distance of eight or nine yards. "If you will recall, I was an invalid until only this evening."

Her previous solicitude seemed to have vanished. "You look well enough to me," she observed acidly, waiting as he caught up to her. The September moon was low in the sky, but there was enough diffused light on the road for him to see her face. She was fuming.

"Hmmm . . . what was it you said last night about temper tantrums?" he goaded her intentionally. Best to have it out now.

"I don't have tantrums," she retorted.

"Then I wish I knew what's put you so out of countenance. The turkey's not off, by any chance, is it?"

She stifled a chuckle before it could emerge from her throat. He wouldn't get around her that easily. She raised her head and looked him square in the eye.

"I'm going to say this once, my lord, and hope that will suffice. You are a belted earl; I am a factory worker. You speak in Parliament as your hobby; I count pins for a living. I should not need to point out the differences between us, but in fact it appears I do."

She stopped to assess the effect of her speech so far. He was gazing at her intently.

"Never once, my lord, have I forgotten those differences between us. Never once have I acted out of my place. But back at the inn, while we waited for Kenny, you treated me in a manner that can only lead me to believe that you have forgotten your place. And it won't do."

He rubbed his knuckles across his upper lip. "Are you through?"

She nodded. She couldn't tell if he was angry. His face had taken on a remote expression, and he was gazing, almost pensively, over her head.

"Tell me something, Evelynne." His voice was like a sigh when he spoke at last. "Who kissed you and made you so afraid?"

"I'm not afraid," she said testily. "I'm merely annoyed. And confused. One minute you ask leave to call me friend, and the next you're trying to have your way with me up against a chicken coop."

"Fairly enthusiastically, I might add." He grinned. "No, don't hit me. Ach, my little Mouse, if you could have only seen your face, like a deer at bay. You *were* afraid, and I'd swear it wasn't me you feared. And whatever man did that to you, well, I suppose that's your own business—though I wouldn't mind having at him in a back alley."

Beat you to it, Evelynne said smugly to herself, recalling the satisfying vision of Ollie Hooper's nose down in the dirt.

"As for myself," the earl continued, "I told you I wouldn't say I was sorry, but I can promise not to bother you that way again . . . so long as you don't encourage me."

"And how did I encourage you this time?" Evelynne bristled.

You have no idea, he muttered under his breath. "It doesn't matter, Eve. But if you'll stop talking claptrap about our 'places,' I'll endeavor to act like a gentleman—a proper Puritan gentleman."

"Well, I'm sure that's how you behave in the *ton*. You are, after all, the 'dour Scot.' I can't credit how you came to act so out of character."

"Must have been a blow to the head," he murmured. He handed her a drumstick, and, amity restored, they continued side by side down the country road.

Chapter 6

❧

Near dawn, when the eastern sky was showing the first hint of pink, they came to an abandoned apple orchard. The trees were stunted, the grass long gone to seed. But there were apples for the taking, and the earl suggested this might be a good place to break their fast.

"Not that you haven't been eating all night long," he observed to Evelynne, who had only just finished off the last of the filched currant cake.

They were both bone weary. Several times during the night Evelynne had staggered, and she hadn't demurred when the Monteith finally put his arm through hers and guided her along the unlit road. Once or twice, at a crossroads, they'd referred to the small map that Smits had drawn, using the tinderbox from the inn, which Evelynne had wisely kept in her pocket, for a light. The Monteith was sure they were heading in the proper direction to reach his friend's home.

They hadn't met up with anyone ominous during their journey, though late that night they did come upon a string of gypsy caravans moving almost silently alongside a field of uncut wheat. The Roms ignored them.

"I guess we're fellow outcasts," the earl had mused as they stood and watched the hump-shaped carts trundle out of sight.

"Maybe we should have asked to travel with them." Evelynne said wistfully. Surely gypsies would know all the secret byways in the county. And how lovely it would be to ride in a wagon after walking for so long. But it also meant more awkward explanations, and, anyway, the caravans were clearly headed north.

"I think we'll save that for our next adventure," the earl remarked dryly, and they had continued on down the road.

Evelynne agreed with the Monteith that the orchard would be a good stopping-off place, but the high split-rail fence that separated the field from the road proved a distinct impediment to them both. The earl, taller and longer-legged than his companion, managed to scale the fence on the third try, but lost his hat in the process. Evelynne couldn't seem to make her legs and arms coordinate properly. She soon found herself hopelessly tangled in the wooden rails, still on the wrong side of the fence. She choked out one of Edgar's favorite oaths, and the earl, who was watching her struggle with a fondly tolerant expression, said reprovingly, "Such language, Evelynne."

She glared across at him, and then laughed. "This is the greatest come-down of all. To have outwitted the evil Lord Skelton, and then to be foiled by a mere fence."

"Here, Mouse." He crouched down and loosened her left foot, which had become wedged in the junction of two rails. He then reached over and hoisted her up, with very little effort it seemed to her, and sat her on the top rail. She was above his eye level for the first time in their acquaintance.

"Better?" His head was cocked to one side, and the early morning breeze was ruffling through his thick hair. A stray lock had fallen over his brow, and he looked young and vital, and so incredibly handsome. *This is how I'll remember him,* she thought, *in all the years to come. Robert MacIntyre, gaunt and unshaven, with my silly bandage on his head, and the first light of morning on his dear face.*

"Yes, much better," she responded. "But whatever are you doing?" He had bent down and was removing one of her heavy brogues.

"There's blood on your stocking, Eve."

"It's nothing really." He was rolling down her thick woolen hose, and she shivered in spite of herself as his hands ran down the length of her calf.

"Stop fidgeting," he commanded sternly, and then uttered, "Good God, Evelynne, why didn't you say something?"

"They're only blisters," she protested, trying not to look down at her rather swollen foot, which had been rubbed raw and bloody in several places. "Those shoes never did fit properly. They were Gilly's."

There was anger, and something more in his voice as he rose.

"You're so damned busy taking care of everyone else, has it never occurred to you to look after yourself?" He pulled at her hair, not roughly, but with purpose. "Do you own a comb? Do you possess a mirror? And why in God's name are you wearing your brother's clothing?" He turned from her, his righteous anger propelling him away.

"Don't you have any idea how damned beautiful you are?" He spoke over his shoulder. "Oh, you're so surprised when a man sees through your boyish disguise. I certainly saw through it—I suspect Wenders did, as well. Christ, Evelynne, even Kenny saw through it!"

She clung to the fence rail and tried not to pitch backward from the effect of his words. He thought she was beautiful! Unkempt, but beautiful.

"I'm sorry about the blisters," she called out to him. "But I kept up with you tonight, didn't I? I didn't slow you down."

He turned back to her and said less combatively, "That's exactly my point. You're still worried about *me*. When are you going to take care of Evelynne?"

"I don't know," she said haltingly. "I've been acting this way for so long now . . ."

"Like a managing little chit, do you mean?" He had picked up her discarded shoe and stocking, and, stuffing them in his coat pocket, he proceeded to sweep her off the fence and into his arms.

"No, don't fight me. My intentions are strictly honorable—murderous, but honorable." He carried her partway across the orchard to where a shallow stream ran through a small declivity. "Now," he barked, tumbling her onto the long grass, "take off your other shoe. And your stocking."

She gazed up at him, feeling very small indeed. "I haven't always been like this, you know. Managing, I mean. And I do look after myself—Oh! Your bandage." The earl had begun unwinding the length of linen from his head. "I really don't think you should—"

He gave her a quelling look, and she shut her mouth. He was right—she had turned into a fishwife. *How distressing.*

She obediently removed her footgear and sat watching him while he dipped the two pieces of cloth into the stream. He came and knelt before her and began dabbing the wet linen on her tender feet.

"On the Peninsula," he said quite conversationally, as if he hadn't just been furiously railing at her, "a soldier learns very quickly to look after his feet. An army may march on its stomach, but it won't get very far if its men are limping along. Which reminds me of one time in Salamanca, we were expecting a shipment of boots . . ."

The top of his dark head was inches from her face; she could have leaned forward and laid her cheek against those midnight locks. He smelled of cider, and camphor, and crisp night air. His hands were so gentle as he bathed her blistered skin . . . and his voice was so soothing as he went on speaking about his time in Spain. He was lulling her and caressing her with his words. She leaned back in the grass and closed her eyes. "Go on, Robbie," she murmured, "I'm listening."

When Evelynne awoke, she was lying under the earl's greatcoat, her head pillowed on his folded jacket. Her damp stockings and the two linen strips hung drying on a nearby bush. The sun was full up, the sky overhead was a sea of azure, and the stream beside her seemed to be chuckling its delight at the prospect of such a glorious day.

She lifted herself up on one elbow and looked about for the earl. He was in his shirtsleeves, halfway up the trunk of a gnarled tree, gathering apples, the shabby hat clutched under his arm in lieu of a basket. He saw she was sitting up and waved.

"Breakfast," he called, holding up the brimming hat, and almost losing his balance in the process. He swung down from the tree, one-handed, and came to her side, tipping all the apples onto her lap. "There, that should keep you for an hour or so."

He threw himself down beside her.

"I'm sorry I fell asleep during your story. Although I gather I wasn't the only one who dozed off." She pointed meaningfully to the flattened patch of grass on her other side, where he'd apparently stretched out to sleep.

"The silent prayer?" he teased, a smile curling one side of his mouth.

"Oh, I see. Still, it was rude of me to nod off while you were speaking," she said, examining the apples before her with a critical eye. She chose one that seemed to be fairly free of spots. The earl reached over and plucked the fruit from her hand. He buffed it with the edge of his sleeve until it shone like a fat red gem, and then handed it back.

"Actually, that's exactly what I was hoping you'd do. My

war stories always seem to have that effect on people." His eyes crinkled with mirth. "One of my lieutenants always said they were better than a rum toddy for inducing sleep."

"Which lieutenant was that?" she asked. "Not Edgar Marriott, by any chance?" It sounded just like something her brother would say.

"The same." He rolled onto his side, facing her, and propped his head up with one hand. "It occurred to me that night in the library that you had some connection to Edgar, but lately we've been too busy outrunning Skelton to discuss our mutual acquaintances. I gather then you are related to my Lieutenant Marriott."

"He was my brother," she said, looking down at her bare toes.

The Monteith, well bred as he was, couldn't hide his shock. Young Marriott had been a fashionable, well-heeled officer, with a fine horse and spare guineas to spend on gambling and drink. This girl beside him was from a poor family, her clothing old and threadbare.

When Edgar spoke of his sister to his fellow officers, he gave the impression of a young lady out in county society. His gypsy belle, he'd called her, relishing the tales of how she could outride most of the men in Devon during the day, and hostess parties for the hunt club that same night. Monteith was sure half of the young officers in his regiment had been secretly in love with Marriott's high-spirited sister, sight unseen.

She looked at him with solemn eyes. "I know I'm not very like him."

"It's not that . . ." He fought for the right words and opted for plainspokenness. "Evelynne, your brother gave the impression of some wealth—he wasn't a Croesus, but he always had cash at the ready. You seem to be, if you will forgive me for being so blunt, not very well up in the world."

She sighed. "My father mortgaged some land to buy Edgar his commission and to keep him in the proper style. There were other, earlier mortgages as well, and when my parents died, I couldn't repay all the debts."

"So you lost everything?" His voice was beyond gentle.

"Only the farm and the land." She shrugged. "My younger brothers and I managed to keep ourselves together. The vicar offered us a place in a church-run home, but we went to London instead."

She told him of her new home in Camden Town, her long search for employment, and the eventual need that drove her to seek work, dressed as a lad, in the pin factory.

He touched her shoulder with his hand. "Evelynne, when we are through with this adventure, as you call it, I vow I will look after your family."

"There's no need . . ." she protested. The more time she spent with the earl, the less she could afford to take from him.

"I told your brother I would take care of his family. He must have known how your father's finances lay. You can't let me renege on a promise."

"Then do something for the boys. I could accept that."

"What? And nothing for you? Isn't there anything in your heart that you desire above all else?"

This was getting into very dangerous territory. Evelynne fell back on the one thing guaranteed to distract the earl from his benevolence—horses.

"Little Georgie, my favorite mount. I would so love to have him back again."

"Ah, was he your first pony?"

She gave a gurgle of laughter. "Heavens, no! Little Georgie stood seventeen hands without shoes. Edgar named him that because even as a foal he was enormous. He was a cross between an Exmoor pony and a draft mare. The oddest dun color, and a head like an ox." She said it quite fondly. "He could jump a six-bar fence from a standstill and hunt cross-country long after all the high-bred horses were in their dainty stalls."

The earl whistled. "Most impressive. And do you know where he is at present?"

"Squire Cosby bought him when our livestock was auctioned off. He'd always coveted Georgie. The Cosbys were all hunting mad, you know. His son started courting me the minute I turned seventeen, but I suspected it was only so his family could get their hands on Little Georgie. When I told him the horse wasn't part of my dowry, he up and married someone else. Quite broke my heart." Evelynne's eyes danced as she watched the earl over her half-eaten apple.

"I'll take a cross-bred horse over a pure-bred any day," the earl pronounced, anxious to move the subject away from Evelynne's ruptured romance. He felt a pressing urge to not only recover her hunter for her, but to go a few rounds with the squire's whelp as well.

"According to Gilly," she pointed out, "you were riding a high-bred stallion yourself the morning you rescued him."

"Oh, Jupiter's my town horse. Good for impressing society misses and stripling lads. Now, for a proper mount, I have Gaitan. He's up in the Highlands at present." He tugged at her hand. "God, I'd love to show him to you, Eve. He got me through more rough times in Spain."

"He was your campaign horse, then?" She tried very hard to disregard his warm fingers upon her wrist.

"They'll never see his like again on the Peninsula." There was a distinct Gilly-like tone of besotted adulation in his voice. "He was part Arab and part French cart horse. I'd bought him from a gypsy in Lisbon, thinking I wouldn't mind having such an ugly beast shot out from under me. He saved me more than once. God, he was a terror in battle—used to lunge at the French soldiers with his teeth bared. I think some Frenchman must have abused him as a foal.

"Oh, and there was one time—an evening when I was out riding him alone. A French sniper picked me off his back, just like that. I was too dazed from the bullet that creased my head to remount or to even know where I was. Gaitan just politely turned back toward camp, and when I realized *he* knew where he was going, I grabbed onto his tail and he led me back, calm as you please. The other officers thought it was great sport. They said I'd followed him home, just like Mary's little lamb."

"Oh, so that's where you got the name." Evelynne gave a pleased gurgle. "Edgar mentioned you several times in his last letter, you know. Called your 'our Lamb.' But you didn't sound very lamblike to me."

"Edgar was more than just one of my staff, Eve, he was also my friend." The earl had both his hands around hers now. "We didn't serve together for very long, but that didn't matter. Sometimes you meet someone and know, almost instantly, that you're bound together. It was like that with your brother. He saved my life at Busaco—no, he didn't die saving me—just got me back behind the lines before I bled to death. As for the rest . . ." He looked at her cautiously. "Are you sure you want to hear this?"

She nodded calmly. "Very much, Robbie."

"It was sometime later in the battle. The French were still firing volleys, but we'd taken their measure, and they knew it. Edgar was leading the rout, always the headstrong boy, and he was hit by a piece of shrapnel. My sergeant swears he was gone in an instant. No pain, Eve, just a soldier's death, with his men all around him."

For some moments the earl looked up at the trees, a faraway expression on his pale face. For the life of her, Evelynne couldn't understand how men could crave to engage in war, and then be so scarred by it afterward. Women, wise creatures, only let love do that to them.

The earl suddenly recollected himself and swung his gaze down to Evelynne. There was fervor in his voice as he spoke. "And don't you dare say you're nothing like him, Evelynne. I've never seen a family with so much courage to spare, and you're likely the bravest of the lot."

"No," she said, disconcerted as usual by his fierce praise. "I'm just stubborn. There's a difference. But thank you for telling me about Edgar. I've always wondered how it happened."

"Just before the battle, Edgar took me aside and asked me to look after his family, in case anything happened to him. I meant it, you know, when I wrote that I was at your family's service. But I never received any response."

"Not until the other night." She grinned a little. "I actually went to Cavendish Square because of something you had written in that letter. I believe the phrase was, 'What I wouldn't give for another lad as fine as Edgar.' I was going to give you Gilly."

The Monteith looked both startled and amused. "You were going to turn that hell-born child over to me?"

"He's the image of Edgar at that age. Headstrong, as you said, and full of himself. But he's decent, too, Robbie, and very, very brave. But Gilly's become too much for me to handle alone—"

"He's probably too much for a Highland regiment," the earl interjected.

"So I thought of what you'd written in your letter, and, well, you know the rest." She looked at him earnestly. "Was I daft to believe you would do it?"

He pondered her words for a minute. "I daresay the lofty Lord Monteith of two nights ago would have turned you from his door with such a preposterous request." He stopped speaking to brush a catkin from her hair, and then continued with a burr in his voice. "But the Robbie MacIntyre, who is here beside you in this overgrown meadow, can deny ye nothing. What do ye want from me, Evelynne Marriott?"

He was leaning over her now, quite blocking out the sun. His face was so close she could see the white, trailing scar above his temple where the sniper's bullet had struck him. His eyes were hooded, obscuring some emotion he wouldn't or couldn't let her see. But his mouth was not obscured, and it compelled her.

"Tell me," he breathed, "your heart's desire . . ."

His hand was on the placket of her shirtfront, tracing the line of her collarbone. She thought of Ollie Hooper's hand doing the very same thing, and she almost smiled. This was much larger game, indeed. And she doubted she had the strength to best this opponent—or even the will.

"Robbie," she said, "am I encouraging you again?"

"Yes, love," he crooned, pulling her shirt open a little and running one finger along her bared throat.

"How, then?" She needed most desperately to know.

"You're breathing." He grinned shamelessly and pushed her firmly back onto the grass. And, God help her, she let him.

When Evelynne embarked on her factory job in boy's clothing, she had counted herself lost to genteel society. She would never wed a man of good birth, would never reclaim her station as a gentlewoman. But that which she had relinquished so easily then, reared up to taunt her at this very moment. She could never have Robbie. Even as a country gentleman's daughter, she was barely suitable as wife to an earl, but it wasn't unthinkable. This, however, was totally unthinkable.

"So quiet, Mouse?" She realized he had stopped touching her and was leaning over her with a puzzled frown.

"I was thinking." She frowned back at him.

"Not very flattering." He sat up and shifted away from her. "My war stories put you to sleep, and my lovemaking sets you to thinking. You're quite successful at keeping me at bay."

"Well, you're not very tenacious . . ." Oh, Lord! She couldn't believe she'd said it.

He had her down, flat on her back in an instant, and his voice was like a searing brand against her ear. "Don't toy, Eve! There's only so much I will stand for."

"I was just trying to encourage you," she said in a small voice. It was hard to speak with the full weight of Robert Mac-

Intyre resting upon her chest, delightful though it felt. "I'm apparently not very good at all this."

He gave a husky laugh. "Then I could teach you, my dearest Evelynne. I haven't always behaved as a Puritan, you know."

"I didn't think so." She gazed up at him, wishing she could guard her eyes as he had. Her heart must be just brimming out over her lashes.

He lowered his mouth to hers. "Lesson one," he murmured, whispering soft kisses along her lips. She tentatively reached up to caress his hair. She had been waiting to touch him forever, it seemed. Now she reveled in the texture of the dark waves. His hair grew long in the back, and she captured it in her fingers and tugged. He groaned slightly and moved against her, hands hard on her shoulders, gripping her, kneading her. His rough growth of beard abraded the tender skin of her face, and yet it was an oddly thrilling sensation.

She wanted to kiss him—to kiss him back, not just be on the receiving end, and she started to ask him how to go about it. She was shocked, and then incredibly stirred, when he slipped his tongue into her open mouth. Something hot seared along her spine, and she arched into him, aching and burning, somehow needing more than just touching or kissing.

"You're trembling, sweet," he said against her mouth. "Are you still afraid?"

"It isn't fear, Robbie . . ." Her voice had a strange, husky timbre. He drew back from her. Her eyes were diamond bright. But something in her face must have given him pause, for he sat upright suddenly. She thought with dismay that he had done with her, but instead he pulled her up and took her into his arms.

"It's safer this way." He gave a hoarse chuckle. "If I lie beside you, I fear we'll get quite far beyond lesson one."

"This is still lesson one?" she asked breathlessly.

"And in what distant kingdom were you raised?" he baited her softly.

"Oh, my." She laid her poor, dazed head beneath his chin as his arms tightly encircled her. "And to think the dairy maids and the chambermaids all know of this."

He rocked her back and forth slowly, letting her catch her breath, and reminding himself to breathe, as well.

He'd only wanted to kiss her, to feel her saucy, clever mouth beneath his own. He never thought to seduce her, or even touch her beyond the normal manner of casual flirtation. Now he wanted to scorch the earth with lovemaking, to set the very trees ablaze with the flame of his passion. She was unschooled and unskilled, awkward even, in his arms, but there was such a fire burning inside her, and he was no more than dry tinder, completely at her mercy.

"I can't kiss you anymore, Evelynne . . ." His voice was muffled against her tangled hair. "I can barely stand to hold you like this." But he tightened his grip, in spite of his words.

"Why?" She tipped back his face, letting her fingers wander from the scar on his brow to his finely drawn lips. He shuddered.

"Because now *I'm* afraid." He set her gently away from him, drawing his arms almost reluctantly from her as he stood up.

"Afraid of what?" Her voice was plaintive and held an edge of pain.

"I can't explain it. I've honestly never felt like this before." He roamed a little distance away, toward the edge of the stream. "I don't know what to make of this whole bizarre adventure. It's been like something from a dream . . . you climbing through the window, and then all the hours in that stuffy closet, Kenny and the turkey . . . the gypsies . . . and the night all around us, holding us safe. But always you, Evelynne, beside me—the best part of the dream." He looked at her, his eyes for once unguarded, and said softly. "Remember the first night, when you had half carried me out of that wretched room? I asked 'Who are you?' and you answered, 'I don't really know any more.' "

"Of course I remember." As if all the words they had spoken to each other weren't forever engraved in her heart.

"Well, that's how I feel now, Evelynne. I'm an earl, a member of Parliament, with responsibilities and binding obligations. I have rank, privilege, money—" His hands clenched into fists at his sides. "And I'd chuck them all to be able to stay right here."

He ran his hand distractedly through his hair and gazed down at Evelynne, sitting there bare-legged on the long grass. She'd never looked more disheveled—or more lovely.

"But I can't, we can't."

"Yes, I know that." She began pulling on her stockings, unable to look at him any longer. "But don't fret yourself. We'll soon be at Levelands, and there's an end to it." *Good.* She sounded brisk and almost matter-of-fact. He'd never guess how her heart was twisting inside her chest, a small animal wounded with words and thoughtless, careless deeds.

He watched her assessingly as she fiddled with her footgear. "Here, Evelynne, put these inside your shoes, they may help." He was holding out the two pieces of linen.

She didn't want to so much as touch his hand. "Just put them on the grass," she muttered, unbuckling one shoe. He did as she asked, and then pulled on his jacket, slinging his greatcoat over one shoulder, for the early afternoon had come on warm.

She wadded up the pieces of his neckcloth and tucked them into the toes of her brogues. It seemed to do the job; the shoes were now quite snug on her feet.

"Old army trick," he said as he reached down to help her up. She shifted away from his hand.

"No." She shook her head. "Don't."

He had the audacity to look hurt. "Eve . . ."

She was stashing apples in her coat pockets. If she was going to be miserable, at least she wouldn't be hungry.

"I think you misunderstand," he continued. "We need . . . I need time to sort things out."

"Oh, I understand just fine," she said beneath her breath as she searched through the high grass for a particularly plump apple that had rolled from her grasp. "We simply go on from here as if nothing has happened. Now—" She stood up and faced him. "I'll thank you not to mention it again." She strode off toward the road.

He caught up with her at the fence. She was gazing up and down its length, looking for a break in the timber. For such a rundown orchard, it certainly was an imposing fence. The earl placed one hand on an upright post, and she watched with chagrin as he easily swung himself over the top rail. He bowed to her from the road, his eyes full of challenge. The man excelled at placing barriers between them.

"Well," he said, "are you coming?"

Evelynne narrowed her eyes, took twenty steps back, and then ran at full tilt toward the barrier. She saw a look of alarm flash across the earl's face as he anticipated her imminent crash into the timber. She stopped short, only inches from the fence, slipped neatly through a space in the rails, and with a look of triumph, joined him on the road.

"You underestimate me, my lord," she said.

"Always," he replied. "It's a bad habit."

*   *   *

They walked together in complete silence for several miles, but the beauty of the day and the realization that they had most likely eluded their pursuers eventually returned them to some level of cordiality. The earl recognized several landmarks along the way, and he pointed them out to her: a burnt-out barn standing bleak on a hillside, and a bustling posting-house called the Terrier's Chase, which they skirted, just to be on the safe side.

As they drew closer to their destination, the road traffic increased; they passed a group of farm women returning from market and a troop of young boys frolicking along with fishing rods slung over their shoulders. Whenever they heard a farm cart or wagon coming, they ducked into the roadside trees; Skelton could still have spies anywhere along the road.

"It can't be above six miles to Levelands." The earl sounded relieved. "I'm known in the village there, so we can send a message up to the house for a carriage. It will save us the long walk through the estate."

"Is it a large property?" Evelynne thought this a safely neutral topic.

"One of the largest in the south of England. Three miles of woodland before you even reach the park. Arkady sets himself up there every autumn in baronial splendor, with shooting parties and the like. I am almost certain he's in residence."

"And who is Arkady?"

"Arkady Pelletier." He gave the name the French pronunciation. "Marquess of Mitford, Viscount Stowe, and about a dozen other tiresome titles."

"It's an odd-sounding name, Arkady Pelletier." In truth, Evelynne thought it had a rather melodic ring.

"He's half Russian. His mother was the Princess Druzgovna; married his father while he was ambassador at Catherine the Great's court."

"How romantic! And is this Arkady as dangerous and exotic as his name sounds?"

"Lord, no!" the earl hooted. "At Cambridge we used to call him the Debutante's Delight: 'All airs and graces, and don't muss my laces.' " He sang out the rhyme.

Evelynne laughed. "How disrespectful. And he a marquess."

"Yes, well he wasn't a marquess yet, and I wasn't an earl either, back then. We were just two young sprigs who somehow shifted along together."

"So, he wasn't one of those people you felt instantly bound to?"

"Arkady? I should say not. I never did understand how the two of us got on as friends. He's possibly the most infuriating man in Great Britain. At times you put me in mind of him."

She cast him a dark look, but merely asked, "So then how did you come to know him?"

"I met him at Cambridge when he fell off the roof of the dispensary. He'd been rescuing a kitten."

"How dreadful! Did something break his fall at least?"

"Yes, the don I was walking with," the earl drawled. "Arkady came tumbling out of the sky, like Icarus descending. Fortunately for my friend, the don was a cat lover and forgave Arkady the broken arm. The don took the kitten back to his rooms, named it Pelly in his honor, and started taking it with him to all his lectures. Arkady followed me back to my rooms, we shared a bottle of claret, and, somehow for the next four years, we were never far apart.

"My family doesn't indulge in Yuletide celebrations, so I'd spend Christmas at Lavaliere—and he'd come up to the Highlands with me for the summer holiday."

"Where is Lavaliere?"

"It's what we call his home. When the Princess Druzgovna came to Hampshire with her husband, she first saw the house from her carriage at night, with every light blazing to welcome her. She proclaimed that 'Levelands' was much too staid a name for such a shimmering place, and that it should forthwith be called 'Lavaliere.' The marquess humored her. Well, everyone humors her."

He stopped dead in his tracks, a look of sudden awareness on his face. "How the devil do you do that, Eve?"

"Do what?" She was quite at sea.

"You somehow get me talking, and I end up telling you things—things I haven't thought about in years. I used to be a man of very few words. Now I rattle on and on."

"I like your stories," she said simply. "You've had a very interesting life. Why doesn't your family celebrate Christmas?"

He glared at her. "You're doing it again. I should start asking *you* questions and see how you like it."

"Well, I've had a singularly dull life. Until now," she added. "Yes, well, my family is not exactly anything to inspire excitement." The earl had continued walking, the dust from the road scuffing up over his boot tips.

"And they don't celebrate Christmas?" she persevered, trotting to keep up. "No wonder you turned out dour."

"My mother's family are strict Presbyterians . . . a throwback to the old Covenanters. They were most distressed when she wed my father—an Anglican. But after Father died, when I was twelve, she was soon drawn back under their influence. No festivities, thank you. No singing, no dancing. Christmas to them is a day of solemn prayer. Well, almost every day calls for solemn prayer. Unfortunately, I was never very pious." He wrinkled his nose at her. "Beatings were almost as regular an occurrence as prayer meetings."

"How shameful " Evelynne declared, biting into her third apple.

"What? That I wasn't properly devout?" The earl eyed her with some amusement.

"No, of course not," she said, then added heatedly, "it's shameful that a family that pretends to godliness can beat a child."

"Spare the rod?" he offered helpfully.

"Nonsense. I'm quite sure I would dislike your family exceedingly." She had uttered the words before she realized what they implied. Her gasp of awareness resulted in a large chunk of apple lodging firmly in her windpipe, and the earl had to pound her soundly on the back for several minutes before they could continue on their way.

He knew precisely what thought had set off her coughing jag. He envisioned presenting Evelynne to his family in Scotland. His mother, Lady Ursula, would not be able to see past the girl's unsuitable bloodlines to the gallant heart within. She'd take to her perpetually gloomy bedroom and pray for her son's soul. His straitlaced, self-consequential cousins would sneer at his choice and think him lost to all sense of familial obligation.

"You might say my family's the reason I attended Cambridge," he explained to Evelynne, once she was breathing normally again. "The University of Edinburgh has been a tradition in my clan, and I was expected to follow suit. But my mother's family has a house in the Old Town, near Holyrood Palace, and she had determined I should stay there with her while I was at school. It was a hellish thought."

"I expect that's why you're so attached to the princess," Evelynne pointed out. "She sounds like a proper mother to me."

God, she was frighteningly acute at times, the earl thought with dismay. He'd never mentioned how much he adored the princess, who was gay and sparkling, and the very antithesis of his own dam. Whenever he traveled to Lavaliere with Arkady, it never felt like a mere visit. After the first time, when he was rapidly enfolded by the princess in a haze of French perfume and spangled gauze, it always felt as if he was going home. It felt that way now.

"Will she be there? At Levelands?" Evelynne knew she was stirring something up in the earl with this line of questioning, but since she was quite churned up inside herself, she decided turnabout was fair play.

"No, I'm afraid you won't get to meet the princess. She travels on the Continent a good deal these days. Russian royalty speaks Parisian French, you know, like natives. So she's been in and out of France, in spite of Bonaparte."

Evelynne looked impressed. "Is she a spy?"

The earl crowed. "Dear Lord, not Nadia! She's almost as feather-witted as Arkady. Let us rather say, she knows a great many influential gentlemen. She has always gone her own way and hasn't let a little thing like a war keep her from her pleasures."

The princess sounded altogether wonderful to Evelynne. And even if she wouldn't get to meet her, she *would* get to meet the intriguing Arkady. And she'd be able to see Lavaliere, their 'shimmering' home. That was, unless the earl sent her posting immediately back to London. She sighed. Best not dwell on that.

Close to sundown they stopped at a crossroads. The trees above them, beech and ash, were a gleaming shade of copper in the gloaming light. The earl knew they were only minutes from Levelton, the small village that lay to the east of Mitford's estate. Every landmark they now passed was like an old, welcoming friend.

He wasn't sure why he stopped. Evelynne hadn't questioned his decision, but had gone to sit on a weathered stile that edged the road. She was watching an angry squadron of crows chase a large hawk through the sky over her head.

The Monteith needed to speak to her, but had no clear idea of how to put his feelings into words. He could easily order his thoughts when addressing a chamberful of politicians, but his brain went on a repairing lease when it came to confronting Evelynne Marriott.

It was over. That was what he was feeling. Their fly-by-night adventure was at a close. They would be whisked away to Lavaliere, and—he knew this, though Evelynne couldn't—they would never be together again. Not as they had been in the last two days. Arkady would have a houseful of guests, probably many people the earl knew himself. The strictures of propriety would descend on them. They'd be lucky if they even had a chance to converse across the dinner table.

He looked at Evelynne with her boy's clothes and impossibly untamed hair. How could he even introduce her into the group? She'd have to be hidden away until he could make arrangements to send her home. God, it was hopeless.

"You're scowling again," she remarked pleasantly from her perch. "You actually haven't scowled like that since you left London. I thought the country air must be agreeing with you."

He started to reply, when there was a clattering noise in the road ahead. A vehicle was approaching at a rapid clip from the direction of Levelton. The earl needed only a glimpse of two gray horses, harnessed abreast, and the hazy outline of a man at the reins, before he tumbled Evelynne backward off her seat on the stile.

"Run, Evel!" the earl cried in a low voice, his hands urgent against her back. "Get to Levelands. Go!"

Evelynne didn't need to be told twice. She'd seen those horses once before, in similarly ghostly lighting. She turned and ran, skirting the low bracken at her feet, heading for a copse of lilac shrubs that stood ten yards from the road. She dove into the center of the bushes, bracing herself for the impact of the earl crashing in behind her. She waited in vain.

She steeled herself to peer out at the road and saw the earl locked in writhing combat with two very large men. They were dragging him down off the stile, while Lord Randall Skelton sat in a four-seater curricle, quite at his ease as he watched the proceedings. Once the two men got the earl under control, Skelton climbed down from his seat, and as he approached them, he pulled a long-barreled dueling pistol from his waistcoat.

Evelynne had leapt from the bushes and thrown the apple, quite before she realized she was doing it. It struck Lord Skelton smartly on the side of his coiffured head. He turned with an oath, and she lobbed another one into his arm. She then fished in her pockets and realized she had eaten the rest of her ammunition. *Drat!*

Skelton appeared unperturbed. "You, lad, come here!" he ordered, brushing the wet residue of the second apple from his sapphire blue satin coat. "Come here, or I will shoot him where he stands."

"No, Mouse!" the earl called, twisting around. "He's bluffing."

"Come here! Now!" Skelton barked, raising his gun higher. "Or I will shoot *you*. It's an easy shot; you make a rather nice target with the sunset at your back."

Evelynne walked slowly back to the road, head down, thinking furiously of how to handle this turn of events. The earl was seething.

"You should have stayed put," he hissed at her as she climbed the stile and went past him.

The men holding him by the arms were not the two from the inn, she noted. They were taller even than the ginger-haired coachman, and much burlier.

The baron pulled her roughly by the shoulder, up close, so he could see her face.

"So you're the boy from the inn? The cook told us there'd been a lad and a tall Irishman who passed through her kitchen last night. Never occurred to her that he was my runaway, foolish woman. Almost as daft as that addle-pated boy."

"Kenny!" Evelynne cried out. "You didn't hurt him?"

Skelton smiled. It was not what Evelynne would have called a pleasant expression.

"I *thought* he'd helped you two get away. Alfie couldn't get anything out of him, but—"

"If your thug harmed the boy—" the Monteith uttered, his head straining forward toward the baron.

"The father intervened, unfortunately, with a shotgun." There was a note of chagrin in Lord Skelton's voice. "But it was enough that the word 'Levelands' was scrawled on a slate in their parlor. The lad had apparently been practicing his letters, and his father had written the name for him to copy. It was then only a matter of waiting, my dear Monteith. We knew you'd be along eventually."

"This has gone a great deal beyond politics, now, Skelton," the earl said through clenched teeth.

"How remarkably observant, my lord. It's gone further than you will ever know." Skelton's voice was silky. "But I think I'll keep with my plan to discredit you. Murdering one's peers is just a little too unsavory, even for a man of my disposition. But you'll keep your long Scottish nose out of my business from here on, or there'll be the devil to pay."

"I wouldn't go talking about long noses if I were you," Evelynne muttered under her breath. Lord Skelton, who was understandably sensitive about his gargoylelike profile, took immediate umbrage at her words, especially coming as they did from a raggle-taggle urchin. He turned to cuff her, and she launched herself at his pistol hand. She got a good grip with her teeth on the fleshy part of his thumb, and with a foul oath he swung around, trying to shake her off.

The pistol flew out of his hand and landed beneath the gray horses, who started to prance and fidget. The carriage moved forward several feet. Skelton called out, "Curry, get the horses, you fool!" to one of the men holding the earl, who quickly ran to grab the harness reins.

The Monteith managed to shake loose from his sole remaining captor, and with great science neatly dispatched him with a left uppercut that felt, the fellow swore later, like something akin to a thunderbolt. The earl started forward just as the baron pried his hand loose from Evelynne's bulldog grip.

"No-o-o!" the Monteith cried out as Skelton landed a crashing backhand blow upon Evelynne's cheek. She reeled back six or seven steps, then collapsed in a tangled heap at the edge of the road.

The earl dove toward Skelton, but the remaining henchman left off holding the horses and intercepted him. The earl ducked under his roundhouse swing and in a bloodred rage turned and pounced on the man. He, too, was quickly overcome by a few well-placed blows to his chin and chest. The earl had clearly not been wasting his time at Jackson's.

He swung to face Skelton, who was crouched alongside his curricle, groping for the missing pistol.

The earl was all Highlander now as he bore down on his enemy.

"Ye puling cur. I'll have the hide off ye. All ye're fit for is frightening the simpleminded and hitting unarmed lads. Let's see how ye account for yerself against a man." The baron appeared to be taking refuge under the carriage. "Can't find yer wee gun, eh?"

Skelton had barely grasped the pistol where it lay, far under one of the front wheels, when the earl pulled him abruptly up by the skirts of his fine coat. The gun skittered from his hands.

Skelton turned to fight—not every sniveling bully folds in the face of opposition. But even the bravest man would have quailed before the Laird of Monteith in a towering Scottish rage. His dark blue eyes were blazing, his lean jaw hard-set, and his face almost ardent with his desire to engage the enemy. Many a French soldier had fled before that look.

"I'm sure we can work this out, Monteith," Skelton said, walking backward and holding up both hands appeasingly. Then, quick as a flash, he darted around to the far side of the carriage, where a holstered horse pistol hung against the door.

The Monteith didn't hesitate. He leapt into the carriage and flung himself at Skelton across the seat, knocking the weapon aside as it discharged. The force of his charge carried them both away from the curricle. Skelton tried to run, but the earl caught him and spun him around. With a lightning left hook he broke Skelton's beak of a nose and followed that up with a punishing right to the jaw, which lifted the man several inches into the air. Randall Skelton, his face bloodied and broken, drifted slowly to the ground and settled gracefully in a pool of blue satin.

"Maggot!" the earl growled.

He was kneeling beside Evelynne's tumbled form in the next instant. She was out cold, a large welt already spreading across her right cheek. He drew her carefully into his arms. Her head lolled back, and he captured it in the crux of his arm.

"Ach, my dearest girl," he breathed against her hair, "I would have spared you this." He touched her injured cheek, and then tenderly kissed the spot where his fingers had lain.

He carried her to the curricle and lifted her gently onto the front seat. He collected the dueling pistol from under the front wheels and tossed it next to the horse pistol on the floor of the rear seat. Skelton had certainly come armed into battle. The earl wondered that there wasn't a blunderbuss secreted somewhere in the carriage.

He climbed into the rig, settling Evelynne against his chest. She moaned slightly, and he drew one arm protectively around her.

"Hold tight, sweetheart," he whispered, taking up the reins

and turning the fractious grays back toward Levelton. "I'm going to spring 'em."

The wind whipped through his black hair as he sent the horses careening along the dusk dark lane. He knew this road, every turning, every bump, every grade and incline. He and Arkady had raced their carriages along this particular stretch times past counting. But never had he felt such a sense of exhilaration before, and never had he carried such precious cargo.

He'd see her safe home now, safe at Lavaliere. And God help any man who tried to stop him!

Chapter 7

❧

Arkady Pelletier, Marquess of Mitford, adjusted his neck-cloth in the gilt-edged mirror above the white marble fireplace. He gave the elaborately tied waterfall at his throat one final tweak, and then stepped back to assess the total effect. It was almost time to go down to supper, but he was suffering grave doubts about the color of his evening coat. The particular shade of pomona green silk certainly did play up the celadon highlights in his large green eyes, but he thought perhaps it also gave the hint of sallowness to his pale face. He wagered he'd appear positively bilious in the brightly lit dining room. There was nothing for it. He'd have to change.

He made a rude face at his reflection. The fair-haired, bullet-headed dandy in the mirror responded in kind. It was deuced hard work being a tulip of fashion, he observed, as he turned to peruse the other five coats that his valet had laid out on the bed.

His valet? Where had the man gotten to? He'd never squirm out of his present coat without assistance from at least one strong man. "Demby?" he called softly.

He looked vacantly around the bedroom. It was a large chamber, furnished with many elegant pieces, but it was unlikely his valet was hiding behind or under the furniture. He peered into his dressing room. It, too, was empty.

Arkady had contorted himself halfway out of the green coat, looking like the loser in a no-holds-barred wrestling match, when Demby emerged from beside the draperies that partially covered one long window at the far end of the room.

"Your lordship," he chided, tugging his master's coat firmly back up around his shoulders. "There's no time for foolishness. I heard a noise at this window, just now while you were adjusting your neckcloth . . . Sir, I think you'd better have a look for yourself."

Arkady gave a little moue of impatience. "But my dinner guests are waiting below."

The valet looked stern. If it pleased his master to act precocious—and it often did—Demby would not throw a rub in his way. But there appeared to be a serious problem down in the drive, and Demby knew the marquess should deal with this himself.

"It's Major MacIntyre—that is, the Earl of Monteith."

"Robbie? Here? Why, of all the jolly luck. Have him come up, Demby."

"I think your lordship had better attend him outside. He looks rather badly used . . . and he's not alone."

"What's that?" Arkady had taken the bait like a trout rising to a mayfly. He made his way to the window embrasure and drew back the heavy, brocaded draperies.

Robert MacIntyre was standing beside an open carriage, speaking with one of Mitford's grooms. Even at this distance, Arkady could see that his friend looked quite disheveled. There appeared to be someone lying on the front seat of the carriage, wrapped in the earl's greatcoat.

"This isn't like Robbie at all," Arkady fussed. With Demby in tow, he made his way along the wide hallway and down the back stairs. They passed through the gun room, where a narrow doorway opened onto the drive.

The groom had mounted one of the stable hacks and was just riding off as Arkady and his valet emerged. As he drew closer, Mitford could see that the earl's face was haggard and bore at least two days' growth of dark beard.

Mitford went to his friend and placed a hand upon his sleeve. "Robbie, what's happened? You look like the very devil."

"I'm sorry to arrive in this state. I saw the light in your bedroom and threw a bit of gravel up at the window," the earl explained. "Thank God, Demby heard me."

Arkady, atwitch with curiosity, craned his head past the earl to see who was lying on the carriage seat. A dark-haired young woman was cocooned inside Robbie's coat, in a complete swoon. She had a nasty-looking bruise on her cheek. Arkady raised one eyebrow. "Are you in trouble?"

"Not if you'll let me stay here. Look, it's a very long tale, but first I've got to get Evelynne into bed—"

"Yes, I don't doubt it," Arkady muttered impishly.

The earl glowered, and Mitford, realizing his friend was not in a funning mood, smiled back placatingly and said, "Sorry. Of course you can stay here."

"That's one problem settled, then. But I'd like to keep all this as quiet as possible. I've sent one of your lads to fetch the doctor, but the fewer who see her, the happier I'll be."

The earl lifted Evelynne from the carriage, still swathed in his coat. Arkady thought he'd never seen his friend handle anything so gently. Demby arranged the folds of the earl's coat around the girl's shoulders, and then gingerly led the gray horses in the direction of the stable.

"Who is she?" Arkady asked over his shoulder as he led the way back through the house and up the stairs.

"No one," the Monteith answered tersely. "Just a factory girl who saved my life."

The earl followed Arkady's winding progress to an unoccupied portion of the great house. Evelynne stirred in his arms and gave a little whimper.

"Hush," he whispered, bending to her dark head. "You're safe now."

The room they entered was small and not furnished in the latest style, but it contained a charming French bateau bed and had a tall window at one end.

"She'll be able to see the park from here," Arkady remarked, apropos of nothing.

The earl laid Evelynne on the bed, pulling his greatcoat from around her as he set her down. Arkady's eyes widened when he saw that the girl was wearing breeches and a boy's homespun jacket. The earl began to open her shirt. He realized with a start what he had been about to do and turned to his friend with a helpless expression.

"She needs a woman to look after her, Arkady. Is Mrs. Lyons still your housekeeper? Can we take her into our confidence?" As he spoke, he drew a coverlet over Evelynne.

"I'll vouch for any of my staff, Robbie. Besides, Mrs. Lyons would probably commit murder for you. She's always had a soft spot for a tall Scot. Shall I ring for her?"

"Hold a minute—" The earl took a nervous turn around the room. "I've got to come up with some sort of explanation. Why we are dressed like this, why we have arrived unannounced."

"How about the truth?" Arkady suggested. It was almost inconceivable that his forthright friend was involved in any sort of subterfuge. That was much more his own line of business.

The earl shot him a look of impatience. "Don't try me, Arkady. I'm in no mood for your banter. I've spent the last two days trying to keep one step ahead of scandal, and I'm damned if it's going to catch up with me now."

Arkady looked a little miffed. "I'd say turning up at a house party with an unconscious woman in your arms is bound to invite some comment."

"I'll go if you'd prefer to be kept out of it," the Monteith said stiffly.

"Oh, no, no, my dear fellow." Arkady went to his friend's side and soothed him into a wing chair. He crouched before the grim-faced earl. "You've gotten me out of dozens of scrapes, Robbie. Don't you think I've lived for the moment when I could return the favor?"

"Hogwash," the earl muttered. "What you live for is meddling in other people's lives."

The Marquess of Mitford gave him a sweet smile. "Well, a fellow does need a hobby, don't you know."

"I won't have you mixing in this business, Arkady. We just require a place to lie low until I can send her back to London."

Ah, Robbie, ever the gracious guest.

Arkady stood up and adjusted his shirt cuffs with white, well-manicured hands. He glanced down at the earl's hands. The knuckles were bruised and bloody. He sat in his chair, twisting those hands, and his eyes never left the still figure on the swagged bed.

"She's going to be fine, you know," Arkady said softly. "She looks like a hearty girl."

The earl gave a brittle laugh. "That is the understatement of the century. But, yes, I think you'd best ring for Mrs. Lyons now. She needs to be out of those clothes before the doctor arrives."

Arkady went to the bellpull and gave it a firm tug. "Mrs. Lyons will make your friend quite comfortable. She'll find her something, ah, more appropriate to wear, and then you and I will have a very large brandy in my library. Oh, heavens, I forgot about dinner. I'll have to send down that I'm indisposed. See now you've got me telling fibs."

The earl grinned in spite of himself. "Much you ever cared for that."

Mrs. Lyons came into the room with a rustling of bombazine. She looked a narrow, tight-faced woman until her glance fell upon the earl. Then her cool blue eyes widened in surprise, and her face took on an expression of great warmth.

"Your lordship!" she exclaimed with a low curtsy. "It is a pleasure to see you again."

He rose and gave her a nod of acknowledgment.

"We have a slight problem, Mrs. Lyons," Arkady began, "and I know I can trust your discretion."

The housekeeper was already beside the bed, brushing the hair from Evelynne's brow and feeling for her pulse. She drew the bedclothes away from the girl's body, and when she saw her masculine attire, she turned to the earl with a stern frown. "How came she to be dressed like this, your lordship?"

Arkady laid a finger over his lips and uttered ominously, "We are not to ask."

"Of course you can ask," the Monteith exclaimed in annoyance. "Miss Marriott is a factory girl who rescued me from a very nasty situation. She is in disguise, as you can see. And she's been injured, as you can also see."

He looked down at the girl on the bed as he spoke; her face was so very white, except for the ugly purple swelling that marred one cheek.

Christ! She should have come to by now. He was pacing again. *Where in blazes is that doctor?*

"I'll thank you two gentlemen to leave us now," Mrs. Lyons pronounced. "No purpose served by fussing and fidgeting." She aimed a sharp look at the earl. "And you, sir, look like you should be in your bed, as well."

Arkady led the earl, protesting, from the room. "We'll speak with the doctor after he's seen to her. And then you're to follow Mrs. Lyons's orders. It's bed for you, old lad."

They repaired to Mitford's library. Unlike most libraries of the day, steeped in their dark woods and leather-clad furniture, the library of Levelands was painted in shades of white and cream. It was airily furnished with faux-bamboo chairs and had as its centerpiece a pale wood refectory table carved with allegorical scenes. It was quite Arkady's favorite room.

Mitford poured a cognac for each of them, and then they settled before the fire.

"I suppose you require an explanation?" The earl sipped his drink slowly, watching his friend with cautious eyes.

Arkady blinked. "Well, yes. You know me, I'm like a cat with a ball of yarn—never content till it's completely unraveled."

"It was Skelton," the earl said. "He had me adducted from my house in London. I've been looking into his business affairs, you know, trying to get some political leverage . . . Arkady, what I'm about to say mustn't leave this room."

"I'm hurt beyond words that you even need to mention it."

"Well, I just wanted to be sure. There's more at stake here than even I realized. I expect you know that Randall Skelton came into a great deal of Scottish property through his mother. Unfortunately, he did not inherit much capital to go with it. He's had to engage in commerce to support the land. I discovered, through a former business associate of his, that he'd lost almost all his money in bad speculations about three years ago. Yet he appears now to be quite flush, if not extremely well-to-do."

"Maybe he just has a good head for business?" Arkady suggested, twirling his glass.

"Maybe he's selling state secrets to Napoleon for French gold." The earl looked intently at his friend.

Arkady knit his brows. "Skelton always was a bad'un, but that's a pretty damning accusation to make against a peer of the realm. Have you any proof?"

"Sir Robert Poole has uncovered some things recently of a very incriminating nature. It was a forged note, supposedly from Poole, that lured me into the coach."

"Ah, the forged-note trick," Arkady murmured knowledgeably. "And you, rash fellow that you are, fell for it."

"Oh, I fell all right." The earl rubbed the back of his head, which was still tender. "And I'd probably still be under guard at the Eel and Barrow if Evelynne hadn't rescued me." Arkady leaned forward eagerly, as the earl continued. "She hid me at the inn until I was well enough to escape. I was being held somewhere near Southampton—"

"That's one of Skelton's favorite haunts. He has shipbuilding investments there, and, if I'm not mistaken, he has an estate there, as well."

"Yes, well it's also close by the Channel. And if Sir Robert's information is correct, my foul friend has been using his own ships to smuggle information into France."

Arkady gave a low whistle. "It's worth an abduction or two to keep that away from the ears of Parliament."

"Treason is a hanging offense," the earl stated. "Especially in wartime. If it comes to that, I'll gladly stand in for the executioner. Skelton showed his hand when he abducted me. Only a man with something serious to hide would go to such lengths."

"So what happened to this girl, Robbie?"

The Monteith looked into the amber depths of his glass. "We were almost to Levelton, almost safe. But Skelton had supposed I would come here, and intercepted us on the road with two of his bullies. He pulled a gun, and Evelynne tried to protect me."

"Plucky chit," the blond man said under his breath.

"He hit her, Arkady!" the earl cried, his eyes flashing up to meet Mitford's. There was an edge of raw pain in his voice. "He struck her down in the road. You wouldn't treat a cur like that." He rubbed his chin with one hand. "I've never felt so powerless. He's lucky I didn't tear out his black heart."

Arkady made a commiserating noise. "Well, I gather you did exact *some* revenge." He touched his friend's torn knuckles. "And unless I'm mistaken, those were Skelton's grays harnessed to that carriage."

"Yes, I took the carriage to get Evelynne away. I'm afraid I left rather a mess of bodies behind me. Skelton probably won't show his ugly face for several days . . . I broke his nose." Arkady gave a little ho-ho of delight. "But he's sure to turn up eventually. Apparently, he was going to set me up in a compromising situation so he could blackmail me into stopping my investigation. I was to be discovered at the Eel and Barrow, drunk, and in bed with a courtesan."

"Well, at least that's a pleasant way to go to the devil."

"Evelynne got me away before anything happened, but, don't you see . . . that's all the more reason not to let a scandal break now. She worked so damned hard. What if it was all for nothing? If it gets about that I spent two nights with her, she'll be compromised, and I'll be ruined politically. It's exactly the kind of scandal Skelton needs to discredit me. And I won't back off now, not when I've almost got the knave cornered. Not for her honor, not even for my career."

Arkady stared thoughtfully up at the serene spaces of the Adam ceiling. "Miss Marriott is a distant connection of your family," he mused aloud. "You were escorting her to visit a relative near here, and were set upon by robbers. Your coach was stolen, and you were both knocked about during the robbery. Then you walked to the nearest town, hired a carriage, and sought refuge here."

He turned to his friend for his reaction to this ingenious fabrication. The earl was scowling. Arkady sighed. "Don't you see, Robbie, it explains everything? Your untimely arrival, your injuries, why neither of you has a change of clothing."

"It doesn't explain Evelynne," he said softly. "Any connection of my family's would be expected to hold their own in this company. How many guests are here at present?"

Arkady waved his hand negligibly. "Oh, not above twenty, twenty-five, at the most."

The earl groaned.

"Lady Philippa is here, with her aunts."

The earl groaned even louder. Lady Philippa Carstairs was the widow of a wealthy baron, a woman of impeccable breeding and heart-stopping beauty. She had been the earl's mistress for a time, when he'd first returned from the war. And she was ever eager to renew the connection and even had hopes, he knew, of making it a legal match.

"It's impossible," the earl said wearily. "I believe Evelynne has been out in county society—you know, hunt balls and village assemblies—but she'd never pass muster in this group."

"She isn't making her bow to the queen, Robbie. We're an informal gathering, as you know. And I thought you said she was a factory girl?"

"She's been working in London, but she was raised in Devon. It doesn't matter. I can't let her loose with your rackety set." Arkady made no attempt to look insulted at the earl's blunt criticism. "However, I do think we can use your story about the robbery. Half the men here would probably recognize Skelton's grays, so I'll send his carriage and horses off to the Terrier's Chase. That way it will appear we did arrive in a job carriage, and no one the wiser."

"Excellent," Arkady said. Robbie was turning out to have quite a knack for scheming. It was a revelation. "And what of the girl?"

"She'll have to keep to her room. As soon as she's feeling fit, I'll send her back to London."

Arkady greatly misliked that part of the plan, but kept the thought to himself.

"Now," the earl continued, "if you'll give me the use of two of your lads, I've some messages to post. I've got to send to London, to let Wenders know I'm safe and to set Sir Robert on Skelton's trail. And there's another piece of business in Devon I need to attend to."

Arkady directed his friend to some writing materials in a drawer, and then watched him scribbling away, seated at the long rectory table. There was something vaguely different about the earl, but he couldn't quite pinpoint what it was. Oh, he was as surly as ever, and as quick to anger. But there was also a look of vulnerability in his eyes that Arkady had never seen before. And he had noticed it most clearly when the earl gazed anxiously upon the unconscious girl in the bed.

Robbie was in love!

Mitford refilled his glass. Now here was something worth drinking to. The factory girl and the earl. *How lovely.* He looked again at his friend's dark head bent intently over his letter. If he knew Robbie, the poor fellow probably didn't have a clue.

I'm going to be very busy the next few days, Arkady mused with a cheerful grin.

Mrs. Lyons brought the doctor down to the library, just as the earl finished sealing up his final missive.

"The young lady is awake and feeling a little better," she said. "But she mentioned that his lordship had been struck on the head."

With an oath the Monteith rose from the table. "There's nothing wrong with me."

"I'd best be the judge of that." The doctor, stout and bewhiskered, rolled his eyes at Arkady. He'd had a few run-ins with the earl during previous visits and knew him for a very uncooperative patient. "Head wounds can be quite unpredictable."

"Let him look, Robbie. Can't have you throwing a fit in the middle of supper."

With a resentful glance at his friend, the earl suffered himself to be examined by the physician. His head was palpated, his scalp wound closely scrutinized, and his torn knuckles dusted with basillicum powder.

"Oh, leave off with that," he snapped at last, twisting away from the doctor's ministrations. "And tell me how Miss Marriott goes on."

"She's just been badly shaken up, my lord. I gave her something to make her sleep. A very compliant young woman," he added emphatically to the earl. "Nothing is broken. Her cheek is merely bruised."

"Merely bruised!" the Monteith fumed. "She was unconscious when I brought her here!"

"She said something about not having slept in a long time. It's my belief she is suffering nothing more serious than exhaustion."

The doctor packed up his bag, and Mrs. Lyons and Arkady walked with him to the door.

"He never saw her clothing," Mrs. Lyons whispered to her master once the doctor had departed. "I had her cleaned up and in one of your cousin Lydia's pretty bed gowns before he arrived. Tomorrow morning she's to have a bath, and Millie's to come in and fix her hair."

Arkady smiled his approval.

"She asked to see his lordship," the housekeeper continued, keeping her voice low. "She was a bit upset to awaken among strangers. She asked me if I was the princess!" She tittered a little. " She's really a lovely, lovely girl, my lord, and I can't think what that Scottish rogue was doing, dragging her about in the night."

"I rather think she was doing the dragging," Arkady responded. "But you've done well, Mrs. Lyons. We are all in your debt." She curtsied, and was about to leave when he forestalled her.

"Oh, yes, one last thing. Miss Marriott is a distant connection of the earl's, and they were set upon by robbers and took shelter here . . . if any of my guests should inquire."

"Very good, my lord. And I will be sure to pass the word downstairs, as well." With a barely contained look of amusement, she made her way from the room. Her master was losing his touch—his Banbury tales were usually much more difficult to spot.

Evelynne was sitting up in bed, looking out at the park beyond her window. She could see white deer grazing on a little hillock, and behind them willows swayed gracefully in the breeze. The edge of a lake was visible, and several fashionably clad couples were rowing to and fro in small boats. There was no clock in her room, but she knew it must be early afternoon. The housekeeper had woken her at ten, carrying in her tea tray, and leading a procession of footmen, who hauled in a copper hip bath and then proceeded to fill it with hot water. Mrs. Lyons had scented the water with verbena and sandalwood, and helped her to bathe. Then, while she sat before the fire, swaddled in a fleece robe, a pert young maid came in and attacked her hair. She snipped and trimmed, humming while she worked, as Evelynne's dark locks fell onto a sheet placed beneath her.

"It's called *a la Circe,* miss," Millie explained as she ruthlessly scissored. "It's all the crack. And, if I may say, you do have a rare head of hair . . ."

Rarer now than it was before. Evelynne eyed her shorn ringlets, scattered in profusion on the floor.

"No curling irons for you, miss, not with all these lovely curls."

I'm going to be bald if she keeps this up any longer. Evelynne watched in dismay as another sheaf of her dark hair fluttered down.

But when Millie brought her a hand mirror, she couldn't believe what she saw reflected back at her. She looked almost pretty, in spite of her discolored cheek. Millie had left the back and sides long, thinning them into dainty tendrils. She had then shingled the rest of her hair to form soft curls that hugged Evelynne's scalp and showed off the refined shape of her head.

"Th-thank you, Millie," she stammered. "It's most amazing."

"Very nice, indeed." Mrs. Lyons was nodding with approval. Miss Marriott cleaned up surprisingly well.

They left Evelynne alone then, with orders to sleep. She did fall into a fitful doze, but kept waking every time she heard a noise. She finally gave up on sleep and passed the time gazing out at the park, all the while wondering fretfully why Robbie hadn't inquired after her.

When she'd returned to a hazy sort of consciousness last night, lying in a strange room, being fussed over by people she'd never met, all she could think of was the earl. She had last seen him being held at gunpoint by a sneering Lord Skelton. And as she lay half swooning upon the road, she was sure she'd heard the report of a pistol. Her disordered mind had convinced her that he had been shot. But the housekeeper had informed her that the "Major," who had brought her hence, appeared to be in quite good health. But, surely, if he was feeling better, he'd have come to see her.

She was beginning to fall prey to the dismals when there was a scratching at her door.

Robbie, her heart hammered. But when she called "Enter," a stranger walked in, bearing a covered tray. He set it down on the bureau and turned to face her.

He was probably not much taller than she was, and he was slight, as well. His hair was the pale blond of winter wheat, and poker straight. Though very well-cut—she now knew a good haircut when she saw one—stray wisps fell in a boyish feathering over his high forehead. His face seemed quite commonplace, until she noticed his eyes, which were jade green, large and very expressive. He wore a brocaded jacket the color of apricots and smallclothes of deep tobacco brown. His extreme shirt points bespoke the dandy, but if that was the case, this man could certainly give the foppish Lord Skelton a few pointers.

He waited out her perusal with thinly veiled amusement.

"I'm Mitford," he said. "Not much like your idea of a marquess, you're thinking." He cocked his head. "No, don't deny it. I excel at reading minds."

She was taken aback at first by his offhand manner. But when he made a round-eyed face at her, it reminded her so much of her brother Josh that she giggled. He grinned, and she held out her hand to him. "I am Evelynne Marriott, my lord."

"Yes, and a vastly improved Evelynne Marriott, I might add." He bowed over her hand and kissed it lightly. "And you must call me Arkady. No one refers to me by my title." He gave an exaggerated pout, and when she giggled again, he offered her his winning smile. "See, absolutely no marquessly respect. And how do you fare this morning, Miss Marriott?"

"Very well, I think."

"Good." He turned to the bureau and took up a small bowl. "I had to bribe Mrs. Lyons to let me see you—it's not good *ton* to visit ladies in their bedchambers—but to make up for my lapse, I've brought you your gruel."

"My gruel?" she echoed, a look of dismay clouding her face. He held out the bowl. Evelynne surveyed it dubiously.

"Or," he continued, replacing the bowl on the tray and taking up a large plate, "you could have this nice chop with a little apple compote."

"Oh yes," she breathed. "You wouldn't make me eat gruel?"

"No," he replied. "Actually, the gruel is for Robbie."

Evelynne laughed then, laughed full out for the first time in what felt like days. Arkady regarded her with approval. He had a very good feeling about this girl.

"I'd like to see you make him eat gruel," she commented as he handed her a large napkin and set the plate in her lap. "You'd likely end up wearing it. He's not the most even tempered of men."

"Robert MacIntyre, ill-tempered?" He looked incredulous, and that set her off again in peals of laughter.

"Robbie said you were infuriating," she remarked, tucking into her meal. "But I think you are exceedingly nice."

Arkady studied Evelynne as she ate. The earl was clearly off his noodle. This young woman could hold her own in any company. She was charming, self-possessed, and bantered surprisingly well, which was always his measure of how intelligent a person was. *A factory girl, indeed!* It occurred to him that perhaps his dour friend was having him on.

"How is my Lord Monteith?" Evelynne asked between bites. She then added somewhat hesitantly, "I thought perhaps he might look in on me."

"Last I heard he was still sound asleep." Arkady toyed with one of the jeweled fobs that dangled from his waistcoat. Robbie had been up at dawn and had ridden off into Levelton to discover any news of Skelton. And he'd strictly forbidden Arkady to have any contact with Evelynne.

"He's not injured?"

"No, no, just getting his strength back, I daresay. He got himself shaken up a bit last night. You probably haven't heard yet, but he thrashed Skelton and his two lackeys. Pity you were knocked out. When it comes to fisticuffs, Robbie displays something rare."

"I'm sure he does," Evelynne sniffed. Here she was, not able to sleep, worried to a frazzle over him, and he hadn't even bothered to wake up and inquire after her.

"I'm sure he'll be in to see you any time now," Arkady assured her. He hadn't missed the snit that Evelynne was cultivating. "He did mention last night that you would probably prefer to keep to your room indefinitely. He felt that in your impaired state, it would be too strenuous for you to be about in company."

Evelynne's reaction was all he could wish for.

"Impaired! He said that?" Her eyes blazed. "He has no say in what I do! Oh, how I wish I had some proper clothes—I'd show him how 'impaired' I am."

"As for that," Arkady said silkily, "my cousin Lydia, whose bed gown you are currently doing extreme credit to, keeps trunks full of dresses here. She's off visiting some country or other with *ma mère*. She'd be happy, I'm quite sure, if you availed yourself of her things."

Evelynne looked doubtful. "I'm horridly tall," she warned him.

"Oh, Lydia can give me several inches; she's quite a Maypole. So it's settled then? I'll send a maid round with some gowns, and she can make any alterations you might need. By the by, the story we've put about is that you are a distant connection of Robbie's family, and you were both set upon by robbers while he was escorting you from town."

She nodded her comprehension. Thank goodness Arkady saw fit to make her feel welcome. That seemed to be more than the earl could manage.

"Rest up now, and I'll look forward to seeing you later. We meet in the drawing room at half after seven."

Evelynne sighed. The flame of her anger had diminished, to be replaced by a gnawing feeling of disappointment.

Arkady lifted one of her hands from the coverlet. "Courage, Miss Marriott. You can't win the battle without engaging the enemy." And with that cryptic comment he departed her room. Once he was out in the hall, he rubbed his two hands together. This had the promise of being a truly exceptional forum for his talents. And now to track down the earl and further set the stage.

Arkady met his friend coming up the main staircase from the great hall.

"I was just going up to visit Evelynne." He tried to bypass Mitford, who was blocking his path.

Arkady shook his head. "Not a good idea. Mrs. Lyons tells me she's sound asleep. Ate a healthy breakfast, though—just to set your mind at ease—and then she dozed right off again."

The earl looked perplexed. Surely, Evelynne had inquired after him. "Well, I'll just peek in then. Maybe sit with her a while."

Arkady looked aghast. "Not done, old lad! You'd need at

least one tabby in there to keep it respectable, and I'm afraid all the maids are occupied this afternoon."

Mitford drew him firmly back downstairs and into the library.

"So, did you discover anything this morning?"

"Skelton's disappeared," the earl said, taking a glass of sherry from his friend. "No one in Levelton saw him again last night. He didn't stop at any of the posting inns hereabouts. Some of his bullies must have found him on the road and carted him back to Southampton."

"Good riddance, I say," Arkady pronounced. "Have you see Lady Philippa yet?"

"Gad, no! I've only just returned. I did run into Westmoreland out at the stable. He'd been apprised of our little fabrication; told me I should travel with postillions as he did, to 'keep the riffraff away.' " The earl was incensed. "As if I couldn't defend myself against highway robbers!"

"Especially with Miss Marriott at your back," Arkady murmured.

"He's agreed to let me borrow some of his clothes—we're of a size, he and I—so I can return your shirt." The earl had appropriated one of Mitford's fine lawn shirts before he'd set out that morning. "It's a dashed tight fit!"

"Sorry. We're not all blessed with your splendid physique," Arkady said a bit peevishly.

"What?" The earl blinked. "Don't gammon me! You play at being the frail lily so often, I don't wonder you've begun to believe it yourself. I, however, haven't forgotten how you trounced me the last time we were at Jackson's together."

"A mere fluke." Arkady smiled graciously. "I believe I had the advantage of surprise." It was an advantage he'd found useful in numerous encounters, outside of the boxing ring as well.

The earl rose, stretching his hands over his head and yawning. "I think I'll go up to my room for a while. I'll leave Evelynne to her slumbers. Maybe I can check on her later this evening." He gazed down at Mitford, lounging back in his chair. "Look, before I go, Arkady, I want to say that you've been really sporting about all this. I'm hoping that Evelynne will be well enough to travel back to London by tomorrow, but if it's all the same to you, I'd like to spend a few more days at

Lavaliere. I've an inkling Skelton will seek me out here, and I certainly wouldn't want to disappoint him."

"You don't even need to ask, Robbie. My home is yours. And, besides, I wouldn't miss the next installment of this adventure for all the treasures of Cathay!"

Chapter 8

❧

The earl spent the rest of the afternoon in his room, reading a military biography. He was avoiding any more of Arkady's guests until the story they'd fabricated had time to be passed from servant to master. He must have dozed off over his book, for it was close to seven when Demby came in to help him dress, carrying one of Westmoreland's evening suits over his arm.

The drawing room was already full of company when the earl at last made his appearance downstairs. Sir Reginald's suit fit him well enough, but Demby must have tied his neckcloth a bit too snugly. He ran one finger along his collar and tugged at it a little as he entered the room.

There was a subtle din of animated chatter all about him as he took a glass of claret from a footman's tray. The houseguests had formed themselves into small, scattered groups. Arkady was by one window, chatting with a bevy of young ladies; the regally attired Lady Philippa was near the fireplace, surrounded by fashionable sprigs. She was laughing at a remark one of her swains had made, her head thrown back a little, exposing her long white neck. She was wearing the Carstairs diamonds, and they were no brighter than her glistening amber eyes or her golden hair.

Monteith looked about for Westmoreland, wanting to thank him for the loan of his clothing. The earl spotted him near the drinks trolley, talking to a tall, willowy brunette. *Hmm?* Not anyone the earl recognized. Her head was turned toward Sir Reginald so he couldn't quite see her face. She wore an alluring gown, though, the blue of a plover's egg, with pale lace edging the abbreviated bodice.

"Westmoreland." He approached the older man. "I am greatly in your debt."

"Don't mention it, Monteith," Sir Reginald responded with gruff joviality. "We've all been the victim of scoundrels at one time or another, as I was just telling Miss Marriott." He motioned to his companion, who was now gazing at the earl like the cat that licked the cream.

She raised her eyebrows. "Feeling better, my lord?"

"Evelynne," he gasped. "Er . . . Miss Marriott. I hadn't expected to see you here tonight."

"Yes, I can see that." She turned to the older man and coyly fluttered her painted fan. "Lord Monteith thinks only of my well-being, Sir Reginald. He believed it would distress me too much to appear downstairs so soon after my ordeal."

"I never said . . ." the earl sputtered.

"Well, you're a plucky gel." Westmoreland patted her hand paternally. "It's good of him to look after you *now*. It's the least he could do after what he put you through last evening."

Evelynne gave the earl a wicked grin over her fan. "Well, what could he do? The robbers were armed to the teeth"—she gave a theatrical shiver—"and he but one man alone."

The earl's eyes had darkened. "Yes, and Miss Marriott had fainted dead away, so I spent my time looking for her smelling salts rather than holding off the ruffians."

"He gave them everything," she said in a conspirational whisper to Sir Reginald. "He told me I'd better take off all my jewelry and be quick about it."

Sir Reginald gave the earl a disparaging look.

"Well, she was shrieking so loudly once she came to, I was afraid they'd shoot her just to keep her quiet."

"Ah, Monteith, I see you've found our Miss Marriott all recovered." Arkady was at the earl's shoulder. He winked at Evelynne. "Come, Westmoreland, there's a question on bloodstock I need you to answer." He coaxed the older man away from the couple, totally disregarding the black look that his friend shot him.

"That was pretty," the earl said scathingly. "Sir Reginald now thinks I am a craven coward."

"Yes, and he believes I'm a raging hysteric." She wrinkled her nose at him. Did the earl don his bad temper with his evening clothes? Not that he didn't look compelling in his borrowed finery.

"And what is that you are wearing?" He was regarding her gown with apparent distaste.

"It's called a dress. I know you've never seen me in one before, but I believe they are common hereabouts."

"It's practically indecent," he said curtly.

"Yes, perhaps to a dour Puritan." She shrugged away his comment. "I'd forgot you were such a high stickler." He continued to scrutinize the offensive upper portion of her gown, but she refused to blush.

The gown *was* low-cut, she had to admit, but not scandalously so. It was nothing compared to the daring décolletage of the blond woman near the fireplace. Evelynne had doubted, when she'd tried it on in her room, that she had enough bosom to even lift the bodice. However, to her surprise, it was almost snug. It occurred to her that maybe she'd filled out a bit in that area. Which might just explain why lately everyone and his brother had been seeing through her masculine disguise.

"I am concerned only with your reputation," the earl said as calmly as he could, trying not to show his vexation with her. This was one of Arkady's starts, he knew, getting Evelynne tricked out in this stylish gown, setting her here among his friends. But to what purpose? Surely Mitford realized that keeping her out of company was the only safe route.

Evelynne continued to gaze at him as if he were an encroaching toady on the strut. Her face was powdered, he noted, the bruise on her cheek the faintest trace of purple. The blue gown clung to her in graceful, almost provocative, folds, and her arms, in their long gloves, appeared elegant and shapely. And her hair! No wonder he hadn't recognized her at first. It wafted in a cloud of deep brown ringlets about her face, and several stray locks danced against her white throat. She looked quite delicious. He frowned even more ominously.

"I think you'd better plead a headache and return to your room," he said in a low voice.

She gave a trilling laugh. "La, sir, you are peremptory tonight. How odd that you should concern yourself with me now, when you showed so little regard for my state of well-being all day. I'm sure you will be relieved if I remove myself from your presence."

Before he could make any response, Evelynne had swept away and sought out another group of guests. He looked about for Arkady. There was going to be a reckoning, and he had no patience to wait. But Mitford was ensconced with Sir Reginald and several other sporting gentlemen. *Damn!* He'd not get him alone before supper.

"Monteith," a sultry voice purred from a distance. Lady Philippa Carstairs, awash with violet scent, hove into his view. "I was thrilled beyond words when Arkady told us you were here."

"Lady Philippa." He bowed low over her hand. "As always, a glimmer of light in an otherwise drab universe." *God, where had that come from?*

She preened and touched a hand to her elaborate coiffure. He noted that the golden hair had been twisted into intricate coils and looped braids, and he couldn't help comparing it unfavorably with Evelynne's charmingly simple style.

"Robbie, I've missed you so," she whispered, leaning toward him and displaying the depths of her not inconsiderable cleavage. He backed away slightly. "When I heard you'd been set upon by brigands, I almost fainted from shock." She waved her fan languidly. "But here you are, delivered safely to the bosom of your dear friends."

The earl made some deprecating comment, remarking that the situation hadn't been really dangerous, merely inconvenient.

"But what of your coachmen?" Lady Philippa inquired, stroking the jewels at her throat as she spoke. "I had heard that you arrived here alone last night with that young woman. Surely, your coachmen weren't killed?"

Coachmen? The earl looked blank. *Drat Arkady,* he thought. He'd left that little detail out of his story. The Monteith rapidly concocted an explanation.

"We were ambushed at a crossroads." Well, at least that much was true. "The coachmen went off in a different direction. They took shelter at a farm, or so I've been informed."

"And this young woman, who is supposedly connected to your family . . ." Lady Philippa cast her imperious gaze to where Evelynne stood talking with some of the younger guests. "I'd heard she was injured, but she certainly looks quite fit to me. Rather a strapping girl, in fact. Do you know, I can't seem to recall anyone in your family named Marriott. And I am well acquainted with your lineage."

I don't doubt it! the Monteith seethed. She had probably poured over her Debretts the instant he took her to his bed. Had he ever really considered her for his countess? He shuddered inwardly.

"Miss Marriott is connected to me through an army acquaintance." Another truth. "Her brother was one of my lieutenants in Spain."

"But from all accounts you were traveling with her alone at night. Unless her maid went off with the coachmen to that farmhouse?"

Fortunately, the earl was saved from having to answer her when the butler appeared in the doorway to announce supper. The earl bowed and went off to find Arkady, leaving Lady Philippa with an unpleasant look of distemper on her perfect face. When Arkady saw the earl approaching with narrowed eyes and the beginnings of a first-rate scowl, he wisely barricaded himself behind several imposing dowagers. Using them as a screen, he managed to get to his dining room before the earl could accost him.

At supper, the earl was seated between a redheaded young lady with freckles and one of Lady Philippa's aunts, Lady Edwina or Lady Agatha Comstock—he never had been able to tell them apart. Evelynne was seated across from him and a little way down, between Westmoreland and a damned insufferable pup who kept ogling her between the courses. Arkady, sitting in state at the head of the table, never once even glanced in the earl's direction, preferring to keep his eyes on Lady Philippa's remarkable attributes.

After supper, once the ladies departed for the drawing room and the gentlemen were left to relax with their port and cigars, the earl again tried to buttonhole Arkady. But Mitford escaped from the room as the Monteith bore down on him, calling out that he was needed in the kitchen.

"Coward," the earl mouthed to him as he bustled into the hallway.

Arkady went directly to his library, sent Evelynne a hastily scribbled summons, and waited for her to respond. She came in shortly, her color rather high. Mitford took her hand and kissed it gallantly. She snatched it back.

"What's wrong?" he asked, brows lifted. "Wasn't the earl surprised and delighted by your transformation?"

"Oh, he was surprised all right. Delighted is another matter." She paced before the fire.

"He didn't pet you and tell you how fine you looked?"

"He was furious that I was there at all. He said my gown was indecent," she cried and stamped her foot. "He all but ordered me to leave the room."

"Hmm? No wonder he's been trailing after me like Nemesis. The man's a nodcock," Arkady added sagely. "You were quite the prettiest girl in the room."

"I'm not a patch on Lady Philippa." Evelynne looked dismally down at her chest.

"Oh, she's old news to Robbie." Arkady realized he'd just been somewhat indiscreet and almost put a hand over his mouth. "And she's an asp, besides. I invite her only because her aunts are deuced fine whist players. Don't let *her* put you out of countenance."

Evelynne's heart had lurched painfully at Mitford's revelation. Had the woman been Robbie's paramour? She composed herself. She'd deal with her feelings later, when she was alone.

"Well, I'm not really sure I belong here with these people." She frowned at Mitford. "I was all thumbs at supper, didn't know which fork to use . . . and I think I must have said something improper to Lady Beauchamp, she wrinkled up her nose at me so."

"Oh, that's just her normal expression." His eyes twinkled merrily. "Now you listen to me, Miss Marriott—oh, dash it all, may I call you Evelynne? I can't treat you like a stranger when I feel I know you so well. But as I was saying, there's nothing you lack, save a bit of confidence in yourself."

"That's easy for you to say! The earl has told me you're from quite an illustrious family. The son of a princess, no less."

"That's not quite true. *Ma mère* is actually from peasant stock. Her mother was abducted from a potato farm in the Ukraine by my grandfather, the prince, don't you know. She became the belle of St. Petersburg and never let her background stand in her way."

"But she must have been quite beautiful," Evelynne protested.

"I don't doubt it, but that's not the point. You don't need beauty if you have charm. And, if you have both, as you do—"

"No, I don't." She shook her head emphatically.

"Hmm? I suppose Robbie has never told you that you're pretty or charming. But that's just the kind of chap he is."

"You mean because he's an earl?"

"No." Arkady grimaced. "Because he's a boneheaded Scot.

He's never learned to get on with people. It's that prosing family of his, made him think the rest of us were scabby sinners."

"Yes, I know all about *them*!" Evelynne said with feeling. "But, then, how did you come to befriend him if he was so remote."

"Oh, my dear girl," he chortled, "haven't you noticed? I never let people discourage me. I just go barging in where I please."

"Yes, I had rather noticed."

"So take a page from my book, Evelynne. Don't let the famous scowl keep you at bay. It's only kindness the earl needs."

"And are you kind to him, Arkady?"

"Only rarely. It's much more amusing to bait the fellow. But, no, I'm wrong there. I believe if I can get him back in charity with you, it may be the kindest thing anyone's ever done for him."

"Well, he doesn't want to be in charity with me. He's made that very clear by his behavior to me this evening." Evelynne looked uncertain. "Will you explain something to me, Arkady? You rather make me feel as though I'm some sort of pawn on a game board. Why should it matter so much to you how things stand between the earl and me?"

Arkady heard the tremor in her voice. He sometimes forgot that these were flesh-and-blood people he amused himself with. He looked contrite. "Robbie is like a brother to me, and since you saved him from a very nasty situation, that puts me in your debt. So I will share this with you." She gazed at him with undisguised curiosity. "You've changed Robbie, Evelynne. For the better, I might add. When he brought you here last night, there was something different about him. As I said, he's such a solitary fellow and always seems so alone. But last night, when he carried you to your room, I saw that he wasn't alone any longer."

"What are you saying?" Her hands were gripping the back of a chair.

"I believe he cares for you very much."

Evelynne's eyes narrowed. "You mean he cares for his reputation very much. He didn't want me here tonight because he was afraid I'd let something slip that would compromise him. I'm not a fool, Arkady. I know what is forced upon a gentleman who spends the night with a lady, however innocently." Evelynne looked at him with tears trembling on her lashes.

"This"—she held her hands out along the sides of her gown—
"this is as much a charade as the boy's clothing I wore." She
plucked off her long gloves and cast them down on the chair. "I
am not a lady. He will never, ever marry me. Not if I saved him
a hundred times over."

Arkady was shaken. He'd thought her charmingly pretty in
the drawing room, but now, with the intensity of her feelings—
anger and frustration and even anguish—written upon her face,
she was nothing less than magnificent.

"God, I'd marry you myself," he said softly, "if you ever
looked that way over me."

She smiled at him through her haze of tears.

"Oh, that's right, laugh at the marquess," he chided, returning her grin.

"I'm very flattered." She gave a watery sniffle.

"You should be," he said. "I propose to only two or three
women a year."

"Stop making me laugh, Arkady. My heart is in pieces, and
you've got me chuckling."

He held out one hand to her. "I'm sorry, Eve. I won't meddle
anymore. It's rare that my schemes don't work out, but I've no
mind to cause you more pain."

"I'll go back to London tomorrow if you'll kindly see to it."
Evelynne picked up her gloves.

"What and leave the battlefield to Lady Philippa?"

"I'm not in her league, Arkady." She went to the door.

"I'd say not! You're several cuts above her. Robbie deserves
more than that harpy."

Evelynne hesitated. If there was anything for her at Levelands but heartache, she'd gladly stay on. That afternoon she'd
written to tell her family where she was and that all was well.
She had no reason to hurry back to London.

"Do you think there's a chance?"

"Not if you leave. He'll just go back to being solitary and
dour, and, Evelynne, it would be such a shame. And if he re-
fuses to make an honest woman of you, well, I'll . . . I'll just
knock him down!"

She grinned at the notion. "Then I'd better stay—for a few
days, at least. I'd hate to be responsible for you and Robbie engaging in fisticuffs. But I think I'll go upstairs now—I don't
want to face that Scots scowl again tonight. Good night, my

lord." And then she was gone, leaving a faint, trailing scent of verbena and sandalwood.

Arkady was on his second glass of brandy, congratulating himself on bringing Evelynne around, when the earl stalked in.

"I thought I'd find you hiding in here. You've abandoned me to the mercies of the card-sharping Comstock aunts and their predatory niece. I see that you disregarded my request and spoke with Evelynne today." Arkady looked up from his glass and shrugged. "I further take it that it was your idea to dress her up and parade her in front of your guests."

"You do Miss Marriott an injustice. I believe she can hold her own in any crowd. And it was she who wanted to be at dinner tonight. I merely furnished the means. Rather a lovely gown, don't you think?"

"I always thought Lydia dressed a little fast," the earl said. "Do you think I didn't realize it was one of your cousin's gowns? I shudder to think what Evelynne will be wearing tomorrow—probably dampened muslins."

You should be so lucky, Arkady murmured to himself. "I don't mean to pry," he then said aloud. He overlooked the earl's brief snicker of disbelief and continued, "but as Evelynne's host, I do have some proprietary rights. What do you intend to do with her, Robbie?"

The Monteith had been wrestling with that very question since the previous evening and still had no satisfactory answer. "It's clear I'll have to set her up in some manner."

Arkady's eyes widened. "It's to be a slip on the shoulder then?"

The earl glared at his friend. "If I didn't know you from my shirttail days, I'd call you out for that. She's not Haymarket ware, as if you didn't know. I mean to give her family a small house and a modest income."

Mitford looked at his buffed nails and said quietly, "She's top-over-ears in love with you, but I expect you know that."

There was a grim tautness about the earl's mouth. "All the more reason not to get involved that way."

"Oh, and what way is it that you *are* involved?" Arkady purred.

"I'm in her debt. It's as simple as that."

"She's very lovely, I couldn't help noticing." Arkady put his drink on the side table and stood up. "Actually, I didn't see it at first. Thought she was a bit ordinary. But once you get past that coltish look she has, when she smiles and flashes those gray eyes at you . . . well, you know."

"Well, I don't know!" the earl said heatedly, rising to his feet. "She's just a clever, capable young woman who came to my aid."

Arkady toyed with his signet right. "Hmm. So you wouldn't mind if I cast an eye in that direction?"

"As if I could stop you, were that really your intent." The earl also set his glass upon the side table and went to the door. His eyes were dark with anger. "Miss Marriott is her own woman, as I've had plenty of opportunity to discover. I wish you well of her. Maybe you'll have more luck than I've had getting her to listen. God knows she never listens to anything *I* say."

As his friend strode from the room, Arkady responded sotto voce, "Maybe you haven't been saying the right things."

The Monteith went directly to his room. He'd had his fill of cards and conversation. His blasted headache was back, and he was feeling blue-deviled, as well. The premonition he'd had at the crossroads near Levelton was coming true with a vengeance. He would never be alone with Evelynne again. What a mournful statement that seemed. He should have gone to see her first thing that morning instead of haring off to look for Skelton. She thought he hadn't even asked after her. Poor Mouse.

And now Arkady was expressing interest in her. Not that he was any threat. Women never seemed to take him seriously, in spite of his illustrious title. With his foolish face, languid airs, and cowherd's shock of pale hair, most young ladies thought him the safest of escorts. No, the Debutante's Delight wasn't the problem. It was his own inability to decide.

And Evelynne deserved better from him. She deserved his honesty. He scrutinized his feelings. They were like foreign soil. He hadn't a clue how to find his footing. He'd thought himself confused in the orchard, torn between wanting her so desperately that he ached from the need, and heeding the harsh voice of familial responsibility. *Lineage or lust?*

But that was before he'd seen her in Arkady's drawing room, looking as though she was born to be among his peers. God, she'd been a vision in that blue gown. Fast or not, Lydia had impeccable taste. He recalled how the strands of Evelynne's dark hair had caressed her throat; he had longed to blaze a trail of kisses where each of those locks had strayed. And that in-sufferable whelp who had eyed her all through dinner—Monteith had barely been able to restrain himself from leaping across the table and spitting the pup with a meat skewer. No, it had progressed a considerable way beyond mere lust. Top-over-ears, Arkady had said? Guilty as charged, milord.

The Monteith carried his candle out into the hallway. He knew the balance of the guests were still in the drawing room. Evelynne hadn't been there, however, when the gentlemen joined the ladies. He knew where to find her.

With only a few false starts into looming, empty corridors, the earl found the wing of the house where Evelynne slept. He scratched softly at her door. "Open up, Mouse. It's me."

"It's too late." Her voice was muffled through the heavy door. "You missed your chance for cheering up the invalid. Go away."

He tried the knob. It was locked.

"Please, Evelynne." He rarely pleaded for anything, and yet the words came out easily. "Please."

She must have heard the plaintiveness in his voice in spite of the thick door. The lock grated, and the door opened an inch. He couldn't see her face, only the froth of lace on the lapel of her robe. "This is very bad *ton*," she rebuked him softly.

"I wanted to talk to you. There's some unfinished business between us."

"I don't do business in the middle of the night." She threw his own words back at him. "Especially with havey-cavey fellows who cajole their way—"

He leaned hard into the door, opening it enough to slip inside the room. He set his candle down on the bureau and took her into his arms. Her eyes were enormous. She'd been crying.

"I never cajole," he said harshly, pulling her up against him. "Ever." He touched her damp cheek. "Ach, were these tears for me?"

"No," she said with a little choking sound, "they were for me." She pushed against his chest. "Let me go, Robbie. You've no right to do this."

He let her go instantly, but her eyes still reproached him. He went to the window, where the draperies were still open. The full moon that had watched over their adventure on the road was now on the wane. His feelings for Evelynne, however, were waxing, ever more beyond his control and his ken.

"How shall I court you then, Mouse?" he said softly to her reflection in the dark glass. She came toward him, the lace robe flowing about her with spectral beauty. He turned.

"Yes," he said, holding out one hand. "I said court. Shall I apply to Gilly? He is the man of the family, now you've left off wearing your breeches."

Evelynne stood rooted to the ground. A pulse beat in her throat, and her eyes were more stricken than when he'd kissed her by the chicken coop. "Come, sweeting." His hand, held out in supplication now, was insistent. She moved forward, and he enfolded her completely in his arms, turning them both to face the window.

"It's still our night out there, Evelynne. Our bright moon. And we're safe now at Lavaliere."

"Yes," she whispered, looking up into his beloved face. "You promised me we'd get here. But I knew I'd lose you then, and so I wanted the road to go on forever."

"We'll have other roads, you and I." He turned her in his arms and kissed the tears from her cheek. "Will you let me woo you, Evelynne? Properly, as a gentleman should—before the whole world, before *my* whole world?"

She sniffled. "You weren't very pleasant to me in the drawing room," she pointed out, stiffening a little in his embrace. "You weren't wooing me then."

He lowered his head and brushed his nose against hers. "I am a complete fraud, my girl. You *had* gotten under my skin, but it wasn't anger I was feeling. It was the most beastly jealousy. You have no idea what a tempting sight you were in that scandalous dress. And there was old Westmoreland hovering over you, and that young jackanapes at dinner—"

"He tried to put his hand on my leg." She wrinkled her nose in distaste. "And so I speared it with my seafood fork. At least, I think it was my seafood fork."

"My precious girl." He laughed as his arms drew her against him. "You are a never ending delight."

Evelynne burrowed her head beneath his chin and sighed. If this was a dream, she wasn't going to do anything sudden to break the spell. Robbie, in her bedchamber, holding her against his heart. 'Twas a consummation devoutly to be wished for.

They stood so for some time, the earl feathering one hand through Evelynne's hair as he gazed out at the ebony sky.

"I knew last night," he murmured soft against her ear. "When that scoundrel struck you. I knew I would kill for you, Eve, if I had to. And I think I would die for you, as well."

"I would rather you didn't." Her eyes shone up at him. "I'd like to have you around for a while."

He looked deeply into those two gray pools of light, and what he saw burning there stole his breath. He shook himself back to some semblance of normalcy.

"I'll take you for a carriage drive tomorrow and show you all the places where Arkady and I got into mischief. Would you like that? And we'll take a boat out on the lake. I'll let you row—I have a hunch you're better at it than I am, being country-bred, and all." She was laughing against his chest. "And, yes, I forgot, I'll have to call out that young upstart with the roving hands—"

"No," she said with a trilling laugh, "I believe I have satisfied my honor on that score." Her voice changed in tone. "But what of Lady Philippa? Arkady said she was 'old news' to you."

"Arkady has a lot to answer for," the earl muttered. "But, be assured, Eve, she and I parted company a long time ago—at my insistence. Now, I'd better leave before I have to answer for any more of my sins."

Evelynne put a hand on his sleeve, her velvet eyes entreating him. "I feel as though this has been a dream, Robbie. Shall I wake in the morning to discover this was only a phantasm?"

His eyes crinkled as he dug in the pocket of his coat. "Here. I've been carrying this about with me. I'm not even sure why. You shall have it, and in the morning you can look at it and know that this wasn't a dream."

"It's a wishbone." She gazed at it with a puzzled expression. It was polished to a fine sheen. "Wherever did you get it?"

He mussed her hair and tugged at one tendril. "It's from Kenny's turkey, the one you consumed to the very bones."

"You kept it?" Radiant delight filled her face, as if he had handed her a rare jewel.

The earl looked almost sheepish. He'd found the thing in the pocket of his greatcoat that morning and had tossed it onto his bureau. He'd only put it in his evening coat pocket out of caprice.

"Oh, Robbie." She stood on tiptoes and put her arms around his neck. "I can't believe you kept it. Let's wish on it now. Then we will each have a half, and we'll both know this wasn't a dream."

She held it out to him, and he took a firm grip on his half. "If I win," he warned her with a wicked gleam in his eye, "you won't much care for my wish."

"I fear you won't approve of mine very much either." Her eyes danced back at him.

"What will you wish? That all the young bucks pay court to you tomorrow?"

"No," she answered with a grin. "I will wish that you kiss me again, just as you did in the apple orchard."

"That was my wish," he murmured, snapping the frail bone, and then dropping it before either of them could see who held the larger half. He tugged her into his arms in one swift motion.

He kissed her then, on her saucy mouth, feeling her melt, pliant and eager, against his body. And this time she kissed him back, meeting him with her own sweet passion, until he was groaning and she was breathless, and they were both trembling where they stood.

"I didn't come here for this," he protested against her throat as his hands rang along her side beneath the lace of her robe. The bed gown she wore was silk, and it rippled against his palm with a sensuous whisper. "You dove me mad in homespun, Eve. Give a little thought to what lace and silk are doing to me."

She nuzzled his ear. "And you stole my heart in your dented hat and shabby muffler." He winced at the image. "But I think of you most often as you appeared that first night in your library, all in elegant black, as you are tonight, with your eyes blazing at me."

"Ah, that first night." The earl coaxed her toward her bed. She let him lower her onto the spread. He sat beside her, holding her hands captive against his chest. "I have to tell you something about that night, Evelynne."

"What, that you wanted to throttle me? I know that." Her levity dissolved as he leaned toward her with an expression of earnestness in his eyes.

"Remember what I said about meeting Edgar, how I knew instantly that I was somehow bound to him?" Evelynne nodded. "I had the very same feeling when I encountered you that night. It was the oddest thing. Here was this unkempt youngster trifling with my books, and all I could feel was an incredible sense of connection. Before I knew you were a Marriott, before

I even realized you were female." He raised her hands and ran his teeth gently along her knuckles. "Maybe I'm one of those fey Scots who has visions and sees into the future."

"If you had visions," she pointed out, pragmatic even in the face of his exquisite mouth against her skin, "you'd have never let yourself get kidnapped."

He quirked up one cheek. "True. Quite true."

"But since we are making confessions," Evelynne said, "I have one of my own."

The Monteith regarded her with interest.

"Something happened to me that night in your library, as well. I thought you were the most odious man I'd ever met." She put her head against his chest. "But I also couldn't bear the thought of anything bad happening to you. I know now why I leapt onto the kidnapper's coach. At the time I couldn't fathom how I came to do such a rash thing."

"And it's a good thing you did," he said stoutly. "Actually, I'm rather relieved by that confession—I was afraid you were going to tell me you'd been kissing the redheaded coachman, after all."

"Don't be impertinent, Robbie." She tugged playfully at his thick hair. "You're the only man who has kissed me. Well, the second, actually."

"Ah." He grinned. "The truth comes out."

"I suppose I can tell you, but it's very mortifying. The same day I met you, a rude fellow at the pin factory, named Ollie Hooper, discovered I wasn't a boy, and he tried to force himself on me. I couldn't go back to Tillery's after that, which was why I was so desperate to see you. So that at least I wouldn't have Gilbert to worry over, you see."

"So that's why you were so frightened the first time I kissed you." He stroked her soft hair. "You thought I was just another Ollie Hooper having at you. Poor Mouse."

She drew his hand from her hair and placed her lips against his palm. "You are not in the least like Ollie Hooper, my lord."

"Did he muss you about horribly?" The earl was trying desperately to disregard the effect that her lips were having on his already overloaded restraint.

"He tried to. He kissed me and put his hands on me. But then I hit him several times with a board until he fell down. But I don't think I killed him." She looked at the earl intently.

"Do you know, Eve, you quite frighten me at times? I wish

I'd known about Ollie Hooper before I kissed you by the chicken coop."

"Why? Would it have stopped you?"

"No." His mouth twisted. "But at least I would have armed myself."

"Robbie!" She flung herself at him in a flurry of lace and silk, trying to topple him off the bed. "I'll make you pay for that!"

He fended her off, laughing, as she attempted to wrestle against his greater strength. She managed to grasp his hands, but he twisted away and threw himself backward upon the mattress, pulling her down with him, so that she was leaning on his chest, their clasped hands trapped between them.

"This was another of my wishes." His voice was hoarse and so soft.

"You get only one wish," Evelynne chided him gently. He raised his head slightly and touched his mouth to the rise of her breast, where it spilled above the neckline of her silken gown. He felt the tremor that rippled through her at his touch, felt his own passion rolling over him like a burgeoning tide. It wasn't burning through him as it had in the apple orchard. No, it surged now, and seethed in his blood. Not so much hot, as molten. He had transcended the fire into the very core of the volcano.

"You are *all* my wishes, Evelynne." He drew his hands slowly from between them, letting his fingers linger an instant beneath the sweet weight of her breasts. She moaned softly, deep in her throat, as his arms circled her waist beneath the lace robe. He ran a hand along her arched spine until the silk cloth gave way to the velvet skin of her shoulders. He caressed her there, moving his hand in a circular motion, until she relaxed against him.

Her fingers twined in his dark hair, and she raised his head, drawing his mouth to her own. She ran her tongue along his lips, feeling the jagged release of his every breath. She bit at the fullness of his lower lip, and he arched up beneath her, with an inarticulate sound of longing. His arms tightened around her, like bands of steel. She gasped that there was such pleasure amid the pain, then gasped again as he rolled her onto her back and took her, openmouthed, with a fierce, hard kiss.

His hands were insistent now as they stroked her, demanding a response everywhere they touched. From hip to shoulder she felt the fevered play of his fingers through the silk, felt her body move eagerly beneath his caresses. He covered her face with urgent, scalding kisses as he traced a searing path from her brow to her chin. His eyes were wild and deep, the blue turned to liquid black, drawing her will from her like the all-consuming center of a whirlpool. He bit at her neck and shoulders, worrying the skin with his teeth, and then, as she cried out, he lowered his mouth to her breast, tasting her through the silk. She tore at his hair, shifting violently beneath him, fighting against this new conquest. But she couldn't fight the fluid, undulating feelings that swelled inside her. She was enveloped and overcome. *Robbie* . . . she keened his name in her soul, as she caught at his hair and drew his head full against her.

The earl had worked Evelynne's gown half off her shoulders when he suddenly drew back and said, "No," and again, "No," in a strained, distant voice. He slid the furled sleeves back up her arms and sat up, looking away. She watched him, a cryptic expression on her bruised mouth.

"You would have let me . . ." He didn't need to finish the sentence. She knew where they'd been headed.

"I can't fight you, Robbie." She ran the back of her hand along his cheek, and he turned to look at her. "No, that's not fair. I can't fight myself, or how you make me feel."

"You steal my resolve, Eve, every damn time I'm with you." His hands were clenched on his thighs.

"You must see that I feel the same way. My upbringing certainly didn't allow for this, and yet, when you touch me, I forget everything—my resolve, my beliefs . . . my virtue."

He tugged at his constricting neckcloth. "We've got to get beyond this if we're going to be in company together. I meant it when I said I'd court you as a gentleman, all present behavior to the contrary notwithstanding."

Evelynne pulled herself up beside him and leaned her head against his firmly muscled shoulder.

"Then I must remember to behave like a lady. I think that's the problem. Our situation the past two days allowed us a great deal of familiarity. We've never had to be really proper with each other. But now we are back to normal, back in the real world. I thought I'd lose you in this world, Robbie. I can certainly stand not to be kissed by you if I know you are still beside me."

"I'll always be beside you, Eve. At a proper distance, of

course." He nuzzled the nape of her neck and sighed. "You are surely the most complicated woman I've ever met—and the most desirable. At least we know we're in tandem there." He touched a finger to her rosy, swollen mouth. "And that's as good a beginning as I could wish for.

"Now, Mouse, you'd better sleep. I'm going to wear you out tomorrow recounting all the wild escapades of my youth." The earl rose and went to the window, where he retrieved the pieces of the wishbone. He carried them back to the bed. "See, I'm giving you the larger half—you got your wish. I have to wait a while for mine." He tucked the fragment into his waistcoat pocket and picked up his candle.

Evelynne lay back against her pillow. She really didn't need the wishbone any longer to reassure her. She had the marks of Robbie's strong hands and hungry mouth upon her body. She had his sweet words in her heart. They were all the testament she'd ever need.

"Good night, Evelynne. Sleep well." He spoke from the doorway, his face ardent in the flickering candlelight.

"Good night, Robbie." *My dearest love,* her heart echoed.

Chapter 9

❧

The next day brought the promise of rain. The sky above Levelands hung thick with dark clouds, and a gauzy haze covered the park and the grounds. The earl was up before most of the other guests and went off on his own for a brisk ride across the downs. He didn't want to face Arkady's probing questions so early in the day. And he hadn't wanted to see Evelynne just yet.

The night before, he'd thought her need for a talisman an almost childish start—how could she wake in the morning and doubt that what had transpired between them was real? But he had awakened from his restless dreams hungry for her arms, and with such a longing in his heart that he was strangely reassured to see the little piece of turkey bone lying on his night table. *God, she really cared for him!* It was the benediction he had yearned for his whole life—that one person in the world could put aside her own pious concerns and cherish him above all else.

He reined in his horse on the crest of a rolling hill, facing north. The plains of Salisbury were a faint, blurred expanse in the distance. He'd take Evelynne to see the Druid stones. It was the perfect day to view the somber, hulking monoliths. In the sunlight they appeared to be the abandoned game pieces of some giant's silly pastime, the mumblety-peg of the gods. But in the watery half-light of a damp, cloudy day, they conveyed all the awesomeness and mystery of England's long distant past. Evelynne would adore them.

He turned his mount from the crest and spurred down again to the parkland. He needed to steel himself before returning to the house. In spite of his vow to behave in a proper manner, he was quite sure anyone who saw him with Evelynne saw the burning desire that she evoked in him, would know instantly what was between them. He'd have to guard his expression, even if he couldn't guard his heart.

Evelynne was wandering through the terraced garden, a high-poked, straw bonnet over her curls. The earl saw her as he came trotting into the stable yard, and he waited a while, still astride, watching her clipping autumn blossoms for the large basket she carried.

He imagined her in the gardens of Leithness, his home in the Highlands. His gardens grew wild, the flowers and shrubs un-pruned, shaped only by the wind and the seasons. Would she clip and trim them into respectable orderliness, or would she revel, as he did, in their untamed beauty?

He dismounted and handed his reins to a stable lad, and then climbed the path of pale bricks that led from the stable to the raised gardens. No one else seemed to be outside. He'd have his Mouse to himself then, for a while.

Off to his right, Lavaliere rose up, appearing—like the Druid stones—quite bewitching in the eldritch fog. It was built of native limestone, in the E configuration so popular in Elizabethan times—three wings built out from a long central structure. The passing years had weathered the house to a soft amber hue. It sat nestled in a small valley, with the green hills of the parkland rising on all sides. It had beauty that transcended mere architecture, as if the witty, charming people who had lived within it had imbued the house with some of their own character.

Evelynne was wrestling with a stubborn briar rose when he came along the path toward her. "Oh, Robbie," she called out with brightening eyes when she saw him. "I'm so glad you're here. I've mangled this branch quite badly with my shears, but I still can't get it loose."

The earl still wore his riding gloves and so was able to rend the thorny stem, with its deep crimson blossoms, from the rose bush. He handed it to her with a flourish, noting how lovely she looked in a day dress the color of cream tea and a spencer of olive green velvet. The bonnet ribbons that fluttered loose beneath her chin were also of a mossy green shade.

"That's a very dashing hat, Eve." His eyes regarded her with open approval. "Even if it is a pity to cover your hair."

"My hair?" She put a hand to the crown of her head. "I thought you disliked my hair excessively."

He resisted the urge to remove her bonnet and prove to her

just how very much he liked her hair, especially the feel of it tangled in his hands just before he kissed her. *Gentlemanly courtship*, he reminded himself. He merely said, "I can't imagine what could have given you that notion."

Evelynne pulled a face. "Oh, can't you? As if you haven't constantly teased me about it . . . oh, well, never mind. I'm relieved that you approve of my hair, even if there is a good deal less of it than before."

She smiled up at him, and the earl had the sensation of the fog suddenly lifting, and of an enormous sun filling the sky, casting its gilded beams down on the garden where they stood. He felt almost giddy. He smiled back at her, and they stood there, not speaking for a time, haloed in a shimmering aura that only they could perceive.

Evelynne broke the spell, She dropped her flower basket—quite on purpose—for she knew that there were times when her beloved was not the master of his emotions. And as much as she wanted him to fulfill the promise that blazed from his eyes, they were, after all, standing beneath at least two dozen windows.

He bent to help her gather the scattered blossoms.

"How do you find Levelands, now you've had a chance to see it from the outside?" He dropped a handful of asters into her basket, holding one aside in his gloved hands.

She looked up at the nearby west wing, her brow furrowed. "It's smaller than I imagined. It seems large and grand on the inside, but from out here it's very welcoming and almost soothing." She glanced at him. "It fits perfectly in this setting, doesn't it? It doesn't sprawl or meander."

"No." He teased the flower along her throat. "That's one of its main attractions. For such a beautiful house, it's not at all imposing."

"It really is like a gem; the princess was right on that score. But," she added as she gazed around the rigidly designed garden, with its geometric flower beds and espaliered fruit trees, "I must say, I find this garden to be very prim. I've always liked a garden with a bit more gumption, if you know what I mean . . . What? What have I said?" She stood there, quite befuddled, as the earl's eyes brimmed with laughter.

"Oh, Mouse, don't look at me so. You've merely answered a question of mine. Don't try to puzzle it out. It was a good answer. A very good answer. Walk with me now through this prim garden, and I'll tell you of my plans for the afternoon."

They did go off to visit the Druid stones in Mitford's laudelet, with another couple along for propriety's sake—a certain Colonel Craft, a hearty man in his late fifties, and his wife, Julia. They proved to be an amiable couple—the colonel and the earl spoke of the war and of politics, and Evelynne and Mrs. Craft, after a few awkward starts, discovered they were both avid readers, and then chattered away like the best of friends.

They'd gotten a late start after a prolonged luncheon, where Evelynne and the Monteith tried to put Arkady off the scent by glowering at each other at every available moment. Lady Philippa also noted this behavior and was smugly puffed up for the entire meal. The earl had the cook pack a light picnic; he knew better than to take Evelynne too far afield without some comestibles at hand.

They drove first to Salisbury, spent some time poking around in the stately cathedral, and then went on to the famous circle of prehistoric stones.

The colonel and his wife had been to Stonehenge several times before and opted to wait in the carriage while the younger couple strolled around it. Evelynne was duly impressed, and was attempting to calculate the meaning of the stones by having the earl count his paces between each one, when the sky opened up and a chilling rain began to pelt down on them.

They raced, laughing and shrieking, back to the carriage, where the driver and Colonel Craft had just raised the canvas roof. They tumbled inside, still laughing, and Evelynne knew if the other couple hadn't been there, Robbie would have kissed the raindrops from her face. It didn't matter, though, for the look that dwelled in his eyes since they'd met in the garden that morning was better than any kiss.

They ate their picnic during the ride home, well satisfied with the day. Evelynne was especially pleased with her budding friendship with Mrs. Craft.

It turned out to be a providential connection for Evelynne. That evening, when they were all assembled in the drawing room before supper, several of the young ladies who had been cordial to her the night before were now barely civil. A few even turned from her without a word when she tried to speak with them. This cattish behavior was not lost on the colonel's wife, who placed herself at Evelynne's side until they were called in to their meal. It had not been lost on the earl, either, who suspected it was the work of Lady Philippa.

After supper the group adjourned to the music room, where the more accomplished of the guests were to entertain their fellows.

Several of the young ladies played at the fine piano that stood at one end of the room. There was Mozart and Handel and badly rendered Bach. The guests sat scattered in delicate chairs, and a few of the men lounged against the columns that lined one wall.

There was some dispute as to who should perform next, a horse-faced lady who played on the harp or two middle-aged gentlemen who wanted to perform an operatic duet. Lady Philippa's voice rose above the genteel squabbling.

"Why not let Miss Marriott entertain us next? I have heard she is accomplished beyond anything."

The earl, propped up against a Doric column fully across the room from Evelynne, was not too far away to see the look of alarm that flashed across her face.

"Oh, no," she said, fluttering her hand dismissively. "I am much out of practice. There is no piano in the house where I live . . ." *Oh, that was not a wise admission.* Everyone in society had a piano, whether they played or not. "That is," she continued, "it's been out of tune for some time. The damp, you see . . ." *Yes, that really gave the right impression.* She looked about for Robbie or Mrs. Craft, or even Arkady to come to her rescue.

"We're waiting, Miss Marriott," Lady Philippa fluted, "with bated breath."

Evelynne shrugged. There was nothing for it but to go up. She unbuttoned the wrists of her long gloves and tucked the mitts back under the sleeve as she walked to the instrument. Robbie had come forward, closer to her. *You don't have to do this,* his eyes said. Or did they say, *Don't make yourself ridiculous in front of my friends . . . ?*

Arkady appeared at her side as she slid onto the bench, settling the folds of her gown around her. "Which sheet music would you like?" He proffered a sheaf of selections to her.

"I don't read sheet music," Evelynne said in a carrying voice, looking straight at Lady Philippa as she spoke. Her host still hovered over her; his expression of doleful concern was doing her confidence little good.

"It's all right, Arkady." She smiled at him in a reassuring manner. "You can sit down now. My fingers will probably be a little stiff at first; it's been a while. But with such a lovely instrument, I'm sure my lack of practice won't matter."

Arkady went to stand beside the earl; Evelynne saw them exchange a look of shared trepidation.

It was a song that her scots co-workers at Tillery's had sung during their luncheon breaks, a Scottish lullaby with beautiful, sad lyrics and a haunting melody. They had sung it in harmony; she sang it now alone in a low, clear contralto. She had never played it before, but she knew the notes in her heart, and her fingers, as out of practice as they were, followed her heart's lead. She sang it for Robbie and for his home in the Highlands, and as she sang, she hoped she might one day sing it to a child of her own.

When she finished, there was total silence in the room. She looked about in dismay. Was it totally improper to sing a folk ballad in society? Then the room burst forth with applause— not the staid clapping of a politely bored audience, but the enthusiastic response of true appreciation.

One young buck jumped up. "Let's have another, Miss Marriott. Something gay this time, for I believe we are all drying our eyes after that one."

Evelynne looked to the earl. He was grinning at her triumphantly, nodding his head. It was proper to play again, he was telling her. Lord, she'd play until dawn if they let her.

She played and sang two more songs, the first a merry Devonshire love song, and the second a somewhat naughty tavern song that Edgar had taught her when she was first learning the piano.

When she got up from the bench at last and went to retake her seat, she passed close by Lady Philippa's chair and murmured low, "How nice that we were both able to display our particular talents this evening."

She didn't have a chance to speak with Robbie for the rest of the night. Arkady carried her off to partner him in whist against the dreaded Comstock sisters, ignoring her protest that she was a very indifferent card player. He merely pronounced that anyone who could thump a piano with such feeling had to be dashed good at cards. She failed to see the connection, but suffered him to lead her to the card table, nonetheless.

When at last they got up to rejoin the guests, having been soundly trounced by the two elderly ladies, the earl was no longer in the room. He had apparently retired.

Evelynne herself left the group after a short while, managing to avoid Arkady's repeated attempts at a tête-à-tête. She was under orders from her lord and had no intention of letting Mitford's guileless green eyes weasel any information from her.

There was a sealed note under her bedroom door. She perched on the side of her bed and quickly opened it.

"Mouse," it read, in handwriting that was dark and sprawling, "once again I made the mistake of underestimating you. Forgive me. You could not know it, but that lullaby was sung to me by my nurse, Aileen, who was a crofter's daughter. You will meet her some day soon, and I believe she is the one part of my family that you will like very much. I bid you good night, and hold you dear in my thoughts. Tomorrow cannot come soon enough. Robbie."

Evelynne clasped the note to her breast. She was crying, but she wasn't sure why. There was a reassurance in his words that she hadn't realized she'd even needed.

The night before, in this very room, Robbie had spoken to her of courtship; he had not mentioned marriage. He had told her that he desired her, that he would kill for her, but he had not said the word "love." These things she knew without assessment. For all the bounty that was between them, she also knew what was lacking. In time, she fervently hoped, her plate would be filled. And his tender note did speak of a future time when they would visit his home in Scotland together. She needed to have faith. She needed to trust.

Evelynne set the note beside her half of the wishbone and got ready for bed with a luminous smile on her face. *Tomorrow cannot come soon enough*.

The next day the weather cleared, and the earl was coaxed into joining a group of guests who were going riding. Unfortunately, cousin Lydia's treasure trove of gowns did not include a riding habit, but the earl had agreed to be one of the party before he realized Evelynne could not accompany him. When he had started to offer excuses so that he could remain behind, she shot him a look of stern rebuke.

She watched from the front portico as the group rode by. The Monteith trotted past her with a salute and a rueful smile. He rode with a relaxed, easy grace, acquired from years of soldiering on horseback. Lady Philippa, clad in a dashing habit of cerulean blue, jockeyed into position beside him before they had come to the first turn of the drive.

Evelynne sighed as she stood on the porch steps. The one arena where she felt truly accomplished was to be denied her. She knew she was the equal of anyone on horseback, and longed to be beside Robbie in Lady Philippa's stead.

"I rarely ride any longer—" Mrs. Craft spoke from the doorway behind Evelynne. "But I always have the maids pack my habit. It would be a shame to let the lack of a proper riding dress keep you from his side."

"What?" Evelynne turned in surprise. "I'm sorry, I didn't—"

"Hush." Mrs. Craft took Evelynne's arm. "Let's walk down to the lake. I daresay our slippers will stand the damp."

They were some way from the house before the colonel's wife continued. "You can tell me if you'd rather not speak of it."

Evelynne brushed the tops of the meadow grass with her hands as they walked toward the still, blue water. "You were very kind to me last night, Mrs. Craft, and I thank you. But I'm under orders not to discuss this situation."

"Orders? Ah, yes. I'd forgotten he was a military man before he got his earldom."

Evelynne said with earnest conviction, "We are really just friends."

Mrs. Craft gave her a dubious look. "Those may be your sentiments, my dear. You didn't see the expression on his face as you played that beautiful lullaby last night. The man was enraptured. Even if the colonel and I had not spent the day with you yesterday, I'm sure I would have known how it was. It's the way he looks at you, you see. My husband even commented on it last night, and he's far from observant in matters of the heart. 'Monteith's fixed his interest with the Marriott girl,' he confided to me. As if it wasn't quite obvious." She gave a low chuckle. "Men are often so infuriatingly dense, don't you think?"

"Oh, dear. Is it really that obvious? I'm not of his station, you must know."

Mrs. Craft thought for a minute. "I believe the nobility needs to marry down every so often. It enriches the blood. Otherwise, we'd have nothing but a collection of jug-eared halfwits running the country."

Evelynne giggled. "My Lord Monteith is neither jug-eared nor half-witted."

"No," Mrs. Craft agreed. "He's quite an impressive fellow. I'm not surprised the Carstairs woman has her nose out of joint. But you spiked her guns last night in the music room. And if you will let me outfit you for riding, I suspect you'll put her to shame in the field, as well. She dresses up like a proper horsewoman, but handsome is as handsome does, and the woman has no bottom. The colonel himself has pronounced this, so there's no arguing the point."

Evelynne laughed and impulsively hugged her new friend. "You are very good, Mrs. Craft, and I will gladly accept your kind offer."

They walked slowly around the lake, chatting about less intriguing topics, and at one point Evelynne stopped to look back at Levelands across the serene expanse of the lake. Soothing, she had called it, and it truly was. It was an enchanted, hallowed house, the place where Robbie had given his heart into her keeping. She would always love it for that reason alone.

While she awaited the return of the riding party, Evelynne occupied herself in the music room, trying her hand at some of the easier classics. She drifted her hands along the piano's keys, picking out a slow waltz. There was to be an impromptu party with dancing later that night. Arkady had hired a small ensemble to come and play, and Evelynne wondered dreamily what it would be like to sweep around the ballroom in Robbie's arms.

She had a sudden, lowering thought. What if the earl didn't dance? He'd said his religion frowned on it. But then Robert MacIntyre seemed to do a great many things lately that most religions frowned on. And so had she, if the truth be told. *Just a pair of old sinners*. She grinned happily. No, there could be no sin where there was such caring.

His hands were on her shoulders before she'd even known he was in the room.

"Did you enjoy your ride?" She craned around to look up at him. He was quite windswept, and his face was getting back its tanned, healthy coloring. He wore a dark brown jacket and beige buckskins.

"I would have enjoyed it more if you had come along to fend off Lady Philippa," he said.

Evelynne rolled her eyes. "What? You can't defend yourself against one paltry siren?"

He grinned. "Short of knocking her off her horse and into a ditch, there was very little I could do to keep her at bay. She clutched my arm so often, I shall probably show bruises by this evening." He rubbed his sleeve distractedly. "She's convinced herself that I'm using you only to make her jealous."

"No!" Evelynne swung about on the bench to face him. "What could I possibly have to cause her envy?"

"My heart?" the earl said simply. He sat beside her, facing the keyboard, and coaxed out the first slow notes of a nocturne.

"You play!" She spoke in pleased surprise. "I thought your family frowned on such frivolous displays."

"S'truth. My mother dislikes all forms of music. It was Aileen who first taught me, on a little spinet in her cottage, and then the princess finished the job. She plays like an angel. I practiced on this very piano. Arkady was quite out of temper with her for tutoring me. He always wanted to be larking off somewhere, and I just wanted to stay here and wrestle with Mozart." He was leaning slightly against her as he played, and she pretended not to notice.

"Who taught you to play, Eve? You don't read music, and you hold your fingers all wrong, and yet you make the piano croon like a songbird."

"Oh, I tried to learn at Mrs. Cooperall's school. But I never could make sense of the sheet music. Edgar always played by ear, so I guess you could say he taught me."

"He taught you a good many things, didn't he?"

"Nothing a young lady needs to know, I'm afraid." She looked down and laced her fingers together.

"But many things *my* young lady needs to know. How to bounce an apple off a wicked baron's head, how to tie a sailor's knot—your bedsheet rope was quite nautical, you know—and how to sing a rowdy tavern song to a roomful of stuffy aristocrats. Yes, I know Edgar taught you that song—he used to sing it for the officers. It became one of the mess tent favorites."

He finished playing with a crisp, sweeping arpeggio, his head thrown slightly back. "I want to kiss you, Evelynne." His voice flowed into the lingering *sustenudo* of his final chord.

"It's never just one kiss," she reminded him softly, trying to ignore the quicksilver delight that lanced through her at his words. "One is never enough for either of us." She was returning the pressure of his shoulder now.

He picked up her hand and whispered his lips along her

palm. He felt the shiver that rippled through her at his touch, and increased the pressure of his mouth.

"Oh, there you both are." Arkady, clad in a coat of lemon superfine, sauntered into the music room. The earl slowly released Evelynne's hand. "I've been looking everywhere for you. I've finished seeing to tonight's entertainment, and now I'm just longing for a game of billiards. Though you might like to join me, Robbie, although I wouldn't blame you if you'd rather stay here and kiss Miss Marriott."

His green eyes fairly danced with wicked glee. "Stop glaring at me, Robbie. I won't pretend I didn't see you. This is my house, and I like to be beforehand with all that goes on inside it." He rocked slightly back and forth. "And it's about time you kissed her if you ask me." He flicked a finger over his neckcloth. "Nobody's been taken in by your little charade. You snarl at each other over lunch, and then go jaunting off together to Salisbury. I admit I had my doubts this morning, Robbie, when you went trotting away with Lady Philippa, but then I realized our Evelynne doesn't have a riding habit."

"She's not your Evelynne," the earl said, trying to maintain his temper in the face of Arkady's provoking chatter.

"What? Oh, just a figure of speech, old lad." He shrugged and glanced at Evelynne. "You don't play at billiards, do you?"

Evelynne shook her head and looked at the earl. "I'll come and watch the two of you play if you like. It will be quite proper—Arkady can be our duenna."

The earl laughed at that and got up, drawing Evelynne to her feet. He tucked one of her hands through his arm.

Arkady eyed the two of them skeptically. "Yes, I have a feeling a duenna is exactly what you do need if you're not to set the gossips' tongues clacking." He took Evelynne's other hand, making a snide face at the Monteith as he did so. "I'll stick close to her side, you'll see."

"Oh, blast!" the earl muttered as they walked from the room.

The dress was of orchid *gros de Naples*, trimmed with spangled white gauze. The short, full sleeves were slashed in the Spanish style, revealing insets of silver lamé. There were silver slippers that matched it and a silver-flecked parchment fan as well. Evelynne sat on the bed in her chemise, kicking her long legs against the bed frame, and looked at the gown like a hungry child before a bakery window. Millie held up the dress against her pinafore and swirled the skirt in a wide circle. "It was quite Miss Lydia's favorite gown until she got taken with a mortal craving for comfits and ballooned up like a toad."

"Oh, how dreadful." Evelynne tried to look suitably horrified, but giggled instead.

"She ate nothing but potatoes and vinegar for two weeks, just like Lord Byron, but by the time she was back to her normal size, she'd lost her heart to a new gown of Delft blue crepe." Millie glanced at the brunette on the bed. "I do think this gown is more *your* color, miss. I always liked orchid on a dark-haired lady."

Evelynne hopped off the bed, and the maid lifted the flowing gown over her head and settled it about her shoulders. She did up the back, as Evelynne twitched with impatience. "I want to see . . ."

"Is this your first dance, miss?" Millie pushed her down into a low chair and began to arrange her hair.

"My first in such a grand house, with so many elegant guests." *My first wearing such a stunningly beautiful gown. My first with Robbie here, to dance with me, and laugh with me, and gaze at me with desire in his eyes . . .*

"All done, miss."

The maid guided her over to the full-length cheval mirror that fronted the armoire. Evelynne peeped cautiously at her reflection. Was this the unkempt young woman who had tramped beside the earl in boy's clothing only three days before?

The dress fell in myriad folds to the toes of the silver slippers. It glistened as she pirouetted before the mirror, a gossamer gown fit for Queen Titania herself. The bodice was cut low, lower even than the dinner dress that had scandalized Robbie that first night. He'd probably be furious with her again, and she shivered in delight at the prospect.

Millie had placed a small garland of orchid silk flowers set among silver leaves upon her dark curls. Evelynne recalled what Robbie had said in the garden about it being a shame to cover her hair. "Maybe the flowers are too much." She reached up to remove them, but Millie forestalled her.

"Nay, miss. They do make your eyes look quite violet, if I may say."

"Really?" She peered closer at Evelynne in the mirror. In truth, her eyes had taken on a strange, deep color, but she suspected the alteration owed more to excitement over the upcoming evening with Robbie than to any mere hair ornament.

Against Evelynne's mild protests, Millie applied some cosmetics to her pale face: a dusting of powder to cover the faint bruise on her cheek, a touch of kohl beneath her lashes, and a hint of carmine to her lips.

"There." Millie stood back, quite satisfied. "My Miss Lydia in all her glory never looked better than you do tonight, miss."

Especially when she was ballooned up like a toad. Evelynne bit back her irreverent mirth. She owed the absent Cousin Lydia an enormous debt of gratitude. How ill-bred to be laughing at her expense.

Evelynne picked up the silvery fan, draped it from her gloved wrist, and with a deep breath to compose her racing heart and a warm word of thanks to Millie, she launched herself out into the passage.

Arkady had filled out the numbers for his impromptu party by inviting several members of the local gentry. They and the house-party guests were milling about in the great hall that lay between the drawing room and the front parlor. In the ballroom on the first floor the small orchestra could be heard tuning their instruments. Evelynne peered into the ballroom as she passed by its swagged doorway on the landing. Arkady had outdone himself. The room was bedecked with potted trees, garlands of fall fruits, and silver ewers brimming with autumn bouquets. The light from hundreds of candles blazed from the twin chandeliers that graced the painted ceiling. The lights were reflected countless times in the night-dark French windows that traversed one side of the long room. It was heavenly—the golden core of this most magical of houses.

"I waited for you." The earl approached her from the opposite side of the landing, from the wing where his own bedchamber lay. "I thought we might go down together." He held out one hand to her.

Evelynne thought he looked almost austere in his black clothing, like the sober prophet of a bleak and wrathful god. But there was nothing sober about the hungry expression that burned in his deep blue eyes.

"I expect you just wanted to examine my choice of costume for this evening?" She teased him over her fan.

His jaw tightened as he took her hand in a strong clasp. "I wanted to catch my damn breath before I went down there.

You've stolen it again, Eve. Taken it quite away. My Mouse has turned into a nymph, I think. It's that dress . . . well it's . . ."

"What Robbie?" she urged, as breathless as he was.

"I can't even begin to tell you. Ask Arkady. He'll give you pretty speeches. But I warn you, if any of those young bucks so much as look at you twice, it'll be pistols at dawn. I swear it." He grinned down at her, and she threw her head back and laughed.

"Ready to face the perils of society with me?"

"Yes, my lord." *Always.*

Arkady, playing host beside his front door, watched them as they came down the wide oak staircase together. The factory girl had been transformed into a fairy princess. It wasn't just the gown—she'd been wearing Lydia's fripperies for days now. It was the otherworldly light that shimmered around her. It made him think of woodland glades and elfen revels. And Robbie was the ardent prince, in jet black, his eyes turned to hers and a constant smile hovering on his usually somber face. Arkady sighed. He really ought to fall in love himself. It gave one such an air!

Mitford's impromptu party was a great success. Country squires, village vicars, London nabobs, and the cream of society mixed and mingled without thought to station or rank. They danced and drank, danced and dined, and then they danced again. The golden ballroom rang with laughter and sweet, flowing music. The footmen cast open the French windows so that overheated dancers could walk out onto the narrow balcony that edged the ballroom, and breathe in the cool September air.

Evelynne lost the earl, once the party began in earnest, for she was quickly absorbed into the fray. One gentleman after another sought her hand for the series of country dances. She whirled and curtsyed, promenaded and pranced until she was sure she had worn through the soles of her delicate sliver slippers.

When the orchestra began a lilting waltz, she looked about for Robbie. Surely he would claim her for this most intimate of dances. There were many men in black evening clothes, but none so tall as her lord, none so wide-shouldered, or so darkly handsome. Arkady was coming toward her through the crowd, wearing a suit of heavily embroidered lavender satin with silver lace at his cuffs.

"It's a pity you're not with me tonight, Eve." He touched her spangled sleeve. "We match something extraordinary."

"I'm not with anyone tonight, Arkady. In case you haven't noticed, Robbie had disappeared." She tried not to sound peevish.

"Oh, that's why I'm here. I've got a message from him. You're to get yourself down to the stable. Such mysterious goings on, I've never seen. And in my own home." He grinned, then wandered away toward the open widows. He turned and saw she was still standing where he'd left her. *Go on,* he motioned.

She flew to her room to get a shawl, wondering what in blazes *was* going on. She hadn't exactly expected Robbie to sit in her pocket all night, but neither had she expected him to abandon her totally. And now this mysterious summons to the stable.

She found a shawl of pink cashmere in a drawer, and, tossing it over her shoulders, she went rapidly down the back stairs, through the darkened music room, and hurried out onto the veranda. The night was chill, the full essence of autumn in the air. Wood smoke tickled her nose, fallen leaves crackled beneath her feet, and the frosty ghost trails of her breath danced before her as she ran.

Something inexplicable slowed her, and she turned to face Lavaliere. It was ablaze with lights, as it had been that legendary night when the princess first arrived. *Go slowly, Evelynne.* It was as though the house spoke to her. *Savor this moment. Don't spoil it with haste. This is your one night to be the princess, to dress in royal purple and dance in enchanted silver slippers. But it won't last . . . it is only a bridge in time.*

Evelynne gave a little shiver; she must have had too much champagne punch. But she did continue on at a more leisurely pace, following the gardens down to where the stable yard began. Two low slate-roofed buildings lay before her where the bloodstock was housed. The first of these buildings showed some light at the stall windows. Robbie was standing silhouetted inside the main doorway at the center of the building. He still wore his evening clothes, though there was now straw on his coat and in his hair.

"Shh." He put a gentle hand over her mouth as she reached him. "No questions. Close your eyes."

Evelynne did as she was bid, surrendering herself to the firm guidance of his long-fingered hands upon her shoulders as he led her along the interior passage. She heard the puzzled nickering of sleepy horses in their stalls as they passed by. There was the subtle sound of great weight shifting from four feet to three as they relaxed again and nodded off back to their dreams of spring pastures awash with new grass.

Finally, the earl drew her to a halt. She could tell there was a brighter light beyond her closed eyes. More nickering, louder now, and insistent. A velvet muzzle touched her face and blew a feathering of warm, hay-scented breath against her cheek.

"Now, Evelynne," the earl crooned, "open your eyes and see who's come to see you all the way from Devon."

She was afraid to open her eyes. She was already crying, the tears seeping between her tightly shut lids. "I can't," she whispered. "I dare not."

The horse took a lock of her hair gently in his teeth and tugged several times. It had been the first trick she'd taught him, and it proved her undoing. She opened her eyes, wailed, "Oh, Georgie," and pitched herself forward onto the horse's great, arched neck. She hung there sobbing in dry, breathless bursts.

The young groom who stood holding the horse's lead shank and who had, in fact, himself ridden to Devon to bargain with the stubborn squire on the earl's behalf, was not the least embarrassed by Evelynne's display. He'd felt that way about certain horses since he'd been a sprat.

"Here, I'll take that." The earl removed the lead from the groom's hand and replaced it with an impressive gold coin. "You've earned your bed, Jim Darby. I'll see that the old fellow gets settled in properly."

"He's a right 'un, he is." The groom smiled, nodding to Little Georgie. "Not much to look at, ceptin' for his size, but the manners of a gent, and that look in his eyes, like he can see miles beyond anything else. All the good'uns have that look." And with that sage pronouncement, he took himself off to his quarters.

The Monteith watched Evelynne, still sobbing against her horse's throat. As his first attempt to make up for the wrongs she'd suffered, it offered an uncertain outcome. Had it brought back to her painful memories of all that she had lost in Devon? How could a mere horse make up for the death of a beloved brother and both parents? How could it replace the home of her childhood that she had seen auctioned away? He cursed himself for a fool.

"I'm sorry, Eve." He cradled his arms around her. "Please don't cry. I didn't think . . ." He heard himself choke in pain. "I didn't think it would hurt you so."

She turned to him slowly, a look of wonder on her face. "Hurt me? Hurt me? Dearest Robbie, this is the most blessed gift anyone has ever given me." She took his face between her hands, her gray eyes brimming with unshed tears. "Something, anything of mine from the past. It's all I ever wanted. I packed up every belonging of Edgar's, every book of my father's, every beautiful drawing that my mother made, and brought them all to London. But they were just things . . . things. I still had the boys with me, of course, but everything else that was *in my heart* was gone. Until now."

She pulled the earl's head down and kissed him gently on the lips. There was no passion in her mouth, no desire. Just giving and warmth and comfort. The earl learned something in that instant—that kisses were not only tokens of passion, they were also pledges of faith and trust. And so he received a gift, as well.

"I love you, Robert MacIntyre," she murmured, looking up into his midnight eyes.

He tightened his hold on her and drew her close against his heart. "And I love you, Evelynne Marriott. Before God and man, I do."

"And before horse," she said, chuckling wetly into his cravat.

"How can you joke?" He pulled at her hair, tipping her head back. "My Mouse," he said, just before his mouth found hers. He kissed her in wonder and joyful completion, holding her dear face in his hands. It would always be like this, he thought. Twenty, thirty years from now, even when the fire of passion had passed, there would always be the warmth of Evelynne's face between his hands.

Little Georgie decided it was time he received a bit more attention and proceeded to pluck the garland from Evelynne's head. She turned from the earl's arms with a fond smile and gently removed the flowers from the horse's mouth.

"Everyone's a chaperone, lately," the earl remarked with a wry twist of his cheek. "Even your horse."

Evelynne leaned her back against the earl as he wrapped his arms protectively about her. "Does he live up to your expectations, my lord?"

"He's quite something to behold. A man's mount, I'd say. Not fit for a scrap of a girl."

Evelynne smiled at his baiting. "Oh, he can be a handful, all right. But he knows when to stop misbehaving, as well. Unlike you, my lord—" She was rewarded for her temerity when the earl bit tenderly at the nape of her neck. "You need schooling, it appears. Little Georgie always minds his manners."

"It's a daft name, Eve. And quite typical of Edgar's sense of humor. Luckily you're not part of the Prince Regent's set, or you'd have a lot to answer for."

"Well, at least Edgar didn't name him 'Fat Georgie,' " she protested, and the Monteith crowed with laughter.

They settled the horse in for the night; the earl covered him with a woolen blanket as Evelynne drew him a measure of oats for his feed bucket.

"We'd best be getting back before Arkady sends the hounds after us." The earl took the lantern from the wall bracket.

Evelynne plucked some straw from her beloved's hair. "Yes," she teased as she twirled it beneath his nose. "He'll think we were being indiscreet in the hay."

They had gone some paces along the passage when the earl stopped. "Hold a minute, Eve."

She watched in puzzlement as he walked back to the horse's stall. He unlatched the gate and went inside. She followed quietly in his wake, then scurried back to where he had left her.

So he never knew that she had seen him put his arms about the great beast's neck and heard him murmur fervently into the black mane, "Thank you, old fellow, and bless you for making her so happy."

Chapter 10

~

They had missed the waltzing and a good deal of the late supper by the time they returned to the party. The earl led Evelynne into the supper room on his arm—the front parlor had been set up with a buffet and small tables—and he didn't leave her side for the rest of the evening. Arkady bribed the orchestra leader to play one last waltz at the very end of the night, and nearly every guest, even those who had sworn they would not consider dancing another step, found a partner and swept onto the dance floor.

The earl took Evelynne into his arms and spun her around and around until she was dizzy from the dance, as well as from the hard, sweet pressure of his hand at her back. His eyes no longer blazed at her through a veil of heat. There was a softer look now in their blue depths, and she felt as though her plate, at last, was filled.

He loved her. He'd said it and kissed her with reverence and joy. She felt as if they had passed safely through a warren of self-doubt and misgiving and dwelled now on a protected plateau.

This is but a bridge in time. Evelynne shivered, and the earl tugged her closer.

"Mouse?" He lifted her slightly as they whirled past another couple.

"It's nothing." She smiled serenely up at him. "Just the breeze from the windows."

Lady Philippa Carstairs lay in her bed, drumming her pointed fingernails on the coverlet. She was not pleased. Not one bit. The Monteith was carrying his game a little too far. It was one thing to flirt with that lanky, dark-haired chit. A little outside flirtation added spice to a seduction. She was not above using it herself, with most gratifying results. But he had carried it beyond good taste. He had practically been dancing attendance on that girl last evening. She was beginning to lose patience.

He knew where she slept. He knew her maid was in a distant chamber. He knew she was not encouraging any other gentleman to pay her court. So why, then, hadn't he come to her?

Her French maid entered, carrying a cup of chocolate and some pastry on a tray.

"The earl has called for his horse, madame. He is riding out later this morning. And the young lady is to ride with him."

"Thank you, Yvette. You'd better lay out one of my riding habits. I think perhaps the red one?"

"*Oui,* madame. The red is *parfait.*"

"See that Sir Gideon and my other friends are informed that we are all to go riding this morning. And tell him I'd like to speak with him before he goes down to breakfast."

Lady Philippa sat up and tumbled her long golden hair behind her shoulders. It was time to stop playing games with the Earl of Monteith. Or perhaps it was time to start playing them. But from now on, she would be making the rules.

Evelynne came slowly down the stairway into the great hall, where the servants were still tackling the job of getting the house back into post-party shape. She carried the long skirt of her habit draped over one arm. It was not a very fashionable riding dress; Mrs. Craft was a dear person, but not a lady in the first stare of style. It was a dark slate color, with black bone buttons that fastened up nearly to her chin. Millie had tucked a bit of white lace at her throat to liven it up and had decorated the rather flattened velvet toque with a curling white feather, filched from Cousin Lydia's favorite summer bonnet.

Evelynne had almost convinced herself that it didn't matter how she was dressed, but when she entered the breakfast room and took one look at Lady Philippa, wearing a most stylish habit of brilliant red with black frogging, her heart sank.

Vain, vain creature, she chided herself. *He doesn't care how you look. He said he adored you in homespun. He told you you looked beautiful sitting on a fence rail in the middle of an apple orchard, with two days' worth of tangles in your hair.*

She smiled grimly at the group assembled at the table as she went to the sideboard for her breakfast. Except for Sir Roland

and Colonel Craft, all of those seated for breakfast were the fashionable gentlemen and ladies of Lady Philippa's particular claque. And they were all dressed for riding. Evelynne felt like Daniel in the lion's den.

"Miss Marriott," Lady Philippa greeted her with glib cordiality, "what an interesting riding costume. It puts me in mind of one my mother used to wear. And gray is such a suitable color for you."

"And red is such an apt color for you, Lady Philippa," Arkady observed as he and the earl came into the room. "Or should I say scarlet is. Yes, very apt."

Lady Philippa smiled at Arkady with clenched teeth, and then winged her most seductive smile at the earl as he passed by. He sat down next to Evelynne and bent to speak with her, the two dark heads almost touching.

"Do you ride with us today, Mitford?" one of the sprigs called out. Evelynne looked up. Arkady had forsaken his brilliant coats and high shirt points for a simple, exquisitely tailored coat of bottle green melton, worn with beige buckskins. Evelynne had the oddest feeling she was looking at a total stranger. In place of the languid, world-weary dandy of the drawing room, there appeared here a well-set-up young man with a trim figure and a rather good leg. His face even had a different cast; the vacant, mooncalf expression had given way to one of candid alertness. How very intriguing.

Arkady had gone to the sideboard and was filling his plate. "One gets a little housebound, if you must know. And I want to see Miss Marriott taming the wild beast." He grinned at the earl, who merely returned him a withering glance. "I am referring, of course, to her new horse."

"A new horse? How nice for you, my dear," Lady Philippa remarked, buttering a scone. "His lordship and I missed having you on our ride together yesterday, didn't we, Robbie? I hope you've acquired a compliant mount. My own Desdemona is quite full of herself at times, but she knows who is the mistress."

"I believe we all know who was the mistress," Arkady said to no one in particular.

Once they had finished their breakfast, the riding party wandered out to the front drive. Liveried grooms held the reins of the high-bred horses, who danced about in anticipation of their morning outing.

Evelynne hung back from the rest of the group.

"What is it, Mouse?" The earl slowed his step to keep pace with her. She looked absolutely miserable.

"I wanted to do this with you. Alone. Not with these people all about." She stopped at the doorway. "You go on, Robbie. I'll ride Georgie some other time."

"No," he said firmly. "You'll ride him now. I've told you, you're worth ten of Philippa or any society miss. I'll wager that on horseback, you're worth two dozen of anyone. And look at Arkady, all dressed down for the occasion. You can't disappoint him."

She gave a little snicker of amusement. "He dresses down rather well. I almost get the feeling that there's a flesh-and-blood man in there somewhere."

"Well, the less you focus on that subject, the better. I'm still not convinced he doesn't want you for himself."

She opened her eyes wide. "Arkady? Oh, you're bamming me, my lord, and now you've made me laugh."

"Yes, I have. And just in time, too. Look, here comes Jim Darby with that behemoth of yours."

The young groom from the night before was leading Little Georgie up from the stable yard. The horse was tacked with a sidesaddle and had been brushed until his scrubby dun coat almost shone.

"Oh my, have you ever seen the like!" Lady Philippa shrilled out from atop her black mare. "Miss Marriott, I fear you have been taken in. It looks like the pachyderm from the Tower Menagerie. All it wants is a trunk." She tittered. "I hope you didn't pay for him by the pennyweight!"

Lady Philippa's friends were guffawing and jeering as Little Georgie was led through their midst, and that was all it took for Evelynne to march resolutely up to her horse. The earl was right behind her. He caught her about the waist and tossed her lightly up into the saddle.

"Stout heart," he whispered. "We'll soon leave them all behind."

He quickly mounted the strapping bay hack he had ridden the morning before. Arkady was sitting, quite composed, on a beautiful gray mare at the edge of the group.

"She's an Orlov trotter," he remarked when he noticed Evelynne studying the horse. "More than a touch of Arab, you know. My mother's family breeds them in Russia." He looked

Georgie over with an appraising glance. "Your fellow there seems a capable beast. He could probably walk over most of the fences we have hereabouts."

As the group turned and headed for the park, Evelynne moved Georgie next to Mitford's mare. It felt wonderful beyond words to be riding again. Little Georgie jigged a little as they first set out, just to remind her he was happy to be with her, but he settled down quite nicely once they moved from the drive to the grassy parkland. Beside her, Arkady urged his mare effortlessly into a smooth, ground-covering trot, and then drew her up just as effortlessly as they crested the rise of a hill.

"You are a sham, Arkady!" Evelynne laughed accusingly, coming up alongside him. "For such a delicate dandy, you ride as if you were born in the saddle."

"Tartar blood." He shrugged his narrow shoulders and looked a tiny bit smug. "Best cavalrymen in Europe, don't you know."

"Why were you never in the war?" Evelynne asked artlessly.

"He's never cared for *armed* combat," the Monteith said with a wry grin as he guided his horse between them.

"Oh, little boys and their tin soldiers." Arkady made sour a face. "Not for me. I value my own neck, thank you."

"Yes," the earl said. "He values it so much, he's three times disappeared into France without a word to anyone. And after each visit, the Home Office has mysteriously received critical information on troop movements and armaments."

"You shouldn't believe all you hear, old lad," Mitford cautioned quietly. He leaned forward to address Evelynne. "His lordship likes to pretend I am not the worthless fribble that I present to the world."

"His lordship has friends at the Home Office, in case you have forgotten," the earl responded smoothly.

Evelynne pondered this. Could the foppish Arkady be involved in wartime intrigue? She'd always felt there was an element of shrewdness behind his languid manner. And he didn't lack for wits—he was, after all, the overseer of a large and thriving estate. So Arkady hid behind masks, did he? No wonder she felt such a kinship with the marquess. Gentlewoman disguised as factory boy meets up with wartime spy masquerading as preening tulip. And then there was her lord, straightforward and stalwart, in between the two grand charlatans. *Poor Robbie.*

Lady Philippa, her mare foaming at the bit, came riding up and forced her horse between Evelynne and the earl. As they were now riding along a narrow country lane, Evelynne had to fall back slightly. The rest of the group lagged even farther behind.

"Desdemona wants a good gallop, my lords. There's a lovely flat field over there—ideal for a bit of racing." She pointed with her whip as she turned to Evelynne. "I'm sure Miss Marriott won't mind if we leave her behind for a few minutes." She gave the towering Georgie a pointed look. "Her new beast doesn't look up to much speed." She then urged her mare toward the level meadow, which was guarded by a high five-barred gate.

"I lease this pasture out to Farmer Patton," Arkady remarked to his companions. "But I believe he won't mind if we make use of it." He then rode after Lady Philippa and gallantly leaned from his saddle to open the wide gate. The balance of the riders caught up with them and filed into the grassy field.

A clutch of brown-and-white cows stood in one corner of the meadow, near the gate, and—hoping this invasion might signal time to return to their barn—they began to low plaintively. Several of the horses took exception to this noise. They caracoled and shied, bumping and jostling one another.

Evelynne sat there on her calm, stoic Georgie; he seemed almost disdainful of these equine hijinks. He laid his ears back as one chestnut gelding swung against him and bucked its male rider half off. As the fellow—Sir Gideon, Evelynne believed he was called—cursed and clung to his beast's mane, the horse again knocked into Little Georgie. The dun took a half step back, just as Lady Philippa cried out. "Desde . . . mona!"

The black mare rose on her hind legs, and then shot away from the group, tearing up great gouts of sod with her steeled hoofs. "Robbie!" the lady wailed. "Robbieeee!"

The earl instantly spurred his bay stallion in the direction of Lady Philippa's flight. He crouched low in the saddle and tried to stay on Desdemona's tail. The mare was at least setting a straight course. He heard a thundering coming from behind him and flung a look over his shoulder. Evelynne was flying in his wake, her horse's powerful, long-reaching strides eating up the ground. He almost grinned. *God, she could ride!*

Up ahead of them, Lady Philippa was making the mistake of leaning into her horse's neck, urging the animal on, instead of setting her weight back in the saddle to slow it down. The mare

ran as if possessed, her head flung up, flecks of spittle tearing
away from her open mouth.

The earl had almost come abreast of the crazed mare and was
reaching for her bridle when she stepped into a gopher hole.
Desdemona went down violently, tail over top, in a screaming
tangle of thrashing legs. Lady Philippa was thrown high into
the air, a flash of scarlet against the morning sky. She landed on
the turf with a sickening thud.

The earl leaped from his saddle and ran to where she lay
sprawled on the grass. "Phil!" he said urgently, taking one of
her limp hands. "Philippa? Can you hear me?"

She groaned softly, raising her head. "What happened?"

"You took a nasty spill. Lie still until I see if you've broken
anything." He began running his hands along her body. Evelynne had jumped down off Georgie and was trying to get the
foundering mare back on her feet. She watched as the earl's
hands tenderly probed Lady Philippa's limbs and torso, and felt
quite ill.

Arkady came riding up to them, just as Desdemona scrambled awkwardly to her feet.

"I saw what she did," he said softly to Evelynne with a dark-
ling look. He dismounted and crouched down to examine the
trembling mare's legs. "How is Lady Philippa, Robbie?" he
called over his shoulder.

"Not badly hurt, I think. Just winded." The earl lifted her into
a sitting position. Evelynne left the mare to Arkady's care and
went to kneel beside them on the grass.

"Can I do anything?" she asked, touching the Monteith's
sleeve. "I could bring her a damp cloth from that stream along
the fence."

Lady Philippa looked up at Evelynne and cringed back
against the earl's chest. "Sh-sh-she did it! It was all her fault!"
she said in a throbbing voice as she pointed a shaking finger at
the girl kneeling beside her. "She slewed that great unmannered
beast into my mare and made her bolt."

Evelynne sat back on her heels as if she'd been slapped.

"Send her away, Robbie," Lady Philippa sobbed, clutching at
his lapels. "Oh, hold me, please! I was so afraid."

"You're safe now, Phil." He clasped her head against his
shoulder. He looked at Evelynne over the bright golden hair
that rested under his chin. "Did you lose control of your horse,

Eve? You've not ridden him in a long while—and all the other horses *were* acting up. It's not shameful to admit it."

As happened on that night in the earl's library, Evelynne had completely lost her voice. *Not my horse,* she wanted to cry out, *not Little Georgie. You foolish man—can't you see what she's playing at?*

"I see you have no answer for me." He looked at Evelynne almost sadly as she rose to her feet. "You could at least own up to it."

Lady Philippa's friends came riding up just then, looking shocked and dismayed. Most of them dismounted and crowded around her prone form, asking after her with frightened voices.

Arkady was still beside the mare, patting her neck and trying to soothe her. He looked at Evelynne, standing white-faced and trembling, her hands clenched at her sides.

"I think you should let Evelynne explain, Robbie."

The earl didn't even glance up at his friend. "She had her chance to apologize," he muttered.

"Monteith!" Arkady's tone of voice would have done a sergeant-major proud. The earl's head snapped up. "It's not as it appears."

"This isn't the time or place, Mitford," he snarled, and then turned his attention back to Lady Philippa, who was now moaning softly.

Arkady looked at Evelynne and shrugged. It was obvious to them both that the earl was not in the mood for the truth.

"I think I'd better go back for a carriage, Robbie." Arkady's tone was cool. "It's clear Lady Philippa can't ride, and anyway, the mare can barely walk."

"I'll go back, Arkady," Evelynne said hoarsely, her voice returning in scratchy increments. "You stay here and look after the mare. She's very badly off, but I can see you've got a calming touch."

"Have Jim Darby bring the dogcart round," Arkady said as he boosted Evelynne into her saddle.

"Well, what are you waiting or?" the earl barked at them. "Go and fetch a carriage! She needs to be home. She needs a doctor—"

"She needs a good thrashing." Evelynne almost spat out the words. She urged Little Georgie right up to the edge of the group, and they all sidled away. The earl quickly shifted Lady Philippa into the arms of Sir Gideon and stood up. He set himself firmly between the fallen lady and the madwoman on horseback.

"Have you lost your wits?" There was a look of thunder on the earl's face as he snatched at the dun's bridle. Little Georgie regarded him with a placid expression.

"No." Evelynne returned the earl's look with blazing eyes. "My wits are just fine. My horse is not to blame for this, and neither am I. The mare didn't run away with her. Lady Philippa slashed at her with her whip to make her bolt."

Beware, the earl's expression said clearly. *Beware what you say.*

"It's lucky she didn't kill that poor beast." Evelynne glanced back at the black mare, who stood, head down, clearly favoring one front leg. "She's probably lamed her for good, though. And all for some foolishness." She looked at the blur of faces before her, some standing open-mouthed, others frowning up at her.

"It's a lie!" Lady Philippa cried out feebly. "It's a foul lie! Oh, Robbie, how can you believe someone like her?"

"I know you all wish me at the devil," Evelynne said with a sob in her voice. "But there was no need to injure an innocent animal for the pleasure of seeing me brought low."

"Go back to the house, Evelynne." The Monteith's voice was clipped, his eyes hooded. "I'll attend to you later."

"Let me come with you—" Arkady reached for his horse's bridle, but Evelynne had already reined Little Georgie sharply around. The dun reared back slightly, and then with a mighty leap forward, he surged into a gallop. They raced full out across the wide meadow, the wind whipping the skirts of Evelynne's habit over the horse's flanks. Evelynne didn't slow down as she reached the high gate, but set the bit horse right at the obstacle. As at least two members of the riding party watched with worried eyes, Little Georgie sailed gracefully over the top rail with a good foot of daylight beneath him. Then Evelynne was gone from sight.

"Kind of takes your breath away, doesn't she?" Arkady murmured. The earl scowled and said nothing.

In spite of the terrible pounding in her head and the desire to do nothing more than fling herself onto her bed, Evelynne did her duty by Lady Philippa. She sent young Darby with the dogcart, directing him to Patton's field, and then asked one groom to ride for the doctor, and persuaded another to fetch the farrier for Desdemona.

She covered her horse with a light blanket and, refusing any offers of help from the stable lads, walked him around the yard to cool off. She had ridden him hard those last few miles, and he was covered in sweat, though breathing easily. She, however, was not breathing so easily. In fact, the ache that was constricting her midsection made it difficult to breathe at all.

She was in the right, she knew she was. But then why did she feel as though she'd made a dreadful error. Was it bad form, in the *ton*, to accuse someone of wicked behavior?

You kicked her while she was down, a little voice reminded her grimly, *and that's not very sporting in any circles.*

Evelynne sighed. Whatever her ulterior motive, Lady Philippa had been thrown and badly shaken up. And ripping up at her had been an ill-bred thing to do. It probably gave the earl a complete disgust of her. No matter that it was Lady Philippa's own fault for trying to lure the earl into rescuing her. Everyone in the riding party, except Arkady, had looked at Evelynne as if she were the villain.

"Oh, Lord!" she cried bitterly into Georgie's neck. "I've made a total mull of it all."

Once the horse was cooled down, she closed him in his stall and walked slowly back to the house. There was a black crested coach in the drive with a team of high-bred gray horses in the traces. It was too soon for the doctor to have arrived, so she payed it little mind as she went into the house.

She changed from her habit into a day dress of nile blue jaconet muslin. It was a charming gown, but she chose it only because it was the first one to come to her hand from the wardrobe. She lay down on her bed and wrapped her hands across her stomach. The ache inside her hadn't decreased—in fact, it seemed to grow stronger with each passing minute. She thought if she could only cry, some of the pain would lessen. But her eyes remained dry, and her head throbbed in cruel syncopation with her hammering pulse.

Someone said her name from the hallway, and before she could send her visitor away, Mrs. Craft opened the door and peered in.

"Ah, I thought to find you here. Arkady asked me to come up and look in on you." The colonel's wife smiled pleasantly. "He told me what happened with Lady Philippa. The doctor's seeing to her now. Not but that she deserves a broken neck for such a trick. Are you quite well, my dear?"

Evelynne put a hand to her brow. "My head aches a bit is all."

"I could bring you some Hungary water from my room if you like. It's very soothing."

"I'd prefer hemlock," Evelynne said with feeling. "That would solve everyone's problem."

"Now, now." Mrs. Craft came in and sat on the bed beside her. She patted Evelynne's hand in a motherly fashion. "I gather the earl was a little put out with you. These things happen between people who are, well, attached to one another. Anger is really just the other side of the coin. And it's quite normal, my dear."

"He was odious to me in front of all those people." She rolled on her side and burrowed her head under the pillow. "And I was horribly nasty to Lady Philippa." Her voice was muffled. "I think I embarrassed him, Mrs. Craft, and he's such a proud man. I don't know how I can ever make it up to him."

"Give it time, dear, give it time. I daresay he'll probably be occupied all afternoon, anyway. Once they've seen to Lady Philippa, he and Mitford are to meet with the gentlemen who arrived in the black coach. 'Dashed bad timing,' I believe that's what Arkady said. He wasn't looking forward to the interview, of that I'm sure."

The black coach? Evelynne recalled passing it on the drive— the black coach with gray horses. She sat bolt upright on her bed.

"Did you see the men who came in that coach? Were you downstairs when they arrived?" There was a sudden urgency in Evelynne's voice.

"Well, no. I was out walking with Lady Springhurst. She recognized the crest, though, when the coach passed us in the drive. Stilton, she said, or Shelton. I can't recall—"

"Skelton," Evelynne said, her eyes narrowing. "So he's taken the bait at last."

"What bait?" Mrs. Craft asked.

"Oh, nothing. Nothing." Evelynne trusted Mrs. Craft completely and would have confided anything to her, but the earl's intrigue with Lord Skelton was not her story to reveal. She slid to the edge of the bed. "I'm feeling much better now. I think I'll go downstairs and have some lunch."

"I believe the earl would prefer it if you kept to your room just now, my dear," Mrs. Craft warned her gently.

"Yes, I'm sure he would. But he's not going to deprive me of my liberty, just because he's in a crusty mood."

The older woman shook her head. "My husband, the colonel, would remind you that discretion is the better part of valor. Plenty of time to make amends with him later in the day."

"There's very little time, Mrs. Craft." Evelynne went to the door. "I promise to behave myself. In truth, there's not much more damage I can do, than I've already done this morning." And with that naive pronouncement she headed for the great hall.

Chapter 11

Lord Randall Skelton had been waiting for over an hour. He knew from the spies he had placed in the village that there had been a party at Levelands the night before, and the household still appeared to be all at sixes and sevens. The servants were rearranging the front parlor, and so he and the soberly dressed man who accompanied him had been shown into the back parlor, a midsize room decorated with primitive armaments and weaponry.

Skelton paced restlessly before the fireplace, while his companion, a lantern-jawed, older gentleman sporting a dapper white wig, sat upon the sofa and occupied himself by shuffling the papers in the large portfolio that lay open across his lap.

"Are you certain Monteith is here, then?" the older man inquired.

"He's here!" Skelton barked, turning into the room. The baron's face was a brilliant medley of reds and purples. The swelling in his broken nose had gone down in the last four days, but the residual bruises had left a contused coloring that even the heavy application of face powder could not hide. "He's been making merry, I hear. Squiring the ladies about and dancing the night away."

A footman came in with a tray of Madeira, followed almost immediately by their host. Arkady had changed from his riding clothes into a coat of buttercup yellow brocade, with smallclothes of a rich turquoise. They quite cast Skelton's claret-and-lilac ensemble into the shade.

"Pray forgive me for the delay." Mitford waved Skelton into a chair, and then took one himself. He crossed his legs gracefully, one over the other. "We had a little *contretemps* earlier, while out riding. But everything is now in order." Arkady brushed a minuscule speck of dust from his knee. "And how may I be of service to you this morning?"

"It's afternoon, Mitford," Skelton grumbled.

"Oh, my. Time just gets away from one. Nevertheless, I'm here now, and yours to command, Lord Skelton."

"I asked to see Monteith," Skelton said brusquely. "My business is with him alone."

"He's gone to his room to change, but he'll be along any time now. Wouldn't want to greet an old acquaintance like yourself in all his stable dirt, you know. Please, gentlemen, drink up." He lifted his own glass of Madeira and took a delicate sip. "And by the by, Skelton, I know you won't take it amiss in me to point this out to you, as one man of fashion to another—puce is definitely not your color."

"My coat is claret, Mitford, not puce," Skelton replied testily.

"Your coat?" Arkady started back. "I was referring to your face, old lad."

Skelton jumped up from his chair, but the bewigged gentleman caught at his arm. "Please, my lord. Let us conduct our business in a proper manner."

As Skelton resumed his seat, Arkady remarked, "I have not had the pleasure of this gentleman's acquaintance."

"He's a magistrate from Southampton," the baron muttered. "Name of Todd."

"Bertram Todd, Esquire. I am pleased to meet you, my lord." He bowed from the sofa.

"Delighted," Arkady pronounced as the parlor door opened. As the Monteith stepped into the room, he closed and locked the door behind him. He was attired in the clothing he had worn while on the road with Evelynne, now cleaned and pressed.

"Ah, here is Lord Monteith, at last. Robbie, I've been entertaining your guests for you. You know Lord Skelton, of course, and this is Mr. Todd, a magistrate from Southampton."

The earl barely acknowledged the older man as he strode across to the baron.

"I knew it was only a matter of time till you showed your face, Skelton. And it's a rather impressively vivid face these days." The earl studied the baron's swollen, discolored cheeks with great satisfaction.

"So I have already observed to him," Arkady said smoothly.

"This needs to be a private interview, Mitford," Lord Skelton said, looking at the blond man with distaste. "Monteith will prefer it so, once he knows the manner of my business."

"Oh, he has no secrets from me." The marquess waved his hand in the air, and then added pointedly, "You have brought a magistrate, Skelton, and now the Monteith shall have one, as well. Or didn't you know that I sit for this district?"

"I can fight my own battles, Arkady." The earl flung himself into a chair near the partly opened French window.

"Yes, I know. But this appears to be a matter of law." He raised his eyebrows questioningly at Mr. Todd, who nodded back. "So you would do well to have me present. Shall we get on with it, then? Our luncheon awaits, and I'm devilish sharp set."

Mr. Todd, realizing his moment was at hand, rose to his feet with some trepidation, clutching a sheaf of papers.

"I have here a complaint against the Earl of Monteith for robbery and battery, filed by my Lord Skelton. There are also sworn affidavits from the two men who were also set upon by his lordship. There is a charge of violence perpetrated upon these men, involving pistols and fisticuffs, and, uh-hum, I believe Lord Skelton's face speaks for itself."

"Eloquently," Arkady stated softly.

"This is a farce." The earl lounged back in his chair. "I may be new to the workings of the law, but I know a damned trumped-up charge when I see one. What possible reason could I have for robbing you, Skelton?"

"Yes," Arkady interjected, "I could understand him wanting to have at you, in a general way. But hold you up at gun point? Bah, it's a ludicrous charge."

Skelton bared his teeth. "Read the statement," he snarled to the magistrate.

"It's quite long . . ." Mr. Todd fumbled with his papers. "Well, the gist of it is that Lord Monteith accosted my client on the road and threatened to shoot him if he didn't alter his position in Parliament. When my client refused, they fought. Lord Skelton was injured, and when his coachmen came to his aid, they too were struck down. Lord Monteith then appropriated my client's carriage and horses."

"You've got the events of the case quite right, Mr. Todd," Arkady acknowledged, "but the players are all topsy-turvy. It was Monteith who was attacked at gunpoint, not Skelton."

"That is for the court to decide. These are very serious alle-

gations, my lords," Mr. Todd said earnestly. "The matter will
surely be brought before the King's Bench in London. And as
you are both peers of the realm, it's not inconceivable that the
Regent himself may become involved."

"I doubt it will get that far," the earl pronounced calmly. "I
doubt it will even get beyond this room."

The Monteith could see that Skelton was perplexed by his re-
fusal to be intimidated by the charges. The baron had surely expected him to be at least discomfited by this new threat. But he
couldn't know that before breakfast the earl had received a missive from Sir Robert Poole, informing him that the net was
quickly tightening about Lord Skelton. Sir Robert himself was
expected at Levelands later in the day, bearing his own reports
on the baron's suspected treason. Skelton's scheme to bring
scandal down upon the earl was about to be checkmated quite
thoroughly.

"Oh, it will go to the highest court, I'll see to that." Skelton
was on his feet. "And, if I win my case or not, your reputation
will be in tatters. No man strikes me and gets away unpunished.
You've gotten in way over your head this time, you and that
mincing popinjay." He swung his hand toward Arkady, who
merely blinked innocuously.

"Lord Skelton, please!" Mr. Todd reprimanded him.

Skelton turned swiftly to the magistrate and uttered curtly,
"You've earned your money, Todd. Now get out and await me
in the hall."

The magistrate picked up his portfolio, and after a nervous
bow to the three men, he let himself out.

"Now the gloves come off," Arkady murmured into his glass.

"I warned you not to mix in my affairs, but you, stubborn
Scot that you are, couldn't leave well enough alone." Skelton
walked behind the earl's chair. He leaned over and purred, "You
know what I'm after, don't you, Monteith? You'd hate to lose
your standing in Parliament. Such a zealous reformer, you are.
Such a sterling reputation. You've no idea how you annoy me
with your righteous prosing. And if you don't immediately
cease prying into my private affairs, I'll see that the newspapers
hear of your lawless behavior outside Levelton. Stealing a
man's carriage at pistol point, highway robbery—it's a very serious offense, my lord."

"Don't make me laugh, Skelton." The earl turned to look up

at him with cold eyes. "It's your word against mine. That rather balances things out."

"I have witnesses," Skelton walked to the middle of the room. "Or have you forgotten that?"

"Hired ruffians." The Monteith was undismayed.

"Coachmen who have been in my employ for years. Family men, of good standing in the community. Church-going men."

"Doing it a bit brown, Skelton," Arkady interjected.

"Witnesses!" the baron insisted, his voice rising. "And who will speak for you, my hotheaded Scot. Who will back up your version of the tale? Who, then?"

"I will!" Evelynne tumbled in from the terrace through the opened French door. "I will speak for my Lord Monteith."

"Evelynne!" the earl and Arkady cried out in unison. She darted past the Monteith, who had jumped up and was trying to get his hands on her and ran to the center of the room to confront Lord Skelton.

"I was there that night, at the Eel and Barrow," she said rapidly. "I heard you conspiring with the redheaded coachman. I saw everything." The earl caught her by the arm, but she shook him off.

Arkady had risen slowly from his chair. "Not necessary, dear girl. We've got everything in hand."

"Who is this chit?" Skelton said warily as he surveyed the society miss in her stylish blue gown. "What's she to do with all this?"

Evelynne looked from Arkady to the Monteith. They were both glaring at her.

"I just wanted to help the earl . . ." her voice was tremulous. "Because I was there, you see."

"No, you weren't!" The Monteith stepped forward and shook her twice by the arm. "Stop telling fibs."

He turned to Skelton and said with a rueful smile, "This young lady has been setting her cap at me all week. I imagine she thinks this latest start will put her in my good graces. Now run off, my dear, before you find yourself in the soup." He pushed her firmly toward the hall door.

"No, wait . . ." Lord Skelton took a step back as Evelynne made to depart, and put his hand firmly against the door, trapping her there with his arm. "She puts me in mind of someone."

He gazed at Evelynne's vivid gray eyes and her flushed cheeks. He looked at her stubborn, willful mouth, and then down at his own bandaged thumb. With a challenging glance over his shoulder at the Monteith, he took her chin firmly between his fingers, tilting her head back.

"I've seen this face before, and not in a society drawing room."

"Get your hands off her, Skelton."

Arkady held his friend back from flying at the baron. "Too late, Robbie," he breathed into the earl's ear. "Too late. She's been found out."

"Yes . . ." Lord Skelton brushed one finger along Evelynne's angular cheekbone, where the last discolored remnants of his punishing blow could still be seen. "I wondered what happened to that young scapegrace who bit me. My men have been watching this house and could find no sign of him."

He gave a nasty chuckle deep in his chest. "For such a pretty thing, she made a very convincing lad. How fortunate for you, Monteith, to share your journey with such as this." He ran his hand along Evelynne's throat, where her pulse beat in triple time. "And how forgiving of you, Mitford, to let him bring his trull into your home, among the ladies of the *ton*."

"If you touch me again, you slimy toad," Evelynne hissed as Skelton turned back to her, "I'll make sure that more than your ugly face is swollen." She shifted forward suddenly, and the baron prudently moved himself out of knee range.

"I rarely hit women," he observed from a safe distance, with deadly, narrowed eyes. "But now I'm glad I made an exception in your case."

That was more than the earl's Highland temper could withstand. He wrestled out of Mitford's restraining arms and hurled himself at Skelton. Before Arkady could stop him, he had the baron up against the door by the lace at his throat, and was determinedly cutting off his air supply with both hands. Evelynne had sidled along one wall, away from the combatants, reeling from the sudden awareness of what she had done.

"Stop it now, I say!" Arkady commanded, trying to pry the earl's hands loose. "For God's sake, Robbie, if you kill him in here, the maids will never forgive me!"

The earl's grip loosened, and with a gasp of indrawn breath, Skelton pushed him away. The color returned slowly to his blanched face.

Mitford prodded the earl toward Evelynne. "Take her out of

here before she swoons. I'll deal with this master of intrigue myself."

Without a word, the earl hooked Evelynne by one arm and dragged her behind him through the doorway. Mr. Todd was standing in the hall, suspiciously close to the parlor entrance, a look of consternation on his thin face.

"I h-heard noises," he stammered. "I-I wasn't eavesdropping . . . I was only trying to . . ."

The earl scowled him into silence and muttered, "Don't concern yourself, Mr. Todd. Eavesdropping is the pastime of choice in this household."

He then continued down the hall with a white-faced Evelynne in tow. When they reached the library, he threw open the door and pushed her ungently inside.

"Go ahead and swoon," he seethed, slamming the heavy door behind him. "I'd like to see it. I'd like to see you exhibit some normal female sensibility for a change."

She fell back against the refectory table, a hand to her breast. Her head spun, the floor tilted, and she felt the room begin to close in on her. Dear God, she really was going to swoon!

"Here, drink this—" The earl thrust a half-filled glass at her. "I don't want to be scraping you off the carpet."

She took a sip and felt the thick amber liquid sear a path down her throat.

The Monteith leaned over the unlit fireplace; his hands gripped the high mantel till his knuckles showed white, and his jaw was set in a taut, unforgiving line. Evelynne continued to sip her drink, watching him and waiting for her heart to stop pounding. The silence hung in the room like a thick, stifling shroud.

When the earl spoke at last, gazing down into the ashes of last night's fire, his voice was weary with defeat. "You've done for us, Evelynne. Highway robbery I could easily defend myself against, and never bring you into it. But not this."

"I . . . I only . . ."

"In a few days time I'd have had the means to indict Skelton. I've almost gathered all the evidence I need against him. But now you've given him more ammunition against me than he'd ever dreamed existed. Even if he discovers his treason has been found out, he won't hold back this story. It will be his best revenge. Very soon everyone in the *ton* will know that I spent two days traveling with you. And they will know how you were dressed—Skelton will especially relish that part."

Evelynne blinked back her tears. There was a world of sadness in Robbie's voice as he continued, "It will be said, just as that scoundrel predicted, that I brought my fancy piece into Mitford's home. The *ton* is very unforgiving about that kind of behavior. We'll both be broken on the wheel of scandal."

"I am not your fancy piece," she protested softly. "I am not a trull." The foul name Skelton had used, stung her still.

"They will think it, nevertheless."

"How is it that Lady Philippa may take lovers and still be received in society? I don't understand."

"Yes." He turned to her with a look of new awareness in his hard, blue eyes. "It's very clear to me now that you don't understand anything about my world." He winced inwardly at the naked pain that leapt across her face at his words. "Lady Philippa is a widow," he said a bit more gently. "She may do as she likes if she is discreet."

"Discreet!" Evelynne cried.

"Don't get me started on the subject of Lady Philippa," he cautioned. "Your behavior to her this morning was disgraceful. Such want of conduct—"

"I-I-I was unjustly accused, and you expected me to defer to her? Because she is a lady, and I am not? You may back the righteous causes in Parliament, my lord, but this time you have stood on the side of injustice."

He laughed at her unpleasantly. "Yes, well my parliamentary career is quite likely over, thanks to your interference. I'll have no more causes, righteous or otherwise. Had you been in Skelton's employ, as I thought that first night, you couldn't have brought me to my knees more neatly."

"Oh," she gasped in outrage. "That's not fair, Robbie. I was trying to help you!"

"Help me? Help me?" He bore down on her relentlessly and grasped her roughly by the arms. "You have been nothing but trouble since I first set eyes on you. You are intemperate and improper, and have proven yourself to be a complete liability. You might have been more useful to me, were you a trull."

Evelynne jolted back away from his restraining hands and slapped him hard upon his cheek. The sharp sound of her open palm upon his face resounded through the room. When she drew her arm back to strike again, he caught at her hands, twisting them painfully behind her. She struggled to get free, crying out as she thrashed and kicked.

"Hellcat!" he uttered viciously. "Will you never be tamed?" And then he swooped his head down and kissed her, lifting her off her feet, binding her helpless against him with steely arms.

"No!" she panted against his onslaught. "Don't. Oh, please don't."

His mouth ground upon her lips, and there was no restraining him. He plundered her there, stole her every breath. Fury schooled his own lips into punishing lines as he kissed her savagely, bending her body to his will, even as she fought him. He was panting now, as she was, and murmuring inarticulate words into the well of her throat. They might have been mistaken for the language of tender passion, but Evelynne had seen, through her tears that there was no light of caring in the earl's eyes as he kissed her. Only anger shone there, and the fierce desire to cause pain. He had made a mockery of all his other sweet kisses, and her heart broke that he could use her so.

She went limp in his arms, throwing her head to one side, away from his avenging mouth. When he realized she was no longer fighting him, he pulled back slightly, thinking she had, indeed, fainted. Her gaze looked through him, emotionless and remote, like the limpid face of a medieval martyr. No light gleamed in her clouded eyes—no anger, no fear, nothing.

"Devil take you!" He thrust himself away from her, so she would not see the expression of self-loathing on his face.

Evelynne leaned back against the library table and continued to observe him obliquely. It was over between them. She knew it beyond conscious thought. Any previous accord was hopelessly destroyed. Pain lanced through her at the realization. But she would regain her dignity, somehow, before she was forced into retreat.

"Are you quite finished with your unpleasantness, my lord?" Lady Philippa herself couldn't have improved on the icy disdain in Evelynne's voice. "You apparently regard your kisses more highly than I do."

"And what do you know of kissing?" he snarled from his place before the hearth. "You knew nothing of the world until you met me."

"And I was happy in my ignorance, sir. I now know a great deal about many things."

"Bah!" His gaze swung again to the fireplace. "You have al-

ways gone your own way—don't lay any of this at my door! I
didn't force you into this infernal situation."

"No," she agreed. "You didn't. It was my choice to aid you.
Arkady did warn me, however, not to expect gratitude from
you. 'Not a master of the finer emotions,' was how he put it."

A gratifying furrow appeared on the earl's brow. Evelynne
suspected she was just about to get a bit of her own back.

"Arkady can keep his damned opinions to himself. And what
right do you have to be discussing me with Mitford?"

"Oh . . ." She toyed with a ribbon on her dress. "He's been
showing me how to go on in society. He, at least, has cared
enough to school me where I was deficient."

"Has he been taking liberties with you?" He had begun to
pace before the hearth.

"Taking liberties!" she exclaimed, stepping away from the
table. "Fine words coming from an overbearing bully. And
that's hardly your concern any longer, my lord. *Arkady* does not
find me intemperate or improper."

He crossed to where she stood. His black hair tumbled over
his forehead, above eyes that were hooded and dark. His blue
coat was the very one he had worn during their adventure; Evelynne knew its fabric and weave like her own skin.

"Has he kissed you?" A slight tic had appeared in the earl's
right cheek.

"Oh, no." She widened her eyes. "Well, not above two or
three times."

"So you've set your sights on a marquess?" There was nothing but contempt in his tone. "You're a quick study, I'll give
you that, Evelynne. I suppose an earldom just wasn't up to your
standards."

"I don't recall you ever giving me that option, my lord."

He winced at her words, his features compressing in pain as
he turned his head away. Evelynne knew she had wounded him
at last. She lost her resolve then. It was not in her nature to be
cruel. Impetuous and foolish, yes . . . but never cruel.

She took a step forward and held out her hand to him. "I will
be returning to London tomorrow." She'd only decided it that
instant. "Arkady will arrange it. I'm sure you will be relieved
to see the back of me. I pray Skelton can be silenced, and if not,
I hope you are wrong about the scandal affecting your career in
Parliament. No one will believe ill of you, I think. Your character is the best witness you could ever have."

The earl disregarded her outstretched hand and said nothing. His empty gaze seemed to go right through her; there was something about that look that disturbed her more than all his heated words had done.

She lowered her hand, then walked with studied composure to the door.

"So nothing remains between you and me." He spoke in a deep monotone. Evelynne couldn't tell if he'd meant it as a question or a statement of fact.

"We were friends once." She turned, with a forced, tight little smile. "But we left that part of ourselves behind us, on the road to Levelands. Let us just say that this episode has been . . . a bridge in time. Nothing more." Then she eased past the library door and shut it softly behind her.

Chapter 12

❧

"Well, Skelton, you've nicely put the fox among the geese." Arkady handed the man his own glass and watched as he downed the Madeira in one swallow. The baron's thick throat, where the earl's fingers had throttled him, had begun to match his multicolored face.

Mitford perched upon the edge of his seat, toying with a barbaric-looking small dagger, one of a collection displayed on the table beside him.

"Blackmail is not a pretty world. Extortion is equally unattractive, don't you think?" He looked across at Skelton, who continued to lean against the parlor door, still catching his breath. "What word, then, I wonder, would you use to describe your actions toward the earl?"

"Protection," Lord Skelton rasped. "I'm protecting myself from that pigheaded Scot and his infernal meddling. He is out to ruin all I stand for, with his noble intentions."

"And, what then, if your cause falters in Parliament?" Arkady waved his fingers in the air. "It's all in a day's work at the House of Lords. Yet you have plotted and spied, abducted and threatened. You have achieved a vendetta that is worthy of the Borgias, Lord Skelton, and over what? Economic reforms? I fear there's a good deal more to this than meets the eye."

"It's not your affair, Mitford. Suffice it to say I have had to involve myself in commerce, and have cultivated many wide-ranging connections."

Yes, ranging all the way into France.

"The people I do business with are men of some stature."

Hmm? I'd heard Napoleon wasn't all that tall.

"And they expect complete confidentiality. I will *not* have Monteith poking his Puritan nose into my doings. He was warned off more than once. I have Liverpool's ear on this, if you must know."

"Ah, the prime minister. Then you must be quite legitimate, old lad." Arkady studied the crude rubies set in the hilt of the dagger. "I gather, then, that Lord Liverpool approved of your scheme to abduct the earl, to threaten him with arrest, and to bring scandal down upon his head."

"I am not compelled to explain my actions to the prime minister—or to you, either."

"You cross a dangerous line when you become a law unto yourself, Skelton," Arkady remarked, tapping the dagger's blade upon one finger. "The jackal who no longer runs with the pack is often eaten by his own kind."

"Are you threatening me?" Skelton took a step forward, his fingers white on the stem of his glass.

Arkady raised his brows. "Me? Threaten you?" He smiled lazily. "Fancy that."

"Bah! I waste my time here. I've said what I came to say." Skelton set his glass down on a table and turned back to the door. "The earl has his choice to make. He relents or the scandal breaks."

"Just one more thing—"

"What? You try me, Mitford, with your endless prosing."

"It's only this. Robbie is not without connections of his own, who would mislike it greatly if you continue your course of persecution. Sir Robert Poole, Ardmore, Lord Butley, and of course, myself."

"You!" Lord Skelton laughed harshly. "The little marquess with his pretty kingdom." He raised scornful eyes to meet Mitford's open gaze. "It will be a cold day in hell when I heed the words of such a man milliner."

The jeweled dagger flew across the room, arrow-swift, and neatly parted Lord Skelton's high pompadour. It lodged firmly in the parlor's stout oak door with a precise snick.

"Are you mad!" Skelton stood, both hands raised, trembling, to his hair.

"No." Arkady leaned back in his seat with a satisfied smile. "Not mad. Russian. You would do well to remember it the next time you cross me. My ancestors have been out of the forest for far less time than yours have, my Lord Skelton."

Arkady watched as the baron, after uttering a most ungentlemanly oath, made a hasty exit. He got up and retrieved the weapon from the door, pulling it out with a low grunt. It had been very difficult to resist the urge to aim just a little lower.

He must be peckish. He'd best go and have lunch, and then see whether the earl had done murder to the meddling Miss Marriott. Now, there was a girl after his own heart!

Arkady discovered Evelynne some time later, after a sweeping search of his home, in the farthest corner of the glassed-in garden room. She was in the throes of what seemed to be a combination crying jag and temper tantrum. He watched her dubiously from behind a banana tree as she alternately sobbed piteously, and then pummeled furiously at the cushions of the bench where she sat.

"I had a feeling things wouldn't turn out too well for you," he said in his most urbane manner, coming out of hiding once he suspected the worst of her emotions had played out. "If it's any consolation, Robbie is, as we speak, on the east veranda, annihilating my stock of clay pigeons with a shotgun. I've recommended that my houseguests and servants remain indoors until he's vented his spleen. You've certainly riled him, Evelynne. He usually only gets that passionate about the poor."

Arkady took a cambric square from his pocket and, sitting himself delicately beside her, proceeded to gently blot the tears that still coursed down her cheeks.

"Y-y-you w-w-were wrong," she hiccuped. "He doesn't care for me. He said I was intemperate and improper." She punched the cushion between them savagely. "He called me a complete liability!"

He brushed an errant curl from her cheek. "There's no getting around it, Eve. The man's a sapskull. Did you try to get your own back, at least?" It was a foolish question to pose to the intrepid young woman beside him.

"Of course I did. I told him he was mistaken about Lady Philippa, we argued over Lord Skelton, and then he kissed me."

"And that's bad?"

"Then he looked through me, as if I were a total stranger."

"That is bad."

"I told him you'd been kissing me, Arkady. I hope you don't mind. I thought it would shake him up."

Arkady stared off at something he'd seen through the glass windows and pondered a moment. "Maybe I should."

"What? Shake him up?"

"No, kiss you." He contemplated her tear-stained face, piquant and childlike. She was such a lovely urchin. "Is Robbie the the only man who's ever kissed you?"

"Well, yes." Ollie Hooper had long since flown from her memory.

"Hmm?" He watched the tall silhouette that moved beyond the garden windows. "Then I think it's time I took your further education in hand."

Evelynne was really quite unprepared for the sensation of being kissed by Arkady. She'd come to think of him as quite an appealing man, in spite of his exaggerated airs and graces. But even if she hadn't been completely smitten with his friend, she didn't think him the type of man whose kisses she would find at all stimulating. She was, of course, quite wrong.

Arkady timed his kiss so that Evelynne was a melting, clinging, dewy-eyed sylph by the time the earl came in through the garden door. Mitford looked over the top of Evelynne's tipped-back head and said, quite conversationally, "Out of ammunition?"

"You should count yourself lucky," Monteith muttered. Evelynne craned her head around and gazed at the earl with wide eyes, but said nothing. She'd realized she was way out of her depth the instant Arkady laid his pliant, clever mouth against hers. She wanted desperately to flee from this place, but Mitford's arms held her firm.

"I'm sorry to interrupt this charming tête-à-tête." The earl's voice was icy. "But Sir Robert Poole has arrived from London, and he bring news of Miss Marriott's family."

Snatching at this excuse to depart, Evelynne leapt off the bench, nearly oversetting Arkady in the process, and after murmuring, "I must go, please excuse me," she dashed from the room.

"Will you cease this playacting, Arkady?" The Monteith leaned the shotgun against a nearby tree and stood before his friend. "I know you believe you are doing me a kindness, that you've some strange notion that I need to be married—"

"Loved, Robbie," Arkady stated gently. "You need to be loved. Quite simple really. It's all any of us need—you, me, even Prinny. And here is this wonderful girl, full of grit and courage, and pretty as Jack's cat, besides, who cares for you in spite of your illustrious title and self-consequence. A girl who believes in the same things you believe in, justice and honor—"

"You've certainly discovered a great deal about her in three days' time," the earl observed.

"Because I listen to her, you dolt, which I'm afraid you rarely do. She wasn't lying to you in the meadow today. Philippa, that wasp, did whip her own horse. She engineered the runaway—I tried to tell you, but you wouldn't listen to me either. I wonder that anyone can talk to you."

The earl mulled over this information for a minute. He felt a sharp pang of shame over the way he'd ripped up at Evelynne in the library.

Arkady leaned forward, his elbows on his knees. "I asked you this question once before, Robbie, and got a fairly nonsensical answer. I except a better answer this time. Just what are your feelings for Evelynne?"

"I won't deny I'm drawn to her." He rubbed his chin with the back of one hand.

"That's rather an understatement, old lad."

The earl shook his head. "It was bad judgment on my part to have let it progress this far."

"If you're feeling guilty for having compromised her, Robbie, you could always marry her. Wouldn't that put things right?"

"I can never take her to wife. Even you must see that she's quite unsuitable—especially after her behavior with Skelton this afternoon. No, it's out of the question now—she's placed herself quite beyond the pale." The earl almost seemed to be speaking to himself. "And perhaps the only way I can redeem myself in society, if this scandal breaks, which I'm sure it must, is to marry a woman of good standing, someone also of the nobility."

"Then I'm sorry for you, my friend." Arkady got up, carefully tucking his handkerchief into his sleeve. "For you have just tossed away a creature of enduring, and very real, nobility."

He left the earl without another word, sauntering away between the tropical blossoms.

Evelynne awoke the next morning to a stiff, chill wind blowing through the curtains of her bedroom. They billowed away from the window frame, like spectral visitors, beckoning her with gauzy fingers. *Ghosts,* she thought. That's all this adventure has lacked. We've had abductions, seductions, accusations, protestations . . . everything but ghostly manifestations. She would have laughed at the thought only one day ago. But now, this morning, her humor had deserted her. Life tasted of sawdust.

She'd somehow gotten through the rest of the previous day, her determination overcoming her feelings of numbed shock. Sir Robert Poole had been kindness itself when she met with him. He'd sensed the distress she couldn't quite hide, and treated her with great warmth. He was a very good man, benevolent and honorable. Just the type of man she wanted to look after Gilly. And surprisingly, he wanted to take over that imposing task. He'd come to offer her brother, he told her in his deep, rich orator's voice, a place in a school he funded. Very impressed with Gilbert, he was—very impressed indeed.

"I need young scoundrels like him," he'd proclaimed. "With a good observant eye and a clever brain, to ensure the safe future of this country."

She had been a little dazed as she listened, and wondered if her hearing had gone off. Gilly was going to ensure the future of England?

His school was located in Exeter, Sir Robert told her enthusiastically. Run by a former intelligence officer—read spy, Evelynne thought—named Matthew Frobisher. He tutored a variety of lads from all walks of life in the fine arts of language, weapons, geography, political history—in other words, espionage.

She had her wits enough about her to know that it sounded perfect for Gilly.

"How much money?" she asked timidly. She didn't think Sir Robert had any idea that the Marriott finances were in ruins. She'd have to get a job double quick to pay for this new school.

"Well, I don't pay the boys that much in the beginning—" She looked up in shock. "But they do study hard, and some of them even get to do a little road work now and then. It's fifty pounds a year, which is quite a fair wage to pay an apprentice." His eyes were twinkling, and he was holding out a small leather bag to her. "Gilbert thought you should have the managing of his funds."

Fifty pounds! It was a godsend.

She had thanked him graciously and gone from the room, still in a daze, but with one pressing need removed from her life. The Marriotts were reprieved, and at Gilly's hands, no less.

She pleaded a headache that night at suppertime and had a tray sent to her room.

Arkady had come up to visit her after supper to discuss her journey to London. He had insisted she take several of Lydia's gowns away with her.

"They'll be long out of fashion when she returns with *ma mère*," he'd explained.

So Evelynne had folded her new dresses and placed them in a bandbox, along with a small piece of turkey bone and a creased note.

Arkady had also insisted on accompanying her back to town.

"But what of your house party, your guests? How can you just leave them?"

He had made a rude face at her. "Oh, them. Since Lady Philippa's mishap—which her friends were party to, you'll be interested to know—the spirit has rather drained out of my little gathering. Everyone's planning to leave tomorrow afternoon. Lady Philippa is to go off with Sir Gideon to, ah, recuperate at his home." He gave Evelynne a meaningful look. "And most of the others are heading back to London. I've given Mrs. Craft your direction, by the by. I hope it was all right. She's very fond of you."

So there Evelynne was, the next morning, standing in the great hall promptly at nine on the dot, as her host had instructed. She was still there at nine-thirty, when Mitford's coachman came in and carried out her bandbox. There was no Arkady to be seen, although several of his guests came down for breakfast, wishing her a good morning before they passed on to the breakfast room.

She feared meeting the earl. Her carefully schooled countenance would crumble like the walls of Jericho if she so much as glimpsed him. *Drat Arkady,* to leave her standing there so exposed.

She finally marched out the front door to the waiting coach. Two coachmen stood at the horses' heads, and a third sat behind the coach astride Little Georgie. Her horse was going home to London with her. With the windfall from Sir Robert, she could afford to stable him in Camden Town. On clear days she would take him up to Hampstead and gallop on the heath till they both forgot the dark moors of Devon and the bright meadows of Hampshire.

A coachman came forward and let down the steps for her. As

she settled on the seat, she could hear Arkady's voice coming from the doorway of the house.

"I'm sorry, but all my other conveyances are being repaired. It's wheel rot or some such thing. Well, of course I know you can rent a carriage. But it would wound me deeply if you refused my offer. And we'll be going right across London, you know, practically through Cavendish Square."

Oh no!

"I know you could travel with one of my guests later today, but Sir Robert did impress upon you that you've got to get back to London as quickly as possible if you're to finish off Lord Skelton."

Oh, please, no!

Arkady climbed in, still chattering relentlessly, and perched beside Evelynne. Behind him came Robert MacIntyre, a truly monumental scowl on his freshly shaved face.

"Miss Marriott," he mumbled into his neckcloth as he seated himself across from them.

"My lord," she mumbled into her hand.

"Dashed fine weather for a journey." Arkady tapped his stick against the front of the coach, and they moved forward. "You may say what you like about the Lake District and the Welsh mountains, I'll take my autumn in Hampshire every time. There's nothing like the downs on a fall day, and the New Forest, all come out in reds and golds."

He continued in this vein for the entire first half of the trip, covering every topic on which he was conversant and many about which he knew nothing at all. He nattered on about Russia, China, horses, cows, the sea, the trees, his coat, the earl's coat, Evelynne's book (borrowed from Mitford's library, and into which she futilely kept trying to escape), the English economy, the French style, agriculture, beekeeping, spaniel-breeding, musical composers, Italian Renaissance artists, and American red Indians.

Evelynne was quite sure that if the earl had carried a pistol, he would have put an end to Arkady before they even left the drive of Levelands. Now, as they approached their luncheon stop, she wondered if she could possibly knock him unconscious with her book.

"Ah, here it is, The Merry Bridegroom. A quaint little inn, and a bit out of our way, but such good food. And such a lovely, shaded path to walk along beside that meandering stream. Why don't the two of you have a stroll while I order us some luncheon?"

The earl, who hadn't said another word after greeting Evelynne, hopped out, clapped his tall hat upon his head, and strode away.

"Stop it, Arkady!" Evelynne cried as she at last gave vent to her desire and rapped him on the side of the head with her book. "You are making an already uncomfortable situation nearly intolerable. The more you prattle on, the clearer it is that he has nothing to say. To me, or to you, or to anyone. Let it be over."

Arkady rubbed the side of his flaxen head and grimaced. "God, I'm parched, Eve. You think it's easy, keeping up a stream of dialogue with you two tombstones?"

"I believe monologue is the correct word."

"I do think it's working, though."

"What? That you're driving us both mad. Yes, I'd say it's working beautifully."

"Eve, you don't know Robbie as well as I do. Um . . . that is . . . you haven't known him as long as I have. He's in the remote stage of Scottish rage, the dour part, where he becomes very silent and ominous, drawn in on himself. He needs to be pulled out of it. Otherwise, it can go on for weeks. I've seen it a hundred times."

"Yes, and I've seen it once. And that's more than enough for me."

"You'd better get used to it if you're going to marry him, Eve. Though I daresay he'll be of a happier nature with you around. He was positively giddy at Levelands these past days. Never saw the like."

"I'm not going to marry him." She put her hands firmly on his arms and looked intently into the round, green eyes. "He despises me, Arkady. He's made it patently clear. And I . . . well, I am very disappointed in him."

Arkady dropped his pose for a moment. "I won't be happy until you sort this out, Eve." His voice became almost tender. "I think at this moment, you're the two people I care most for in the world. You belong together. And I'm not going to let Highland pride and Marriott mulishness prevent that from happening."

Evelynne was about to protest that her mulishness had nothing to do with the case when the earl swung open the coach door.

"I am in rather a hurry if you don't mind." The coach's two occupants looked at each other guiltily and climbed out.

They lunched in a private parlor, spoke only when necessary, and were soon under way again. Arkady elected to ride Little Georgie for the remainder of the trip, sending the groom to sit atop the coach. Hoping, Evelynne suspected, that if his presence couldn't bring the two passengers together, his absence might.

As they progressed east, Evelynne became lost in her book of poetry, while the earl gazed aimlessly out the lowered window at the passing scene, his wide shoulders rocking slightly with the motion of the vehicle.

"What?" Evelynne looked up over her book.

"What?" The earl turned from his perusal of the countryside.

"Sorry. I thought you made a noise." She lowered her eyes back to Dr. Donne.

"What sort of noise?" It was difficult to be always looking out at the blasted countryside, which he'd seen a hundred times before, when his Evelynne, in a fetching peach-colored hat and matching carriage dress, sat no more than an arm's length away from him. She smelled of incense and garden spice and God knew what else, and he was going to kill Arkady for torturing him this way.

"Oh, just the usual sort of noise, when someone is about to say something." She turned a page.

"No, no. I wasn't about to say anything." He looked out the window and counted his ten thousandth hay rick. He coughed. "Well, I suppose I was going to say something."

"Yes?"

"I believe I owe you an apology, Mous . . . Miss Marriott. There probably won't be another opportunity for me to offer it." He ground his knuckles together and bit his bottom lip. "I was precipitate yesterday morning during our ride. I made an error of judgment. The Carstairs woman has a lot to answer for."

"So, Arkady told you what he'd seen. Strange that you wouldn't take my word for it," she mused. "And what of yesterday afternoon? Were you precipitate then, as well?"

"I have nothing to say regarding yesterday afternoon."

"Oh." She lowered her eyes again to the page.

"I believe you were the precipitate one in that case."

"Yes, my intemperate behavior has been well documented."

He loosened his neckcloth. He was most definitely not going to apologize again, so he attempted a neutral topic. "I believe you met with Sir Robert yesterday?"

Evelynne nodded without looking up. The earl continued in a purposely casual voice, "It might interest you to hear the news of Skelton he brought me. As I suspected, the landlord at the Eel and Barrow had been abetting him in his plots against the Crown. The fellow's been taken into custody, along with some of Skelton's ruffians. Sir Robert is posting down to Southampton this afternoon, and as soon as he has their signed confessions, he can have papers drawn against Skelton. There's a slight chance it might happen before he can spread his slander about me—about us. Sir Robert has said he will allow the baron to flee the country if he promises to keep his tongue between his teeth. A sort of quid pro quo."

Evelynne regarded the earl with an expression of barely concealed resentment. "Am I correct in assuming you knew of these developments before you met with Lord Skelton yesterday?"

The earl closed his eyes and nodded. "Yes, both Arkady and I knew he would soon be arrested."

Evelynne's voice rose a notch. "Then has it occurred to you, my lord, that if you'd bothered to tell me any of this beforehand, if you'd trusted me enough to confide in me, I would have known you didn't need rescuing from Skelton? That his threats would soon be made meaningless?"

That very thing has crossed the earl's mind frequently since Evelynne's disastrous intervention in the parlor. He hadn't thought to tell her of Sir Robert's heartening message yesterday morning, and then, after the distressing scene with Lady Philippa, he'd been too out of charity with Evelynne to discuss anything.

"I wanted to keep you out of it," he explained. "I knew there wasn't anything Skelton could use against me . . . except you."

She leaned back against the cushioned squabs. In the shadowed interior of the coach his face was half dark, half light. It was an uncanny outer facsimile of his inner nature. Her Robbie, all dour and remote one minute, then laughing and teasing the next. Except that there hadn't been any laughing or teasing for quite some time. What had Arkady said? It could go on for weeks.

"Well, you needn't worry," she said, and then sighed. "I'll

disappear back into the streets of Camden Town, and you will never hear of me again. I'll just be a nameless person you were once associated with. Skelton is very foolish if he believes he can create a scandal with such poor clay."

The look of resignation that Evelynne now wore spurred the earl to more open speaking. "You don't understand, Eve. I never meant for you to disappear from my life." He started to reach for her, but his prudence overrode his desire. He placed his clenched hands upon his knees. "Do you doubt that I was courting you in earnest? Do you think I want to let you go? To let you just disappear?" His voice almost broke. "I wanted to marry you, Evelynne. Marry you! And now, if this scandal breaks, it will place you beyond me, so far beyond me."

"Why?" Her voice was a whisper. He had said *beyond*, but she knew he meant *beneath*.

"They will call you harlot, and hussy, and, yes, trull. They will lampoon you in the coffee shop windows and in the gazettes. A young lady in breeches! The press will have a field day. Lady Philippa will come limping back to London and throw her log on the fire. She suspected something about you from the first." He paused to catch his breath. "I'm sorry for what I said in the library, that I called you a liability. But I felt you had brought this down upon us, and so I spoke in anger at what must now be forever lost to me."

Evelynne rubbed her eyes with the sleeve of her jacket, and the earl's heart almost broke.

"If I let you go, Eve, let you disappear, there will be no subject for ridicule. You can't lampoon a phantom. It's poor clay, as you said."

"And what if you stood by me?" Her voice trembled.

He drew in a breath, and hated himself for his next words.

"I can't," he said. "I can't."

"No," she whispered raggedly. "Please forget I even asked." She picked up her book and pretended to read, pretended to breathe, pretended that her heart had not been ripped right from her breast by his words.

They reached London by late afternoon. The coach drove into Cavendish Square and halted in front of the earl's town house. He climbed out without a word to Evelynne, glancing up the street as Mitford came trotting along on Little Georgie.

"Eve!" Arkady called, jumping down from the saddle. "Evelynne. Come out here!"

The earl lingered on his doorstep, watching his friend with a mixture of curiosity and disdain. Evelynne sighed and climbed out, refusing to even glance in the earl's direction. She walked behind the coach to where Mitford stood slapping the horse's reins against one gloved hand.

"Well," he whispered. "Any progress? Has he declared himself?"

"I'm going in now," the Monteith called from his porch. "Good day."

"No, wait," Arkady called back. "We're coming in for tea. I'm just congratulating Evelynne on this splendid beast of hers." The earl crossed his arms over his chest and leaned against his front door, an expression of long suffering on his face.

"Go on . . ." Arkady prompted.

"Oh, he declared himself, all right!" she said with feeling. "He declared he wouldn't stand by me in the face of scandal. The craven, cowardly—"

"The devil he did!" Arkady dropped the reins and took her full in his arms. "I can see this needs a bold stroke. Kiss me, Eve."

Before she had a moment to consider his peremptory request, she found herself ruthlessly crushed in his embrace. The Monteith leapt from the top step of his porch to the pavement and stalked toward them.

"Mitford, what the devil are you about?"

Arkady looked up from Evelynne's rosy mouth. "I'm about to ask Miss Marriott to be my wife."

"Not while I'm here to prevent it!" And with that, the earl spun his friend away from Evelynne and knocked him down with one blow.

Arkady sat in the street, where he landed, ruefully nursing his jaw with one hand.

"Well, I'll cry quits if she means that much to you."

Evelynne stood over him, hands clenched, a woman at the end of her tether.

"Arkady, this farce has gone on long enough." She spun to Monteith with fire in her eyes. "You should be ashamed of yourself, brawling in the street, in your own street, and taking advantage of a friend's hospitality, and then knocking him down in the gutter."

"I'd rather you didn't bandy that part about," Mitford interjected, but Evelynne merely flashed him a quelling look.

"I will not be the latest amusement in your jaded life, Lord Monteith, or yours either!" This to Arkady, who still sat where he had fallen, almost under Georgie's front legs. "I am not some new toy for you to brangle over. I am a person, not a plaything. I have real feelings, or have you both forgotten that?

"You are spoilt and interfering," she snapped at Mitford, and then turned to the earl. "And you, my lord, are a spineless, hypocritical wretch."

She grabbed Little Georgie's loose reins, dragged him to a nearby mounting block, and threw herself into the saddle, astride. She rode forward to the coach and tugged her bandbox viciously from the luggage rack.

"Wait, Evelynne!" The earl stepped into the street, reaching for her horse's bridle. "Hear me out!"

"No!" She pulled around sharply, her horse dancing to be off. "I'm done with your words." Her eyes were wild with anger and pain, like the mare in the meadow. He thought her an avenging Valkyrie on her mythic steed. If she plucked his heart out with a fiery sword, he would not be amazed.

She leaned down to him so their eyes, stormy gray and deepest blue, were nearly level. Those blue eyes entreated her, but it was much too late. She took a calming breath.

"Robbie, don't you see? We're back in Cavendish Square. This is where it began, and now this is where it will end."

The Monteith stood, arms loose at his side, and watched her gallop away.

It was bad *ton* to gallop in the streets of London. It was extremely bad *ton* for a female to ride astride. His Mouse probably didn't know that, and she wouldn't care if she did. His sense of loss overwhelmed him before she was even out of sight. *Dear God, what had he done?*

"Now you've hobbled it." Arkady had finally picked himself up and was brushing the dust from his riding coat. "She's gone to earth. How ever are you going to find her? It'll be the Runners, for sure."

"Oh, shut up, Arkady!" The Monteith turned swiftly and strode into his town house.

Mitford watched him retreat, and then threw his head back and said to his coachmen, sitting upright and impassive on the box. "They called him 'Lamb' in the war, did you know? Isn't that the damnedest thing?"

And then he followed the earl into the house, wondering what sort of cake he should have with his tea.

Chapter 13

❧

When Evelynne returned from her weeklong absence, she was made much of by everyone at Number Twelve. Mrs. Cooperall fussed over her like a fond parent, and her brothers wouldn't leave her side for more than ten minutes at a time. One and all, they clamored repeatedly to hear the tale of her adventure with the earl. She had glossed over the two nights she had spent alone with him, redirecting their focus to the wonders of Levelands and the sartorial splendor of its owner.

Gilly, who now insisted on being addressed as Gilbert, would be leaving for Exeter after the Christmas holidays to attend Sir Robert's school, so Evelynne especially cherished the time they spent together. He seemed to Evelynne to have grown taller while she was away. And he was careful, she noticed, not to ask her too many probing questions about her journey with the earl. Something about her face or manner must have kept him at a distance. He was truly growing up, she realized a bit sadly, and with each passing day he put her more in mind of Edgar.

Several days after her return, a package arrived for her from Berkshire. It was from Mrs. Craft. The colonel's wife had sent her the slate gray riding habit and a warm note; she promised to come calling when she and her husband next visited London. Evelynne took to her room and cried for the first time since she had pelted back to Number Twelve on Little Georgie's broad back. Her visit to Levelands had not been totally without merit—she had made a friend.

Evelynne read the London papers each day from front to back, seeking news of the earl. There wasn't even the breath of a scandal involving the Monteith, but within a week of her return to Camden Town it was reported in all the papers that Lord Skelton, Member of Parliament, and confidant of Lord Liverpool, had fled to the Continent. He had been implicated, the paper stated, in selling military information to the French. The incriminating evidence had been compiled by the Earl of Monteith and his political mentor, Sir Robert Poole. There was talk in government circles that the young earl might even be rewarded with a cabinet post for his service to the Crown.

Evelynne clipped out one story to save; it was accompanied by a rather good pen-and-ink sketch of the earl. Not that she had a hope of ever forgetting what he looked like.

With some of the money from Sir Robert, Gilbert was outfitted with clothing suitable to a young gentleman. Jem and Josh had new blue coats, as well, and Mrs. Coop found herself the possessor of a high-crowned silk bonnet that made her chortle with delight. So now, when the Marriott family took a turn about the square or shopped upon the High Street, they appeared quite genteel. Some even thought them a particularly handsome group, the raven-haired sister set like a dark jewel in the midst of the golden-haired boys.

In fact, it was Arkady Pelletier who had said those very words to himself as he sat in a closed carriage near the Gatekeeper Tavern and watched the family pass by. He was a bit vain about his own wheat blond hair—he accounted it one of his few attractive features. But when the Marriott lads capered by, their guinea-gold locks shining in the late September sunshine, he sighed and jammed his beaver hat hard upon his head. No wonder Evelynne was uncertain about her own looks. Those three boys were quite dazzling.

Mitford had been keeping an eye on Evelynne since her return home—he felt partially responsible for her falling-out with the earl—if only for neglecting to assure her that Skelton was no real threat to Robbie. He swore, if he could get those two back together, he would never, ever meddle again. Since he had franked at least three letters to her family for her while she was at Levelands, Arkady had no trouble locating Evelynne's house in Camden Passage. Of course, he had refused to share that bit of information with his bone-headed friend—he believed Robbie needed a while to stew in his own Scottish juices before he was given access to the fair Miss Marriott.

Evelynne, happily, had found a very satisfactory position shortly after her return to London. She'd answered an advertisement seeking a young woman of breeding to companion a widowed lady. It required only that she be able to read aloud in a pleasing voice and converse knowledgeably on "improving" topics. Whether it was the stylishness of her peach-colored carriage dress or the subtle lines of maturity that her face now possessed, Evelynne was retained on the spot by the plump, self-indulgent, and very well-to-do Mrs. Allbright.

Now that her family's future was looking brighter, Evelynne determined to put any thoughts of the earl behind her. Enough time had passed since she had been with him for the initial pain to have given way to a sort of hollow numbness, and the pleasure of being back with her family had lessened the ache that dwelled in her heart. She rode Georgie on weekends and reveled in the exhilaration of free flight as they galloped across the wide heath of Hampstead.

But Evelynne knew she would never be totally apart from her loss. It was woven indelibly into the fabric of her life. A tall, dark-haired gentleman turning a street corner set her pulses racing. A Scots burr, overheard in a crowd, brought her near to tears. A waltz whistled by the costermonger sent her flying back into the house. And she would never taste turkey or apples again without a pang of hunger for the man who had fed them to her, laughing, as they walked along a dusty country road.

One afternoon she returned early from Mrs. Allbright's house—her employer had turned peevish after overindulging in pickled plums and had waved Evelynne away with a flick of her fingertips. "Off you go, gel. It's no use reading to me when my head is pounding so." Evelynne suspected the lady's head was not at the root of her problem, but said nothing.

As she let herself in the front door, she could hear Gilly chattering away in an excited voice to someone in the parlor.

"It's in Exeter, sir. Captain Frobisher, the headmaster, was once our most valuable agent in France. I don't know how I'll get on there, but my friend, Mr. Fletch, vows I'll make a proper spy someday. Not that I won't be sorry to leave Evelynne and the boys."

She could hear the deep tones of a masculine response, but could not quite make out the words.

"Gil?" She slid open the pocket door and popped her head into the room. Gilbert was perched on a low stool before the small fireplace. His visitor was sitting in the armchair that faced the hearth. Evelynne could see only a pair of long legs encased in buff riding breeches and gleaming black top boots.

The room was not at all smoky—Mrs. Cooperall had had the

sweep in only last week—but for some unaccountable reason, Evelynne was having trouble breathing.

"Eve!" Gilbert glanced up from his seat, his face lit by more than the flickering flames in the hearth. "Look who's come to call."

The owner of the long legs got slowly to his feet, reaching down to tug at Gilbert's hair as he rose.

"Hardly a proper introduction, my young cockerel. I hope that Frobisher fellow can teach you better manners, along with all the espionage." His eyes shifted then to the young woman in the doorway. "Good afternoon, Miss Marriott."

"My lord," Evelynne managed to rasp out. Now her voice, as well as her breathing, seemed to be totally beyond her control.

"Gilbert, if you would excuse us," the earl said urbanely. "Your sister and I have something to discuss. Something rather, um, private."

"No. Stay," Evelynne uttered feebly as her brother jumped up and came toward the door.

"Go, Gilbert," the earl repeated in a voice that was a shade away from peremptory.

The boy looked first to his sister, who stood white-faced and rigid beside the door post, and then to the Earl of Monteith, who was now leaning back upon the mantelpiece, his broad shoulders nearly obscuring its entire width.

Gilbert hesitated. He owed Evelynne his support, but he was also wise enough to know that something far beyond his ken was happening here in this room. The air positively quivered with tension.

"I'll wait in the hallway, Eve."

As he sidled past her, she grasped his sleeve. "Gil, please find Mrs. Coop and ask her to attend me."

"She's just gone off to the market with the boys, not ten minutes past. Sorry." He looked at her sheepishly for an instant before he darted out and closed the door.

"It appears you've been deserted, my dear." The earl's eyes were laughing at her gently, gleaming in the warm light. Evelynne could see that there were dark smudges in the hollows beneath his lids.

In Mrs. Cooperall's tiny parlor the Monteith was an overwhelming presence. But then he had overwhelmed Evelynne in the grand, lofty spaces of Levelands, just as handily. He was wearing a jacket of melton cloth in a rich shade of tawny gold;

it fit him superbly, without a wrinkle or crease. Sir Reginald's borrowed clothing had never done him such justice.

Since the unsteady fluttering of her heart would not allow her to converse with any semblance of polite normalcy, Evelynne took refuge in anger.

"You have no business here, sir," she said in a low, surprisingly even voice.

His eyebrows rose perceptibly at her tone. "What? Not going to offer me a dish of tea, or a glass of ratafia?"

"I could offer to show you the door."

He made a tsking noise. "Between you and your brother, Eve, it's difficult to know who shows the poorer manners."

Her eyes narrowed. "My manners or lack of them are none of your concern. To those who are welcome in this house, we can be graciousness itself."

"Ah! A direct hit." He gave an exaggerated wince, and then lowered his head so that his next words were uttered through the dark spill of his forelock. "You always knew how to get past my defenses, Eve. But you were not always so loathe to banter with me. I meant you no disrespect just now. You manners have always exceeded mine when it came to suffering fools gladly."

"And do you now play the fool, my lord?" She had stepped a little way into the room, but was careful to keep several pieces of furniture between them.

He gave a careless shrug. "I play whatever role you require of me."

Evelynne's eyes darted to his face. Behind his idly spoken words, she sensed a certain unsureness, but his expression was one of wry humor. His own eyes, black as pitch in the deeply shadowed room, were observing her intently.

"Well?" He flung his arms out on either side of his body, palms up, the long fingers splayed. "Shall I be your fool? God knows I've played the part before. Fooled into mistaking you for a boy. Fooled into thinking you one of Skelton's minions." His voice lowered an octave. "Fooled into believing that you loved me."

Evelynne's head snapped back. "I think I must take the honors for foolishness in that instance, my lord."

"Oh?" The earl approached her, skirting the footstool and the chair, the table and the ottoman. When he halted his progress, he was only an handspan from her. "Then perhaps we can share the title of fool. Since you choose not to share anything else with me—not even your conversation."

Evelynne pushed past him, not wanting him to see the help-less yearning his nearness evoked. She sought refuge behind the loveseat, placing her hands along its back, hoping the carved wood frame would offer her the support that her knees were refusing to supply.

Dear God, why has he come here? To further taunt her? To mock her in these humble surroundings?

Evelynne stifled her panic and drew a deep breath. So he wanted conversation, did he? Good. She would offer him a very nice display of plain speaking.

"My lord," she began, her chin in the air. "I am at a loss to comprehend the reason for your visit. We said everything we needed to say to each other on the coach ride from Hampshire. I believe you made your feelings clear to me on that occasion. Painfully clear."

This time, the Monteith's wince had no playfulness to it. He strode to the loveseat, and kneeling upon it with one knee, he covered Evelynne's hands with his own. His eyes beseeched her as he spoke.

"I can only say, upon reflection, that my feelings at the time were wrong. I was . . . very cruel to you, Eve. Pompous and ar-rogant and . . . oh, god, Mouse—" His voice grew ragged. "When you rode out of Cavendish Square on that bloody behe-moth, all the brightness went out of my life. I'd give the world to unsay the words I spoke in the coach." He ran his hands up past her wrists until he was gripping her just below the elbows. She was trembling violently, and she knew he could feel the tremors beneath the fabric of her pelisse.

"You might unsay them, my lord," she said softly, refusing to look down at his earnest face. "But I will never stop hearing them. When you denied me, when you refused to stand by me, you killed any feelings I may have had for you."

"No!" he cried, shaking her slightly. "Feelings don't die so easily."

"No," she said sadly. "But illusions do. And what is love, without its inherent illusions?"

The earl tugged her toward him, sliding his arms around her back so that his head rested against the rise of her bosom. "I've come back, Eve. Because I couldn't stay away. Not for another hour. I'll stand by you. Whatever happens, I vow on my honor as a soldier and as a Scot, I will stand by you."

Evelynne drew a halting breath, wanting with all her heart to raise her arms around his broad shoulders and cradle his dear head against her breast as she had done that first night they were together, when he needed comforting so badly. But now it was she who needed comforting, and he could never be the one to offer it. Not after the ragged tear he had left in her soul. So her practical mind prevailed, kept her arms inert at her sides, and made her voice sound sure and firm, when, in fact, her insides felt like a blancmange pudding.

"I think you had better leave now, my lord." She carefully disentangled herself from his embrace and went to stand beside the door. "My brother will not like it that you are manhandling me in my own parlor."

"Eve!" he implored her from the loveseat. "I have just bared my soul to you, and in return I receive a lesson in propriety? Now who is being cruel?"

"I will tell you what is cruel." She leaned toward him, her eyes ablaze. "To come to me after letting two weeks pass. To have waited until you were sure no scandal had broken that involved you with my *intemperate* behavior. Now that you feel safe from the gossipmongers and are basking in the glory of your fame as a spy catcher, you tell me that you have changed your mind and will stand by me." She gave a bitter laugh. "The cannons have been spiked, Major; there is no valor now in standing before their muzzles."

"You blasted, pigheaded girl!" He was on his feet now. "It's not over! Nothing is resolved."

"It is to me. By waiting so long to seek me out, you have again proven yourself less than valiant."

"You think I waited two weeks out of caution? Great jumping Christ! Of all the . . . I've been seeking you since the day you rode away from my town house. But no one would tell me your direction."

"Arkady must know it," she remarked blithely. "He franked my letters from Levelands."

"I-I would have franked them for you, Mouse." Somehow that little defection stung him deeply. But it wasn't a patch on the pain of her grossly unjust accusation. Did she honestly believe he was so cowardly, so craven, that he had waited until the danger of scandal was over to declare himself?

Of course she does, his inner voice replied. *And you have no one to blame for that but yourself. And your own stupid pride.*

"Sir Robert also knows my location," Evelynne continued calmly. "He has been a regular visitor here—a most *welcomed* guest."

The earl dragged his hand through his dark hair. "I swear to you, Eve, neither he nor Arkady would tell me where I could find you. Sir Robert humphed and fidgeted and said it wasn't really his place to reveal something you obviously wished kept private. And Arkady, damn him, merely suggested I contact the Bow Street Runners."

Evelynne had to suppress a smile. She wondered the earl hadn't torn his friend limb from limb for such provoking insolence.

"So how did you find me?" she questioned, unable to keep from asking.

His look was reproachful in the extreme. "I had to bribe one of Sir Robert's coachmen. See what you've reduced me to, Eve—cozening servants."

"I haven't reduced you to anything, Robbie . . . er, my lord. And it's a pity you wasted your money. This visit has done nothing but convince me I was right to forget you."

With an oath he stalked rapidly across the carpet to where she stood.

"I won't let you forget me, Evelynne Marriott."

She was too busy framing her next scathing response to see the light of desire flare up in his eyes. He reached for her, his fingers curled in frustrated anger. But then something in her stony face made him stop. His arms fell to his sides as his glance lowered to her stubborn mouth. He realized how pointless it would to be wrestle her into submission. She'd think him a bully, as well as a coward.

Instead, he leaned toward her, arched his body over hers, his head canted slightly to one side. All she needed to do was raise her chin another notch, and they would be kissing. He waited, his breathing arrested, for her to make the next move.

"Tell me ye haven't forgotten me, Evelynne," he crooned, the Scots burr slurring his words slightly.

Her heart twisted at the sound. She felt the whisper of his warm breath on her lips, felt the heat of him and the power of him as he stood so close before her. The merest tilt of her head, and she would find his waiting mouth. All his railing and man-handling were nothing compared to this potent inducement.

She took a half step back. It felt as though a chasm had opened between them.

"No, I haven't forgotten *anything*, Robbie," she said, looking at last into his eyes. They regarded her with anxious entreaty, bluer than any polar sea. "And that is why you must go away now. Precisely because I cannot ever forget. There's no profit in stirring things up between us."

"You won't let me prove myself to you?"

"No." She laid a hand against his chest. "I won't hear another word. I cannot give my heart into your keeping, as much I might desire to."

"But I lo—"

"Hush. Whatever feelings you may have for me now . . . they can never heal the breach that is between us. It's rather ironic, I think—you spent the entire time we were together refusing to trust me. And now I must live the rest of my life, knowing I can never trust you."

He gazed one last time into her gray eyes and saw only firm resolve in their smoky depths.

"Never is a very long time, Eve," he said quietly.

She turned from him then, fisting her hands into the skirt of her pelisse, unable to bear the expression of lost hope that had flickered over his face. She heard the pocket door slide open. There was a whispering touch on her hair, and then he was gone.

Thankfully, Gilbert did not chose to interrogate Evelynne on the matter after the earl had gone. He did not inquire why she left her dinner untouched that evening, nor did he question why she did not reveal the happenstance of the Monteith's visit to Mrs. Coop. Evelynne reflected that she had to agree with Mr. Fletch's pronouncement that Gilbert was going to make a proper spy. It was a more than accurate assessment, if his studied silence where she was concerned was any indication.

Evelynne feared a second visit from her erstwhile suitor, but after several days had passed and there was no further sign of the earl, she started to relax. And she began the healing process all over again.

Stepping back from Robbie had been the hardest thing she'd ever done. But she knew if she had raised her head, if she had kissed him, her emotions would have overcome her prudence, and she would have lost all her resolve.

For some nights afterward, as she tossed restlessly in her bed, she wondered if she hadn't been too harsh with the earl. Perhaps he was not so fickle, nor so despicable as her damaged heart insisted. But she had suffered enough losses in her short life; she would not risk her peace of mind by allying herself with a man who had such enormous power to hurt her.

There were other nights when she wished she had allowed herself to take that sweetly offered kiss. She could have warmed her dreams with the remembered sensation of his mouth upon hers for years to come. Perhaps it wouldn't have been her undoing, only a last pledge between parting lovers. And he had waited so patiently, almost benignly, for her to respond; was it possible he would have let her go afterward and not continued to force his suit? Now she would never know.

Of such regrets are spinster's memories made, she mused sadly.

One October afternoon, nearly a week after the earl's visit, Evelynne was reading aloud in Mrs. Allbright's sunny parlor, slogging through the ponderous sermons of the Reverend Dawson, when her patroness interrupted her.

"Well, Miss Marriott, I expect you have heard that Monteith is not so sainted as we all believed."

"Monteith?" Evelynne echoed her like a parrot. She hadn't seen a newspaper for days; she'd become less vigilant, once she thought the threat of scandal had safely passed.

"Where have you been, gel? It's in all the papers. The Earl of Monteith brought his light o' love to a *ton* house party, bold as anything. Don't blush, gel; we're both past the age of such missishness. My good friend, Lady Cantling, came to tea yesterday, and it seems her cousin's son was actually there—name of Gideon something-or-other. As he tells it, the chit was a brassy piece, and quite free with her favors among the men." Mrs. Allbright sniffed with outrage. "I haven't heard the like of this since Winterbourne was charged with bigamy—and he merely a viscount."

Evelynne said nothing. Well, she thought, what could one say?—"Oh, yes, I was there, Mrs. Allbright. In fact, I was the brassy piece who was so free with her favors."

"There's no clue who the woman was. Some little adventuress, most likely. Who'd have thought the patriot earl would have turned out to be such a rogue? Pass me a sweetmeat, Miss Marriott, there's a good girl."

On her way home that afternoon, Evelynne bought all the London papers she could find, bundling them under her arm. As soon as she was home, she scurried up to her room to read them in private. She scanned the pages quickly. Somehow it wasn't so bad as she had imagined, although the headlines were quite florid.

The *Times* ran a story, "Hussy Invades Hampshire House Party," and the *London Gazette* spelled out "Nobility Nobbled by Cyprian Conquest." "Member of Lords Joins the Muslin Company" was how the *Daily Sun* phrased it.

It was not front-page news, as Lord Skelton's treason and defection had been. No, the slandering gossipmongers never got their stories onto the front pages. Rather, their tattles were placed farther back, beside the ads for hair tonic and age-reducing cream. But every gentleman and lady of the *ton* knew exactly where to turn to sniff out the latest *on dits* and scandals.

"It has been reported by a most reliable source," the article in the *Times* began, "that the recently lauded Earl of M——— was seen at a house party in Hampshire, at the home of the Marquess of M———." *No guesswork required there,* Evelynne observed dryly. "In the company of a young woman quite unknown to those there assembled. She was introduced to the marquess's guests as a connection of the earl's family, and it was his marked intention that she be accepted by those present, and that she further receive the treatment accorded a lady of gentle birth.

"It now comes to light that this woman had traveled for several days with the earl, without benefit of chaperone, and that she was clearly a woman of questionable background. The earl intentionally, and without compunction, overstepped the bounds of propriety. What contempt for his peers he has here exhibited. We do not like to moralize, but it would do well to scrutinize this man, a member of the House of Lords, whose public persona has always been that of a champion for reform. Perhaps the reformer needs to examine his own highly unsuitable behavior."

After she read the items in the other papers, a wrinkle appeared on Evelynne's brow. All the stories were worded almost exactly the same, leading her to conclude the various writers had had the same source. But who? Skelton was fleeing for his life somewhere on the Continent. Surely he hadn't the time for this petty revenge.

She gathered the papers together and thrust them into the fire. "Poor Robbie," she wondered aloud as the last bit of newsprint ignited and curled into ash, "how do you go on, now your worst fears have been realized?"

He would be furious at first, she had no doubt. But were these vague allegations enough to ruin his political career? Important people were forever suing the newspaper for just this type of transparently obvious libel, and they often won in court. But if the earl sued, it would just add fuel to the fire. Any sort of legal case involving a peer wouldn't be kept hidden on the back pages. No, he'd probably just weather it out, scowling and dour as ever.

She imagined he must also be greatly relieved that she had refused his suit; how quickly the gossips would have put things together if he had become betrothed to a "woman of questionable background."

For herself, she felt strangely calm. The other shoe had fallen, and she was quite unmarked. Well, as unmarked as it was possible to be, with an aching heart and an unfulfilled longing in her soul.

Several mornings later, Mrs. Cooperall came bustling into the garden where Evelynne sat reading, undaunted by the mid-October chill. It was her day off, and she was making the most of it.

"You have a caller, Evelynne. A gentleman caller."

Evelynne chided herself for the way her heart pounded at the landlady's words. *Oh, please let it not be him.*

"Mitford, he said his name was. I told him I would fetch you, that you were in the garden—"

"Ah, and so she is." Arkady, resplendent in salmon silk, had followed Mrs. Coop through the doorway.

"Good day, Miss Marriott. I'll join you out here if you don't mind." He settled himself beside her on the stone bench.

The landlady looked about for a place to sit chaperone.

"Oh, it's all right, Mrs. Coop." Evelynne motioned her back to the house. "I'll be quite safe alone with him. We are old friends, he and I."

"I don't bite." Arkady smiled pertly up at the older woman.

"And if Miss Marriott feels compelled to do anything improper, I'm sure you'll be within hailing distance."

Mrs. Coop looked more than a little miffed, but she retired into the house as requested.

Arkady took Evelynne's hands between his own and scrutinized her. "You're looking very well, Eve. In fact you look a dashed sight better than he does." It never occurred to her to ask Arkady who "he" was.

"Never tell me he is ill!" Her hands tightened on his. "Not the head wound?"

"Oh, he's got a problem with his head all right." Arkady nodded emphatically. "He's got marbles rattling around in it, is what. He's become impossible to live with, I can tell you that."

"He's staying with you? At your town house?"

"No, I descended on him in Cavendish Square just after we returned to London. Told him my place in Berkeley Square was being repainted and that the odor was giving me megrims." Evelynne frowned at the mirthful look that glimmered in Arkady's eyes. "Just a fib between friends to get me into his house. He wants looking after, Eve. Someone has to be there for him to rage at, else he'd have no servants left."

"I gather he's very upset about those items in the papers. The scandal has finally come out, just as he feared it would."

Mitford waved a dismissive hand. "What? That bit of tattle-mongering? That's not what's got him worked up. He's been acting like this for weeks. Since the day you rode out of Cavendish Square on that leviathan, if you must know."

Evelynne picked at the cover of her book. So Robbie had been telling the truth—he really did miss her as much as he'd claimed. She looked up at the ivy-covered garden wall, so like the one she had climbed at the Eel and Barrow. She sighed. Was there nothing around her that didn't whisper of Robert MacIntyre?

"Well," Arkady prodded, "don't tell me you've exactly been dancing in the streets since that day." She shook her head. "Has he made any attempt to get in touch with you, Eve? Especially now that this thing has hit the papers?"

"He is not welcome here," she prevaricated. Evelynne had no intention of revealing the nature of her interview with the earl, even to his best friend. And her experience at Levelands had taught her that Arkady was best kept in the dark about certain matters.

"He must have your direction, Eve. I assumed you wouldn't want me to give you away, but Poole is in and out of the house almost daily, and I know *he* has it. It's true that Robbie never mentions you any longer, but I thought maybe—"

"What, that he'd stop being a stiff-necked Scot? No, it's just as well I've gotten past all that. He made it very clear that he values his good name more than my feelings. And even if my name is never publicly connected with his, even if I escape becoming a byword, I can't forgive his cowardice. I . . ." She choked softly. ". . . I want nothing more to do with him."

Evelynne looked away from the marquess; he dabbled his fingers on the edge of the bench as he waited for her to compose herself.

After a few moments she said with some warmth, "I am truly glad to see you, Arkady. You put me in mind of happier times. But if you are to be my friend, you will not ever mention the earl to me again. And you are welcome here only so long as he never knows of your visits. Promise me that you will not ever discuss me with him."

Arkady chewed this over a little. "But, Eve—"

"Never. I mean it.' She held up her hand. That willful Marriott chin was brooking no opposition. He nodded slowly.

"Good. Now come inside and meet my brothers. Gilbert will plague you with questions about your cattle, and the younger boys will make you play at forfeits. Come on, they won't bite!"

By the end of his visit, Arkady was sprawled on the floor before the parlor hearth, playing snakes and ladders with Jem and Josh, while Evelynne and Gilbert looked on in amusement.

Mitford became a frequent visitor to Camden Passage, and he kept faith with Evelynne's request not to mention the earl. But his nimble, devious mind could not adhere to her wishes. He schemed and plotted various ways to get Evelynne and his friend back together, almost as though his life depended on it. And, as he continued his sojourn with the testy, volatile earl, he sometimes believed that his sanity did.

A week after the scandal broke, Evelynne received a letter in the post. Even if it hadn't been franked by the earl himself, she would have immediately recognized the sprawling handwriting. It was a puzzling turn—once the items had appeared in all the papers, she had been certain that he would distance himself from her completely.

Again, her prudence overrode her curiosity—as much as it

wrenched her heart not to read his words, she knew that a glimpse of Paradise only made one long to be inside its gates. She returned it, unopened. Two more letters arrived subsequently, and they received the same treatment.

That was not the end of Evelynne's unwanted correspondence, however. A thin parcel appeared hard on the heels of the three letters from the earl. It was from a solicitor's office, offering her the deed on a small house in Hampstead and four hundred pounds a year. The correspondent, a Mr. Paulson-Smythe, wrote that he could not divulge the name of her benefactor.

"Have you the name of Monteith's solicitor?" she asked Arkady quite conversationally when he visited the next day. "I have something of his that I would like to return. I couldn't ask you to carry it, you must know, for then he would realize you have been seeing me."

"You could post it," he offered helpfully.

"It is somewhat personal in nature. I would prefer his solicitor."

"He uses old Pauly, I believe. Lord, the man's a Methuselah, seventy if he's a day, and his father's closing on ninety-five. Those Paulson-Smythes don't die, they just wither away in a pile of foolscap."

So Evelynne had an answer to her unasked question and promptly returned the parcel to the solicitor's firm with a courteous but firm note explaining that she wanted to be beholden to no benefactors, secret or otherwise.

Several days later, another letter arrived. This time the offer was for a small manor house in Devon and two thousand a year.

"Oh! Does he think I was holding out for an increase?" she bristled, holding the letter away from her as it if were a disgusting insect. "He could offer me Windsor Castle and the Crown Jewels, and I would throw them back in his face!"

She penned another note, this time a bit less courteous, requesting that Mr. Paulson-Smythe inform his client that she was not interested in any offers, regardless of magnitude. "Tell my benefactor," she wrote, "that my good offices cannot be purchased, at any price."

Chapter 14

❦

"I'm going home to Scotland," the Monteith proclaimed to his perpetual houseguest. Arkady looked up from his shot. They were having an after-dinner game of billiards in the earl's spacious game room.

"Scotland?" Arkady sounded a bit confused.

"You know, that damp country just north of here, with all the sheep and bagpipes."

Arkady was so taken aback, he quite missed the cue ball. It was the first time the earl had made anything resembling a joke since the marquess had come to stay at Cavendish Square.

"Leithness," the earl continued. "My home? Where I was born? Where I shall probably die . . . and soon, if the gods are merciful."

Uh, oh! The Scottish dismals had progressed to their morbid stage. The earl was sinking fast. Arkady cursed Evelynne for tying his hands so completely.

"Would you like me to travel north with you, Robbie? It's been an age since I've seen Edinburgh."

"God, no!" The Monteith shuddered, clenching his cue stick. "I've barely recovered from our last coach ride together.,"

"So when will you go?"

"Soon." He leaned low over the green table to make his shot. "Probably Saturday. Yes, definitely Saturday. I'll leave here at ten, and take the post road north to Bedford. Your sister resides near there, does she not?"

"Catherine? Yes, she's at Holystead, just south of Bedford. How long will you be gone, Robbie?"

"It depends."

"You'll want to wait for the scandal to die down, eh?"

"The scandal?" the earl echoed.

"I noticed Bishop and Northgate gave you the cut direct last night at Waiter's."

"Well, yes. I suppose I've lost a few acquaintances in the past week. But it hasn't affected any of my real friends; Bishop and Northgate were hardly bosom bows. And," he added with relish, "the damnedest thing is, the matchmaking mamas have all but burned me in effigy. If I'd known that was what it took to get them out of my hair, I'd have courted scandal years ago."

"You have only to marry, Robbie, for them to leave you in peace," Arkady pointed out sagely. "Can't matchmake a fellow who's already leg-shackled."

The earl chose not to remark on his friend's digression. "Several of my colleagues from the House of Lords have been almost congratulatory. Strange, that." He looked distracted for a moment. "No, that's not why I'm leaving. I miss the Highlands, Arkady. Parliament won't be in session for another two months. London can spare me."

Arkady fairly flew to Camden Passage the next afternoon. Evelynne had just come in from Mrs. Allbright's, flushed from her walk in the brisk autumn air. He waltzed her into the parlor and slid the pocket doors shut.

"What?" she said. "You are all a-twitter today. Have you bought a new coat?"

"Better than that, Eve. My sister in Holystead has written me. She asks if I can recommend someone as governess for her son."

"But I have a position, Arkady. Mrs. Allbright is very congenial, and I still manage to spend time with my brothers. I don't want to be away from home just now."

"That's the beauty of it, Eve. My sister'll be coming back to London next month for the winter."

Evelynne thought this odd; most of the nobility spent their winters away from the dank chill of London. But then Arkady came from a family chock-full of strange starts.

"She won't want you to live in, Eve, just tutor her son. And she's offering a very generous wage." He mentioned a figure that took Evelynne's breath away.

"Is the child so ill-behaved that she needs to pay such a sum?"

"No, no, he's really a very decent chap, uh, child. Look, you've got to come and meet with her. I've already written that you would see her this Saturday next."

"Well, that was a bit presumptuous of you," she complained, her hands at her waist. "I was going to take Georgie up to the heath."

"It don't signify, Evelynne. This is a rare opportunity."

Evelynne was still dubious about the whole thing, but Arkady got around her in the end.

"So I'll be here to fetch you at nine. We can have an early lunch at the Cobbler's Bench, and then go on to Holystead from there. You won't be sorry. I think I can promise you that."

With an oath Arkady brought his pair of bays to a halt. They were somewhere between Billings and Hoopstow on the post road, ten miles north of London.

"What's the problem?" Evelynne asked. "Why have we stopped?"

"It's the near horse. I think he's gone lame." He handed her the reins and leapt down from the high seat of his curricle.

"Walk them a bit, Arkady. Maybe he's just picked up a stone." She tried to sound more optimistic than she felt.

She'd had great misgivings about going off with Mitford that morning. She didn't want another position—silly Mrs. Allbright suited her fine. Still, he had been very persuasive, and it was a lovely day for a visit to the country. But now there seemed to be trouble afoot. Literally.

Arkady was running a hand down the horse's foreleg. "Pulled a tendon, most likely."

"He wasn't limping or favoring it that I could see. Couldn't we try to make it to the next town?"

Mitford flashed her a look of contempt. "Do you presume to tell me how to look after my cattle?"

Oh, no! She'd vexed him. This was too bad of him, to cajole her into this pointless journey, and now to scold her as well.

"I'd best go on to Hoopstow and fetch us a gig. Here—" He motioned for her to come down. "You need to keep them walking."

"But I thought he was lame?"

"He is. He can't pull the carriage with us in it, but he needs to be walked. They both do. Can't leave blooded horses just standing about."

"Then why don't we just *walk* them to the next village." She was getting exasperated.

Arkady was unprepared for the logical progression of Evelynne's mind. "Because, dash it all, it's probably too far . . . and if you even suggest that I wait here with them while you go for help, just imagine how far an unescorted female will get in a strange town."

And with that bit of verbal obfuscation, he turned from her abruptly and set off north. Evelynne watched crossly as his amethyst coat disappeared over a rise in the road.

"Oh, bother," she fussed as she began to lead the fractious horses in a wide circle. She was in a general way quite unafraid of any horses, but these two seemed quite high in the instep. They kept fretting at their bits, and one tried several times to nip her hand. After twenty minutes of leading the headstrong brutes in an endless circle, she was quite willing to risk Arkady's wrath and drive them into Hoopstow herself.

She couldn't detect anything at all wrong with the leg of the horse she was leading. He wasn't favoring it in any way. She was weighing her options when an elegant traveling coach hove into view, coming from the south, the team of black horses heading toward her at a spanking trot.

The driver saw Evelynne and slowed down.

"My lord," he called to the coach's occupant, "there's a young lady stranded in the road ahead."

"Stop, then." The voice was curt.

The coach drew to halt directly across from where Evelynne stood as the isinglass window was let down. The Earl of Monteith leaned out, his gleaming eyes taking in the scene before him. He said languidly, "Is this an elopement I have stumbled upon?"

Evelynne put up her chin, said nothing, and continued to circle Mitford's horses.

"But where is Arkady? Those are his bays, as I should know. They've been eating their heads off in my stable this month past."

"We've lost our near horse," Evelynne replied tersley. "He's lame."

"And has the groom bolted? Or has he just gone to fetch another horse?"

"Arkady didn't bring his groom. The fellow has the mumps or something . . . Oh! You mean the *groom*. Good heavens! You don't really think I was running off with Arkady?"

"Very suspicious, Eve. A man, a woman, alone on the road." He shrugged. "It's a very compromising scenario."

"Oh, of all the infuriating things to say. Especially coming from you."

What she needed, Evelynne decided, was a nice brisk walk. Something to diminish the pounding in her head that was the inevitable result of any conversation with the Monteith. She turned the horses in the direction of Hoopstow and prayed that the earl wouldn't keep pace with her and harangue her all the way into town.

But the pair she was leading had a different idea. Their dinner lay behind them, to the south. It was time they took this slip of a girl in hand.

They both reared up, and the one nearest Evelynne took a sharp bite at her mittened fingers. She hung gamely on, but cried, "Oh, blast!" as they lifted her off her feet.

The Monteith sprang from his coach and was at their heads in an instant.

"Stubborn chit," he said through his teeth as he motioned the junior coachman to come down from the box. "Here, William, mind these troublesome beasts until Mitford returns."

The earl turned to Evelynne. "And now, Miss Marriott, if you will oblige me by stepping into my coach." She looked resistant. "Or are you going to tongue-lash me here in public, like a common fishwife?"

Evelynne bit back her anger and preceded him into the coach. She settled herself in the corner farthest away from the spot where he lounged back against the padded squabs.

He was watching her, his eyes deeply shadowed. He now looked gaunter than he'd appeared in Mrs. Coop's parlor, gaunter even than he'd been after his ordeal at the inn. He looked, in fact, rather like she felt.

The earl spoke at last. "If you weren't eloping with my tiresome friend, then how came you to be here, holding his horses?"

"I suppose you must see yourself in the flattering role of rescuer and think yourself entitled to an explanation." The earl nodded at her. "But it's really none of your business." She crossed her arms.

"I don't want an explanation." His eyes were strangely intense in his angular face. "I want the truth."

"I don't care what you want!" she snapped, looking away.

He reached swiftly across the coach and plucked her from her corner, settling her across from him. She struggled until he caught her hands and held them down against the seat cushion on either side of her.

"Now you listen to me, my fine girl. I will not have you larking about with Arkady on the high road. He can go to the Devil, but I'm damned if I'll let him take you with him. Now, why are you here?"

"We were going to his sister's home in Holystead . . ." she sputtered. ". . . she needs a governess for her young son. Arkady insisted that I come."

The Monteith sat back and regarded her with puzzlement. "You would not take so much as a farthing from me, and yet you place yourself under the dubious patronage of Mitford?"

"I can't take anything from you. You must know that." Her voice shook. "I owe you far too much already, as things now stand."

"I thought it was I who owed you?" He spoke slowly, his brows furrowed.

She twisted her fingers together. "I realize I can never undo the events I set in motion at Levelands. Especially now that the scandalous stories have been published. I . . . I don't blame you for leaving London, my lord. It must be hellish for you, knowing Skelton has had his revenge after all."

To her startled shock, he gave a shout of laughter, darkly hued, but laughter all the same.

"The only hellish thing about this scandal is having Arkady constantly underfoot. Claims he's got to stay in my house to show solidarity. You know—not turning his back on a friend."

He leaned toward her, running his hands up her arms to just below the point of her shoulder. "Eve," he said as he tightened his hold. "Skelton didn't spread the story. He was arrested the instant he set foot in France. Apparently, he was also selling French secrets to *our* government. That was how he got the prime minister's ear."

"Dear God," she muttered. "What a horrid creature he was." She cocked her head. "But if it wasn't Skelton, then who told the newspapers?"

The earl took a deep breath as he let his hands slide from her arms. "I did."

"You!" Evelynne's mouth dropped completely open. "You did?"

He reached over and gently pushed her chin up. "Don't look so shocked, Eve."

She was still staring across at him in wide-eyed disbelief. "It was you who wrote 'Hussy Invades Hampshire House Party'?" Her hands had drawn into tight fists.

"I haven't spent the last fourteen years in Arkady's company without learning how to turn a phrase." His eyes danced as he gazed at her. She looked as if she wanted to slap him again, as she had in Mitford's library.

"No, Evelynne," he said soothingly. "Of course I didn't write that. The blasted journalists added that little touch."

"But why, my lord? Why would you do such a mad thing?"

"You may think it mad, but I had my reasons. When Skelton fled to France, I admit I thought we were out of danger. Then Lady Philippa paid a call on me—she had suspected from the first that you had been traveling with me without benefit of chaperone. I refused to discuss it with her, and she said she would take herself off to the papers with the story, whether it was true or not, unless I resumed my, um, former connection with her."

Evelynne looked thunderous.

"But that's not all. No less than three of Skelton's hirelings have come to me with threats to unleash the full tale of my abduction and subsequent rescue by the girl in boy's clothing if I didn't cough up the ready. Even Mr. Todd, the magistrate, approached me to invest in some gimcrack he's invented. He might be on the up and up, but everyone else who was remotely downwind of Skelton has come sniffing around with their hands out.

"All these things transpired before I visited you in Camden Town. If you'd been willing to listen to me and not put my back up as you did, I'd have told you we weren't out of the woods yet. That's what I meant when I said nothing was resolved. For a woman who proses on about trust, Eve, you've offered precious little to me lately. Considering," he added with a wry grin, "that I have been on my very best behavior."

That was true, she mused, recalling how he had refused to coerce her with his kisses in Mrs. Coop's parlor. It dawned on Evelynne that the earl had offered her a choice that afternoon—he hadn't tried to browbeat her into compliance, but had stepped back and let her make up her own mind. It was a strangely heartening realization.

She looked a trifle ashamed as she said, "You came there to warn me?"

"Yes, my little hothead," he replied, tweaking her lapel with his thumb. "And to offer you the protection of my name. I saw it as a chance to salvage my tattered honor in your eyes. But you were so icy, so distant, and . . . well, I suppose I thought my cause truly lost then, and so I left without ever telling you that the threat of scandal was still hovering over us."

A rapid pulse began to beat in Evelynne's throat as he continued.

"It looked as if the story would break for certain, and I was going to tell my blackmailers, 'Publish and be damned.' But then I remembered something Wellington said to me—that you can't win the battle if you never engage the enemy."

"Arkady said the same to me once," Evelynne interjected with a slight smile. "I believe you were the enemy in that instance."

"Well, Arkady's no Wellington. Anyway, I realized it might serve me better if I sent my own piece to the papers—and neatly put my various extortionists out of commission, to boot. And so I wrote out my version of the story and sent it in. If you read the piece, you know I kept all the details rather vague. And I made any references to you as sketchy as possible. If anyone was to pay the dibs on this, it was to be me."

"You were still trying to protect me? In spite of all the horrid things I said to you that day in the parlor?"

"Horrid, but true, Eve. All you've ever had from me were words: I needed to *do* something to prove myself to you." His voice lowered a notch. "So I purposely broke the scandal, so you would believe, once and for all, that I would stand beside you in the face of any possible disgrace. I put my family name on the line for you, Evelynne. But you, maddening wench that you are, sent back all my letters. How could I stand by you if you wouldn't even acknowledge me?"

"You tried to buy me off with property," she protested. "As if I were a cast-off ladybird."

"No, Eve," he said, trying to retain his patience. "Even if you wouldn't have anything to do with me, I still wanted your family to be taken care of—as I'd promised Edgar. Acquit me of any misconduct on that matter."

"Oh," she said a bit weakly. "It was for the boys then. I never thought . . ."

Evelynne sat looking down at her lap as she mulled over his words. She thought of the belittling analogy she had thrown at him in Mrs. Coop's parlor—and knew now that he had truly placed himself before the cannons, regardless of the cost.

Then her mellowing humor suddenly dissolved at the memory of his viciously worded attack on her in Hampshire. "Oh! But when I think of how you ripped up at me that afternoon at Levelands for placing your precious honor at risk. And now, to discover you have put your own head in the noose." She tried not to let her voice waver. "You still have a great many things to answer for, my lord."

"Yes. And I'll have a very long time to answer for them," he responded. "The rest of our lives, in fact."

She folded her arms and remained unmollified. "So now I expect you are ruined politically. Have they drummed you out of Lords?"

He touched the tip of her nose. "No, Mouse. The scandal raced through London's drawing rooms, and yet here I am, whole and barely marked by it. You were right—my character *was* all the witness I required. Those I care about have not turned their backs on me. One fellow I sit with in the House actually came up to me and said he was relieved to discover that I had some human foibles after all. And several ladies of the *ton*, rather than being outraged, seem now to regard me in a most interesting manner."

"I really don't care," she said.

"You used to care." He looked across at her earnestly.

"Don't remind me!" she warned.

"How puffed up I must have seemed to you, Eve, when I prosed on about my stature and my consequence. Yet, this news coming out has not handed me anything I can't weather. In fact, I received a cabinet appointment yesterday—I'm to be sent as special emissary to Scotland, to make recommendations on land reform."

"How nice for you," she drawled. "But you will forgive me if I do not congratulate you on your good fortune. Things might just as easily have gone in the other direction. And to think what the threat of scandal cost us, what we both lost . . ."

"But that's just the point, sweetheart." He reached out to drift his fingers along her cheek. "I was no longer afraid of what a scandal could take from me because I'd already lost the only thing that was precious in my life. You, Evelynne. Without you, nothing has any meaning."

She looked at him, yearned for him. More than food or drink, more than the air she breathed. And then she recalled how much power he had to hurt her.

"More words," she said wearily. "You still think words solve everything. God preserve me from parliamentary men. You can't win me with words."

"What then?" He took her stiff, resisting hand in his own. "Shall I endow you with all my worldly goods?"

"As if I cared a fig for that!" she snapped.

"What, Mouse? How shall I court you now?"

"Don't start that again! Your last courtship lasted exactly two days—almost to the minute."

The earl looked away, out the window of the coach. She was being difficult. And with every right, he had to admit.

"You have a very uncertain temperament," she continued. "That is not a good thing in a husband. You are moody, quick to anger, surly—"

"And dour, don't forget dour."

The chuckle sneaked out before she could contain it.

"I make you laugh, Evelynne. Doesn't that count for something?"

"This is not the playhouse, my lord. A woman doesn't look to be amused by her spouse."

"What does she look for?"

"A certain restraint. Breeding and ease of manner. An earnest, respectful regard."

He eyed her skeptically. "Oh, God, Evelynne. Don't tell me you've been reading *Mrs. Goodbody's Guide to Marital Bliss?*"

"There is no such book." She glowered at him. "You have just invented it."

He laughed. "Well, if there were, I'd burn every copy. An earnest, respectful regard, indeed. I know what you want, my girl, and, more important, I know what you need."

"Robbie, no. Aaah . . ." He had shifted to her side of the coach and now thrust her back against the seat, pulling her bonnet from her hair. His fingers twined in the dark locks, and he looked intently into her eyes.

"Deny me, Eve. Deny me this, and I'll go away and never trouble you again."

His hand was against her side, and he drew it slowly up until it touched the rise of her breast. He caught her mouth as she gasped, and kissed her hard. There was no other conscious thought in his head but Evelynne. Nothing but the sweet feel of her, and the honeyed taste of her. He drew on her mouth and heard the murmuring response deep in her throat.

He was coercing her now with his hungry kisses, but Evelynne didn't care. She only wanted him to keep on and never, ever stop.

"Deny me this," he breathed against her lips. "Tell me to go."

Evelynne wrapped her arms about him. "Dearest Robbie." She was crying hard. "My dearest, dearest Robbie. How can I tell you to go? How can I tell you anything, but that I love you . . ."

It was more than his insistent kisses that won her over at last. It was the sudden, fierce realization that her fear of being hurt by him paled beside the empty prospect of a life lived without him.

"Ach, my sweet Mouse," he soothed, stroking her hair back from her face. "I have missed you so very much. How did you think I was to go on without you? Can you forgive me for being a pompous fool that day in the coach? I have cursed myself a thousand times for saying those words to you. Marry me, and I will stand by you till Judgment Day. I swear it."

"I forgive you, my love. But only if you will forgive me—for not trusting you enough to give you a second chance."

Trust, Evelynne now understood, was a two-way street. It was disconcerting to discover that she could also hurt Robbie—and had hurt him with her own brand of stubborn pride. But in spite of the pain she had caused him, he still trusted her—enough to lay his heart at her feet.

The Monteith drew her into his lap, snuggling her firmly against his chest. Evelynne tucked her head beneath his chin and sighed, comforted beyond words to be cradled again in his strong arms. She raised his hand to her lips and slid a kiss along his palm.

"You know there will be more talk if we wed, Robbie. It's bound to come out that I was the mysterious house party guest. Could you bear it if I become the laughingstock of the *ton*?"

"I dare anyone to cross swords with you, Evelynne Marriott. Remember Ollie Hooper? And besides, you'll be the Countess of Monteith by then, and I will teach you to perfect a withering scowl."

She laughed against his hand, her tears all fled.

"Say you'll come with me to Scotland, Eve. I will feel as though I'm in exile if you're not beside me. Come to Leithness

and make the Highlands ring with your laughter. You might
even banish the gloom from my family. Yes, I do believe you
might. Look at what a promising start you've made with me."
He grinned ecstatically. "And if that doesn't work, we can unleash your brothers on them."

Evelynne gave a watery, snuffling chuckle. He was clearly
quite daft.

"We can be wed in London if you like—just to thumb our
noses at all the high-sticklers. And then we'll go on to Scotland
for our honeymoon."

"I haven't actually said yes," she reminded him with an arch
look.

"Your mouth has." He kissed her there. "Even if your words
haven't."

The earl called for his driver to turn back to London.

Evelynne watched through the coach window as William and
the bays receded in the distance. She plucked at the earl's waistcoat. "But whatever will we do with Arkady?"

"Wish him in Hades for the rest of our lives, I shouldn't
doubt."

"No." Evelynne grinned up at him. "I mean now. He's gone
off to Hoopstow—and his sister is expecting us."

The earl put her a little away from him. "My dearest girl, if
you studied your Debrett's, like some other ladies of my acquaintance, you'd know that Arkady's nephew, Viscount
Broom, is at least two years your senior. He might enjoy having you about, but not as a governess, I think."

"Arkady would never lie to me," she protested.

The earl raised one brow. "Lies are as necessary to Arkady as
the air he breathes."

"But what reason would he have for making up such a preposterous story?"

"Another Arkadian plot. Don't you see? He's purposely
abandoned you here directly in my path, knowing I would have
to stop for you. But Arkady's not the only one who can run an
intrigue, and he's been a pawn in *my* game this time. I set him
up—told him I was going off to Scotland today and gave him
every last detail of my journey."

"You did?"

The earl nodded. "I know he's been visiting you in Camden
Town, Eve." He tugged on one of her curls. "I happen to have

an accomplice inside your home. Your brother is going to make a fine intelligence officer one day."

"Gilly?" she said in amazement. "No wonder he never asked me anything about you. He didn't need to."

"He came to see me after our unpleasant scene in the parlor. Said you were not at all yourself and that he wanted to get to the bottom of it. I was half afraid he was going to ask me my intentions, and then call me out—the little firebrand. We agreed that he would keep me informed of any unusual occurrences at Number Twelve. So I knew that Arkady had taken the bait, that you'd both be haring off to Holystead this morning, just as I'd hoped. And, since you refused to have anything to do with me, I trusted Arkady's feverish little brain to find a way to bring us together."

The earl looked a trifle smug at the success of his scheme.

"And what if I protested these high-handed doings, my lord?" Evelynne challenged him with a martial gleam in her eye. "Having my own brother spy on me! What if I refuse to be a pawn in *your* game, sir?"

"I am prepared to carry you off to Scotland and marry you at pistol point if necessary," he stated resolutely. "And compromise you in earnest, I might add."

"You were planning to have your way with me?" Her face bore an expression that looked suspiciously like anticipation.

"Yes, and as often as possible."

"Foul beast," she murmured against his chest. "As if I have no say in the matter."

He nuzzled the top of her head. "And what would your say in the matter be, my dearest Mouse?"

"This—" She pulled his face close and kissed him full upon the lips. "Stop scowling, Robbie," she whispered against his hard mouth.

"I'm trying to pace myself," he muttered. "We've got quite a bit of kissing to catch up on."

"As you pointed out, my lord, we'll have the rest of our lives for that." She touched his lips gently with her forefinger and watched as his scowl softened to a tender smile.

The earl held her away from him then, and looked at her with what he hoped was an earnest, respectful regard. "It took me a while to realize how very much I love you, Evelynne Marriott. Arkady, blast his meddling soul, knew it before I did. So maybe he *can* take some of the credit. There's nothing for it, Eve"—he grinned broadly at her—"he'll have to be our best man."

Evelynne gazed lovingly into the laughing blue eyes that she once feared would never smile for her again. "If Arkady brought us together, Robbie . . . well, then he is the best man."

"No, my love." The Monteith took her willful, obstinate chin in his hand. "*I* am the best man."

And then he kissed her, ruthlessly, mindlessly, holding her with all his strength against his heart.

Arkady crept from his hiding place in the bushes near where the earl's coach had halted. He now watched that coach disappear down the road in a cloud of dust. His last glimpse of Evelynne and the Monteith had been most gratifying. Through the lowered window he'd seen enough kissing to almost put him to the blush. But not quite.

Whistling a passage from *The Marriage of Figaro,* he strolled to his horses' heads, brushing bracken from his sleeves as he walked.

"Hop up behind, William," he said with a grin. "I've an engagement party to arrange back in town. It's been a long haul, but I believe we can wish your master happy at last."

He held the horses while the earl's coachman leaped onto the groom's perch. Just before he released the bridle, Arkady placed a swift kiss on the near horse's silky cheek.

"Owe you an extra ration of oats, clever creature. Your little show of temper quite did the trick. But that shouldn't surprise me. Horses have always been throwing those two together, one way or another."

And then, with a dreamy smile lighting his green eyes as he pictured the splendid coat he would order especially for the wedding, Arkady Pelletier, Marquess of Mitford—and sometime meddler in the affairs of others—climbed into his carriage and headed back to London.